FALCONER AND
THE DEATH OF KINGS

Further Titles by Ian Morson

The Falconer Mysteries

FALCONER'S CRUSADE
FALCONER'S JUDGEMENT
FALCONER AND THE FACE OF GOD
A PSALM FOR FALCONER
FALCONER AND THE GREAT BEAST
FALCONER AND THE RITUAL OF DEATH *
FALCONER'S TRIAL *
FALCONER AND THE DEATH OF KINGS *

The Mediaeval Murderers

THE TAINTED RELIC
SWORD OF SHAME
HOUSE OF SHADOWS

The Niccolo Zuliani Mysteries

CITY OF THE DEAD *

* *available from Severn House*

FALCONER AND THE DEATH OF KINGS

A Master William Falconer Mystery

Ian Morson

This first world editi_ _ _ _
in Great Britain and in 2011 in the USA by
SEVERN HOUSE PUBLISHERS LTD of
9–15 High Street, Sutton, Surrey, England, SM1 1DF.
Trade paperback edition first published
in Great Britain and the USA 2011 by
SEVERN HOUSE PUBLISHERS LTD.

British Library Cataloguing in Publication Data

Morson, Ian.
  Falconer and the death of kings. – (A Master William
  Falconer mystery)
  1. Falconer, William (Fictitious character) – Fiction.
  2. Bacon, Roger, 1214?–1294 – Fiction. 3. Edward I, King of
  England, 1239–1307 – Fiction. 4. Paris (France) – History –
  To 1515 – Fiction. 5. Detective and mystery stories.
  I. Title II. Series
  823.9'14-dc22

ISBN-13: 978-0-7278-6977-7   (cased)
ISBN-13: 978-1-84751-310-6   (trade paper)

Severn House Publishers support The Forest Stewardship Council [FSC],
the leading international forest certification organisation. All our titles that
are printed on Greenpeace-approved FSC-certified paper carry the FSC logo.

MIX
Paper from
responsible sources
FSC
www.fsc.org   FSC® C018575

Typeset by Palimpsest Book Production Ltd.,
Falkirk, Stirlingshire, Scotland.
Printed and bound in Great Britain by the
MPG Books Group, Bodmin, Cornwall.

This book is dedicated to
Clare Morson, 1921–2008

PROLOGUE

The Feast Day of St Cyr of Quiricus and St Julitta,
the Sixteenth Day of June 1272

Edward stared moodily out of the narrow window of his Outremer fortress in Acre. The brightness of the Holy Land sunlight contrasted starkly with the gloom of his private room high above the arid lands that rolled away to the horizon beyond his gaze. He squinted, and around his eyes the lines that were now permanently etched in his otherwise young-looking face were furrowed deeper. His holy campaign had been a failure. It irked him that petty feuding, greed and treachery had marked the behaviour of his fellow Christian fighters. Even his position as King Henry of England's son and heir had failed to work in his favour. In despair, he had resorted to sending an embassy to the Tartar khan to the north. Advisers told him these Tartars, who some called Mongols, were the very forces of Prester John, the great Christian lord of the East who it was said would save the Latin Christians at a time of their greatest need. God knows, that need was now. The Tartar hordes had scared the very Devil out of the West some years back, but even they had been turned aside by the forces of Baibars, leader of the Mohammedans. The situation had been so desperate a month ago that King Hugh of Cyprus and Jerusalem had signed a ten-year truce with Baibars. Edward had remained defiant, but he now found himself bottled up in Acre, the last Christian stronghold in the Holy Land.

He sighed and turned from the window, his eyes momentarily unable to penetrate the gloom of the chamber. Slowly, he became aware of his surroundings again. The drab stone walls and flagged floor reminded him of a prison cell. In fact, it might as well have been a cell for all the freedom he had. Suddenly, he was aware of a shadowy presence in the furthest corner of the room. He could discern two people and instinctively felt for his sword, but then remembered he carried no weapon. He was safe in his own chamber deep inside the

fortress of Acre – his own prison cell. Still he tensed, ready
for a fight, until one of the shadows spoke.

'Prince, it is Anzazim. He has a letter from the Emir of
Joppa for you.'

Edward immediately relaxed. The guard who spoke was
referring to an Arab who was a trusted go-between. He often
bore letters from the emir addressed to him. The Saracen
professed an affection for Edward on account of his reputation for valour. He indicated that the guard should go, and
held out his hand for the letter. Anzazim stepped forward out
of the shadows. The wiry young man was dark-skinned, and
his hair was long and oiled. But he claimed to be a Christian
convert, and often dressed in Western clothes. Today he was
clad in the cool, clean white robes of his race, though the hem
where it touched the floor was soiled with red dust. His long
sleeves almost covered the hand in which he held the letter.
Edward took it and turned back towards the window, where
he might have some light to read the message.

He had barely broken the seal on the letter when he was
aware of the rustle of robes behind him. But before he could
turn he felt a sharp pain in his right arm followed by another.
He was being stabbed. He lifted the arm up to defend himself,
only to feel another dagger thrust go in under his armpit. Fully
turned to his assailant, he could not believe it. Anzazim, with
a snarl of pure hatred on his face, was slashing at him with
a knife he must have secreted up his long and loose sleeve.
Edward swung a foot out and swept the killer off his feet in
a manoeuvre he had used more than once in battle. But this
time his opponent was not encumbered with chain mail and
a shield. The lithe Arab leaped back upright and lunged at
Edward again. He grabbed the only weapon he had to hand
– the tripod stand of a small marble-topped table close to him.
The top fell to the stone floor and shattered. Edward swung
the metal tripod back and forth in front of him, protecting
himself from the knife thrusts. Where was the guard who had
left him alone with this maniac? Anzazim suddenly feinted
to the left only to alter his balance and thrust at Edward from
the right. There was nothing else for him to do but grab the
knife blade in his left hand. It sliced through the skin of his
palm, but he held on, blood squirting between his fingers. He
landed a blow with the clumsy tripod on Anzazim's head, and

his assailant fell, the blade released from his hand. Edward turned the knife round, and, using his right hand, he stabbed Anzazim in the chest, sliding the thin blade between his ribs. By the time the guards had responded to the sound of the commotion, Anzazim was lying at Edward's feet. They stood aghast as their prince stood before them, his chest heaving and blood dripping from his hand. He roared at them to get the body out of his sight.

'Take it to the city walls and hang it there by the side of a dog that everyone might see and be afraid.'

As the two men bustled to bear Anzazim away, Eleanor ran into the chamber. Edward's wife and constant companion, she gasped when she saw him, and rushed to his side. He held her with his good arm, wishing to show her he was strong and well. It was barely a month since his wife had given birth to a daughter, and no more than a year since another girl child had been born and died within days. The child they had called Joan must survive, or Eleanor would not bear the agony. And Edward would forever regret bringing her to this arid and unforgiving land. He hugged her.

'See. I am fine. The killer is gone, and I have no more than a scratch on my palm.'

He held his left hand firmly closed so she might not see the nasty gash the blade had inflicted. Suddenly, he felt dizzy and was glad of having Eleanor at his side. He shook his head to clear his brain. How could he be so weak, when he had lost so little blood? The room began to swim around him, and he was aware of small, slim Eleanor attempting to support his manly bulk. The gash in his palm and the pinpricks in his arm began to throb. He realized what was happening to him, and felt cold. The Assassin's knife had been poisoned.

He fell into a black pit.

ONE

The old man lay dying, his breath coming erratically with the desperate heaving of his sunken chest. He was but a shadow of the powerfully built man he had been in his prime. Now he was gaunt, his skin yellow and resembling parchment. His skeletal hands lay limply on top of the ornate cover that was draped over his shrivelled body. Another painful breath rattled in his chest as he sucked air in, only to expel it soon after in a long deep sigh. By the side of his bed stood three anxious physicians, none of whom were able any longer to suggest a remedy. What cure was there for the ravages of old age? But still they argued among themselves.

Master Roger Megrim stood inches taller than his fellow physicians, a stature that emphasized his precedence. At least in his own eyes. Megrim's height made it seem as though he had been stretched on the rack. His limbs were unusually long, his chest concave and his stomach protuberant. He hunched over to disguise his height, and his beak of a nose poked forward like a bird's bill. He was once again pontificating on the causes of his patient's illnesses, though in more uncertain tones than normal. Brother Mark, a Dominican monk of medium height and nondescript features, had adopted his usual pose of dark disdain, half-turned away from the voluble Megrim. The third member of the group, however, was apparently hanging on to Megrim's every word. John Rixe, short, fat and of a jolly aspect, fawned on the Cambridge-educated man. But then he would as easily denigrate Megrim to the Dominican once out of the Cambridge master's hearing. As a mere guild apothecary, Rixe depended on the approval of the educated clerics for his very existence. But that did not mean he was not ready with a strong recommendation for his own pills and potions.

Their patient took another deep and painful breath, and his

eyelids fluttered. He had been recognizable by a lazy, drooping left eyelid that gave him the appearance of always winking conspiratorially with his fellows. Now both eyelids, dark and bruised-looking, were closed, only briefly fluttering at each drawn-in breath. Megrim made a suggestion.

'I could bleed him. Using the phlebotomic method of revulsion – tapping the patient's blood vessel at an extremity – I could relieve the black bile of melancholy.'

For once John Rixe expressed his disagreement.

'Don't be stupid, man. He is barely alive as it is. To bleed him would be catastrophic. No, I have a parchment here with some powerful names written on it. He should wear it around his neck.'

Brother Mark merely sighed at the bickering of his fellow physicians and fell to his knees in fervent prayer. The bedroom's air was thick with the rank and oppressive smell of death and with the sweat of other men's bodies. The room had become crammed with earls and nobles, and not a few prelates in heavy brocaded robes. In its furthest corner, separate and alone, stood another witness to the dying man's struggle to stave off eternity. A grizzle-haired man, in a plain black robe that contrasted starkly with the splendour of those others in the room, hung back in the dust-laden shadows as though trying to distance himself from the events playing out before him. For a time he held his own breath, waiting for the old man to catch another himself. It seemed forever before it came, and it was shallower this time. It was as if the old man was now resigned to his fate, slowly drifting down the darkened vale towards his death. An elderly prelate began to murmur words of absolution, his ear pressed close to the old man's lips to catch his dying confession. The plainly dressed man did not bother to strain his ears to hear what might be said. History would provide the text. Regent Master William Falconer stood silently in the Palace of Westminster and caught his own breath again, as King Henry, the third of that name to rule England, finally gave up his struggle and died.

It would be fully a week before William Falconer found himself back in Oxford. The snow lay heavily on the ground, hampering his journey back to his duties as regent master at the university. And he was to return alone. Saphira would not return with him. She had received a message from her son Menahem urgently requesting her presence in France to sort out a problem with the Le Veske wine business. As Jews, Saphira Le Veske and her son had a rather precarious existence in a Christian world. In England, Jews were supposed to deal only with the lending of money at interest, a business proscribed to Christians and therefore conveniently foisted on to the Jews. In France, matters were a little more relaxed, and when Saphira had taken over her dead husband's finance house in Bordeaux, she had changed the emphasis of the business. Wine shipping became the undercurrent of transferring financial resources between England and France.

When her errant son had been finally convinced to take over the family business, Saphira had been able to concentrate on what had tied her to England recently. Master William Falconer. They had met, and, despite his vows of celibacy, she had made her home in Oxford. Now a simple problem with a ship's captain in Honfleur had ruined everything. The letter demanded she take passage to France. She passed the message to William, who read it in silence. Glumly, he looked at Saphira, her glorious cap of red hair crowning her head like a fiery halo.

'Can't Menahem sort this out himself?'

Saphira pulled a face.

'Don't make this harder than it already is, William. You can see he says that he must stay in La Réole at present. And I am closer to Honfleur than he is.'

'And a whole dangerous stretch of water stands in your way.'

Saphira tilted her head back and laughed out loud, the chimes of her voice echoing down the gloomy corridors of the palace.

'You are being like a protective and overbearing husband.'

Falconer was getting angry without realizing it. Simply because Saphira spoke the truth, it did not make her chiding any more bearable. He returned truth for unpalatable truth.

'And I am just a celibate teacher in holy orders who has no rights over you, I suppose.'

Now Saphira was seeing red.

'Of course you have no *rights* over me, William.'

Suddenly, the natural chill of the room seemed to strike to Falconer's heart. The woman was correct. He was a regent master of Oxford University in holy orders. He could not marry

without losing his position and everything he had cherished for
twenty years. True, each new bunch of students that had arrived
in recent years seemed to annoy him more and more with their
ignorance. But he still loved his role as their teacher and mentor,
didn't he? When Saphira had put in an appearance and diverted
him from his daily tasks, he had managed to find a place for
her. They met when they could, and were discreet about their
amorous activities. What more could he offer?

He looked over at her as she began to pack her chest with
her best dresses. She was worth every risk he took with the
security of his post at the university. And their time away from
Oxford over the last few weeks had been . . . exceptional. It
had all come about because she had given Falconer a curiosity:
a skystone with reputed healing powers. King Henry had got
to know about it and had summoned Falconer to his court at
Westminster. Falconer had persuaded Saphira to accompany
him, and they had taken lodgings together. Perhaps that had
been the problem. He thought maybe she now expected him
to live with her permanently. Something that was an impos-
sibility. Though she had said nothing more, and these thoughts
had been all in his own mind, he found he was ever more
annoyed with her. The trouble was he had already forgotten
what the original argument was about. In fact, he got everything back to front.

'Why can't you just do as I say for once?'

Saphira looked at him, her emerald eyes shafting him like
daggers. But she said nothing, merely sighing and returning
to her packing. Falconer stormed out of the room in disgust.
It was only when he was halfway down the gloomy corridor
that led towards the king's chamber that he began to feel like
one of his own students after a prank had gone wrong. Foolish
and contrite, but with no way back without being humiliated.
He stood beside one of the tall candles that barely lit the
passageway, picking at the runnels of wax, and groaned.

Sicily

Edward sat at the banqueting table, staring disconsolately at
the lavish spread before him. His host, Charles of Anjou, King
of Sicily, had laid on an extravagant feast, served in the highest

of modern style. Each person at the table had their own page standing behind each chair. After Edward had sat down, the page had placed the salt at his right hand and a trencher of dry bread at his left. Then a knife had appeared at his left elbow, along with a spoon wrapped in a linen cloth. Edward had disgraced himself. When the soup bowls had been served, he had raised his to his lips and drunk in the old manner. It was only when he looked around that he saw that everyone else, including Eleanor, was using the spoon to ladle the soup up to their lips. He had blushed, but no one professed to have noticed his mistake. Charles eventually clapped, and the servants brought cooked heron and crane. Then their host had thrown up his hands in delight at the arrival of the central feature of the table. It was greyish meat that Charles had proudly explained was porpoise. Edward's stomach had heaved at the thought, but he had smiled politely, if a little wanly.

He had still not recovered fully from the attack of the Assassin months earlier. He had been close to death for days, as the poison had slowly entered his body. The places where the blade had entered his body had gradually turned black, and finally his physician had insisted that he must cut away the poisoned flesh. Edward had groaned and acquiesced. The pain had been excruciating, and he would have rather faced the slashes of a horde of attacking Mohammedans than the probing slices of the surgeon. He had been bound up, and laid in a daze on his bed for weeks.

'Come, eat, Edward. You look somewhat pale.'

Charles's loud and stentorian voice dragged him back to the present. But not soon enough to prevent a shudder of horror racking his body as he recalled the attack and the subsequent butchery perpetrated on his body. Eleanor, his wife who sat at his side, knew what was troubling him. She gently squeezed his arm – the one that still bore the scars of his surgeon's work – and slid a bread trencher in front of him.

'The crane is a delicious and delicate meat, darling. I will eat some too.'

She slid her hand from his arm and touched her belly. He wondered if she was pregnant again. God knows, she was often enough. Edward counted up the score in his head. In the last eighteen years, Eleanor had given him eight children. And five were already dead, including his eldest son and one-time heir, John. Little Joan had been born in Acre and was not yet a year old. Could she be with child again? The trouble was, she was irresistible. He touched her golden hair, neatly arranged under her fashionable snood. Soon enough he would see it loosened and spread across their pillow. His loins stirred, and he squirmed in his seat. Eleanor's big blue eyes, at once all innocence and knowingness, stared at him. She could always read his mind, and pursed her full, red lips in mock disapproval of his errant thoughts. She pushed a serving of white meat at him.

'Crane, my dear. And try one of these coffins.'

Edward blanched a little at being offered the hard, crusty pastry. He had only just heard of the death of his father, Henry, and the thought of coffins did not sit well with his stomach. He was not yet used to the idea of being the King of England himself. For all his life, his father had been the king. It was a given, an immovable star in his firmament. Now his father lay in a coffin, and Edward was king. The thought, and that of Eleanor naked on their bed later, made him feel a lot better. He smiled and took a piece of crane in his mouth from Eleanor's slender fingers, kissing the tips as he did so.

TWO

Oxford

That winter was a harsh one, with blizzards often cutting Oxford off from its surroundings. Many people, fearful of starving, moved from the frozen countryside into the shanty-town outskirts just below the walls. Some, like the recently widowed Sir Humphrey Segrim, stuck it out in their manor houses. Burning precious stocks of wood, Segrim brooded over the murder of his wife, Ann, and huddled deeper under his fur robes. He had never really got along with his wife. She had ideas that she was better than him – ideas put in her head by that master at the university. But now she was gone, he missed her company. He could not fault her dutiful nature as mistress of the house. Nor could he quite put out of his mind the suspicion that she had had an affair with William Falconer. When her body had been found with the man kneeling beside it, he had been sure that he had killed her. Falconer's trial had been a farce, however, and the regent master had been exonerated. But Segrim still harboured doubts about the real killer. And they grew in his isolation at Botley Manor all through the winter and into the cold New Year.

The object of Sir Humphrey Segrim's misgivings was having a cold, miserable winter of it too. The Christmas celebrations at the university had failed to cheer him up due to the continued absence of Saphira. Even the antics of the King of Misrule – the youngest clerk at the university elected for a brief few days of sovereignty – seemed cheerless. The new chancellor, William de Bosco, stoically bore his time in the stocks at Carfax, and carols mingled in the darkening streets each evening with love songs, and tales of Nebuchadnezzar, and Pyramus and Thisbe. But for William, holed up in his attic solar in Aristotle's Hall, his acrimonious parting with Saphira rankled. More so, because he could not work out what he had said that was wrong. Whatever she thought, he could not give

up his post as regent master, which he would have to do if
he was to share his life openly with her. A master who married
forfeited his degree. Yet all he had suggested was that she
owed him some obligations. What was wrong in that? His
fevered brain was cut in on by a sudden burst of singing from
the main hall of the lodgings. Those students who had not
gone home for Christmas, or who had been trapped by the
snow in Oxford, were enjoying themselves around the
communal fire below. Falconer listened to the words, sung
off-key by Peter Mithian:

'Make we merry in hall and bower
This time was born our Saviour.'

Irritated by the happiness inherent in the singing, he called
out down the stairs to those below.

'It is a week since Christmas, and the New Year is upon
us. I want some peace, and you should be studying.'

The sudden silence was palpable, and Falconer immediately regretted his outburst. He was becoming just like one
of those pompous and solemn masters he ridiculed in his
schools every day. Glumly, he wrapped his blanket around
him and stared at Balthazar in the corner of the room. The
snowy-white barn owl stared back at him unblinkingly, then,
with a silent flap of his wings, flew out of the window and
into the darkness. Falconer hunched even lower into his blanket
and muttered an imprecation.

'Even you desert me, bird, and leave me to my misery.'

*The Feast Day of St Peter of Canterbury, the Sixth Day of
January 1273*

It was the week following Falconer's uncharacteristic outburst
that he received a cryptic message from France. He was
teaching his students in a chilly hall in Schools Lane that a
small fire was failing to heat adequately. Falconer was pacing
around the room, in part to keep warm, and throwing questions at the young men who sat on benches before him.
Recently, the faces before him had become a uniform blur
that had nothing to do with his short-sightedness. He was finding
it increasingly difficult to distinguish one young clerk from
another, and one year from another. He tried to rally his

enthusiasm. The text being studied was Aristotle's *Metaphysics*, and the boys were struggling. Falconer returned to basics and picked out one boy he did know.

'Peter, tell us about Aquinas's interpretation of Aristotle when it comes to natural law.'

The older Mithian brother grinned. He was on safe ground here.

'Aquinas says that natural law is based on first principles and that the first precept of the law is that good is to be done and promoted, and evil is to be avoided.'

He turned to his fellow students in triumph. His teacher, however, was not so impressed. He knew the boy was reciting something he had learned by rote. So much teaching was done this way at the university, and it frustrated him. He threw out a challenge with more of Aquinas's thinking.

'He also says that the desires to live and to procreate are among the most basic human values.'

The young men giggled at the thought of procreation, a concept that was often on their minds. Especially after a night spent in a local tavern drinking ale. Then a steady voice spoke up from the shadows near the street door.

'Aquinas also says that the goal of human existence is union and eternal fellowship with God.'

Under his breath, Falconer groaned. He knew that voice.

'Brother John Pecham, come close to the fire and tell us about your work on optics.'

The Franciscan who stepped into the yellow candlelight of the schoolroom was a small and wiry man with a strict tonsure and an even stricter-looking face. Everything about him suggested cleanliness, and even the hem of his grey habit seemed untouched by the dirty slush outside the door. He shook his head at Falconer's invitation, knowing he was being diverted from his religious teaching deliberately. Pecham was a deeply pious man, but he also subscribed to a belief in the value of experimental science. His field was that of optics and astronomy.

'No, Master Falconer. Let us not stray from your main thesis. Your students are misled if they believe Aquinas advocated sexual activity for its own sake. He went on to say that . . .'

Falconer broke in on the Franciscan friar.

'Alexander Aspall, tell Brother Pecham what Aquinas says about non-procreative sex.'

Aspall, a small and scrawny youth who looked more like a child than his true age of seventeen, blushed. But he stood up and spoke out clearly, as Falconer had drummed into him.

'Thomas Aquinas was vehemently opposed to non-procreative sexual activity, and this led him to view—' here he took a deep breath before he continued '—masturbation and oral sex as being worse than incest and rape.'

With the words out of his mouth he sat down blushing, but to howls of laughter from his contemporaries. Falconer smiled innocently at Pecham, who to give him his due grinned back at the triumphant regent master and nodded in acceptance of his defeat.

'You have obviously schooled your students well in the more solitary pursuits and their dangers. But I am not here for a lesson in procreation, nor in optics. May I speak to you . . . alone?'

Falconer's curiosity was piqued. Though Pecham was a fellow scientist, his religious orthodoxy had not made him one of Falconer's intimates. If he wished to speak to him without any other ears present, the matter was perhaps important. He nodded briefly.

'We were about to conclude anyway.'

He turned to his students and dismissed them for the day. This cheered the frozen students up no end, and they made a dash for the door before their teacher changed his mind. Once the noise of their departure had subsided, he brought Pecham over to the fire to derive what small crumb of heat it offered.

'We are alone. What is it you want to say?'

Pecham stared into the glowing coals for a moment, and when he spoke it was not without a little embarrassment.

'I have a message for you.'

'Then give it to me.'

Falconer held out his hand, puzzled by the secrecy that delivering this missive had entailed. Pecham stared long and hard at the outstretched hand before explaining.

'It is a verbal message that I can only divulge if you can tell two things. First, who is the man who masters the secret of flight in the air?'

Falconer shook his head in bewilderment. What was this

game of puzzles? Looking at the Franciscan, he saw nothing but earnestness in his large brown eyes.

'That man is me. Come, tell me the message.'

'Not until you answer the second question. Who is it has unravelled the secret of sailing under the sea?'

Falconer was beginning to see where this was leading.

'He who is known as Doctor Mirabilis. Friar Roger Bacon. Is this message from him? He alone knows of my little . . . obsession with the secrets of flight, and I his concerning undersea ships.'

Pecham nodded, the glow from the fire turning his face a ruddy colour as he gazed into the greyish-red ash.

'I am sorry to play these games, but my brother insisted I ask the questions of you before I delivered his message. He is somewhat . . . worried just now by the absurd notion he is persecuted by his own order.'

Falconer could see how painful this all was for John Pecham. He was a Franciscan, and deeply religious, and yet he was also a disciple of Roger Bacon's obsession with experimental science. It was a calling that conflicted with the demands of the Church hierarchy, and of the religious order of which they were both members. Bacon had once had the support of Pope Clement and had written copiously concerning knowledge and the world. But Clement had died some years ago, and Roger had disappeared into the depths of the Franciscan order somewhere in France. Pecham, however, must have made contact with him recently. Indeed, as the Franciscan had just returned from the University of Paris, Falconer wondered if that was where Roger was now. He grasped Pecham's arm excitedly.

'You have seen him? Is he well?'

The Franciscan grimaced and extricated his arm from Falconer's vice-like grasp.

'I did not see him as such. He is . . . cloistered away in a cell. I had this message from one who had seen him, however. I am just the bearer of a second-hand missive.'

'And what is this message that must be conveyed by word of mouth only?'

Pecham formed the words in his brain carefully, reciting them just as he had been told them.

'That he who designs submarine ships would speak with he who flies in the air with the purpose of perpetuating knowledge.' He grimaced. 'There. I promised I would pass on the message just as it was delivered to me. But I have to say, it only serves to confirm my fears that Friar Roger has gone mad. He is set on writing an encyclopedia of all knowledge but fears that anything he writes will be destroyed unless he also passes it on to others. It seems you are to be one of those selected to be his memory.'

'But how am I to get to Paris in the first place? There are my teaching duties, my students and the cost to consider.'

Pecham smiled conspiratorially.

'The chancellor awaits your petition to be allowed to study the effect of Bishop Tempier's Condemnations on the teaching of Aristotle at the University of Paris.'

The Franciscan was referring to the results of a meeting of conservative clergy under the guidance of the Bishop of Paris in December of 1270. The tract that emanated from the good bishop's office sought to ban certain Aristotelian teachings in Paris. Thirteen propositions had been listed as false and heretical, but that had had little influence on William Falconer in Oxford. Pecham patted him on the shoulder.

'Who is more suitable to gauge the reaction now than Oxford's most splendid proponent of Aristotle's thought Regent Master William Falconer?'

Falconer's face creased into a wry smile.

'It seems that my path has been laid out for me.'

The truth was that he did not mind at all being manipulated in this way. Hadn't he only just been thinking that his life of teaching had become routine and dull? Here was a chance to travel to Paris and to seek out a meeting with his old friend Roger Bacon. It was dawning on him how much he missed the incisive and argumentative mind of the man. He nodded his agreement.

'In which case, I have no choice but to go.'

His interview with the chancellor was as swift and painless as that with Pecham. William de Bosco was a new appointment to the post, which controlled the administration of the university. He was a safe and secure appointment, made to redress the balance of the previous incumbent, Thomas Bek, who had been deposed due to his overweening ambition. True to the meaning of his name, de Bosco was a short, stocky man who seemed to be firmly planted in the good earth. His demeanour was similarly stolid, indeed almost wooden. He ushered Falconer into his presence and bade him take a seat. In similar circumstances, Bek would have kept his visitor standing. Especially William Falconer, whom he had detested as a disruptive element in the good running of the university. De Bosco looked almost pleased to see the troublesome regent master, and he got straight to the point.

'William, Brother Pecham has recommended you as our envoy to Paris. You understand what you are to do there?'

Falconer smiled and nodded.

'Yes, Chancellor.'

Indeed he did know, but it was not to be the errand that de Bosco was sending him on. The chancellor seemed reassured, however, and not a little relieved that he did not have to enter into a taxing discussion of heretical teachings.

'Good, good. And you are not to worry about your teaching duties, nor the good running of Aristotle's Hall. That can all be managed in your absence.'

'But that is my only source of income. If I am not earning it, how am I to fund my journey and sojourn at the university, sir?'

De Bosco waved a dismissive hand and leaned forward with the air of a conspirator. He gleefully whispered in Falconer's ear, obviously loving his new-found powers.

'I have plundered the university chest to pay for you and another master to carry out your task.'

Falconer frowned. Another master? Pecham had not told him that he was to have a companion. Was he then to be spied on?

'Why do I have to have someone travelling with me?'

De Bosco waved his hand again in a gesture that he obviously found quite satisfying.

'It's nothing. I just need someone to . . . erm . . . ensure that no errors are made in the collection of facts concerning the Condemnations. Someone who can act as your scribe.'

And your spy, thought Falconer. Maybe de Bosco was not as dull as he appeared.

'And who is this secretary to be?'

De Bosco grinned broadly.

'I have already spoken to a young man, newly qualified as

master of the university, who would benefit from such a post. He has no living at the moment, so he is more than eager to assist you. He is fresh, and with a sound if rather conventional brain that will suit the purpose perfectly.'

Falconer was beginning to get worried about who this companion might be. It sounded as though he would be saddled with a conservative drudge who would dog his every step and prevent him seeking out Roger Bacon.

'Who is this paragon of virtue, may I ask?'

'Pecham recommended him. He is one of your former students, Master Thomas Symon.'

THREE

Falconer had a spring in his step despite the icy conditions as he returned to Aristotle's Hall after his interview with the chancellor. Pecham had manipulated the entire project. He had ensured that Falconer would have no impediment to his meeting with Roger Bacon by suggesting Thomas Symon to de Bosco. The chancellor, new to Oxford, was completely unaware that the young man was more than a student of Falconer's. He was learning to assist Falconer with the more medical aspects of the murder cases that came the regent master's way. His cool brain could handle the dissection of bodies to try to understand what caused the person's death, where Falconer shied away from this gruesome task of cutting up flesh.

'Let's hope that your skills will not be needed in Paris, though, Thomas,' muttered Falconer to himself as he skipped over the steaming open channel in the middle of the High Street that was the sewer for the town. A mangy cur foraged at the debris that ran down the channel, and even Falconer's passing by did not deter it from its task. 'On the other hand, you had better hone your writing skills, if you are to record what Roger tells me.'

Having hurried down Grope Lane, and past the brothels that lined the narrow passage, he turned left into St John Street and was soon outside the narrow frontage of Aristotle's Hall. Next to it stood the dingier and more ramshackle Colcill Hall. Here, Thomas Symon lodged with a handful of other impecunious masters still seeking a place in the university and a living of their own. Before returning home, Falconer decided to call in at Thomas's abode and speak to his newly appointed travelling companion. He found him seated at a table in the shabby hall, soaking stale bread in ale to make it more toothsome.

'You will have no more need of such plain fare, Master Symon. We shall soon be living off the fat of the land. French land.'

The young man beamed happily at Falconer, already knowing of his appointment. But still he exercised a note of caution.

'Will there be a stipend from the chancellor?'

'A small one. Perhaps enough to allow a little goose dripping to be spread on your stale bread.'

Symon asked Falconer when they might begin their journey, and whether the bad weather might hamper them. Falconer, looking around the gloomy hall and noting the absence of a fire to take the chill off the air, suggested they had best start soon.

'Before you freeze to death trying to break the ice on the top of your ale. I had forgotten how an impecunious master begins his tenure at the university.'

Symon nodded gravely.

'I will not have much in my saddlebags besides a few texts, and pen and parchment. All the clothes I have you see on my back.' He paused, and with an innocent look asked another question of Falconer. 'Shall I also pack my knives?'

Falconer thought of the cruelly sharp instruments that the young man used to dissect bodies. He had inherited them from Richard Bonham when the quiet little master had died of typhus after being careless with one of his dissections. He had also inherited the man's obsession with studying how the human body worked. Falconer nodded briefly.

'There is, after all, a medical school in Paris. You may learn a lot while we are there.'

Symon did not say that he had suggested he take the knives because murder and the need to examine bodies seemed to follow William Falconer around. He saw no reason why the University of Paris should be any different. Falconer continued developing their plans.

'We will spend a day or two settling our affairs here, and then begin. Monday will be a good day.'

Symon ruefully thought that his affairs would take less than a day or two to arrange. His absence would be hardly noted. But he agreed to Monday as a start for their journey to Paris. It would give him time to hone his knives.

The Feast Day of St Adrian of Canterbury, the Ninth Day of January 1273

It was the day to begin their journey, and Falconer had arranged for the horses to be readied by the innkeeper Halegod at the Golden Ball Inn. He was relieved to see that the dirty, close-packed snow in the streets of Oxford was beginning to melt. Their journey would be long and arduous enough without having to plough through snowdrifts. But as he hurried back towards Aristotle's to collect his saddlebags, the skies turned grey, and a new sprinkling of snow began to fall. He made haste to avoid being caught in another blizzard.

Pushing through the door, he was surprised to find a heavily built figure hunched over the fire in the communal hall. Falconer might have been worrying about travelling through snow, but the large man, whose back was now turned to Falconer, had clearly made his way through it easily enough. A scattering of flakes was thawing off the thick fur collar of his cloak, and his boots were caked with melting snow. Peter Mithian and Tom Youlden, two of his clerks who would now be under the tutelage of John Pecham, stood on the other side of the fire, clearly overawed by the visitor. The bulky figure, enveloped in his cloak and fur hat, which also had its share of the latest snowfall stuck to it, turned to face Falconer. From the furry depths a drawn and ageing face peered out. Falconer was surprised.

'Sir Humphrey Segrim! What brings you here?'

Falconer thought it unusual that Segrim had made this effort to call on him. After all, the man who now stood before him had long believed that Falconer's relationship with his late wife had been more than a friendly one. And Ann's refusal to dispel his doubts, claiming her husband's suspicion was too base to refute, had not improved matters. When Falconer had then been accused of her murder, Segrim must have assumed the worst about their relationship. Even to have a man other than Falconer found guilty of the deed had not cleared his doubts away.

Falconer had not seen Sir Humphrey since the day of Ann's death. Rumour had it that he had buried himself in his manor, the snowstorms only putting the final icy seal on his self-incarceration. Now he stood in Aristotle's Hall facing the very man he could never bring himself to speak to during his wife's life. Falconer observed that his visage, too long hidden indoors, was the colour of uncooked pastry, and just as flaccid and soft. His eyes were dark pools showing no spark of emotion. But his furrowed brow, half hidden by the fur bonnet he wore, betrayed an uncommon level of unease and uncertainty. His lips flapped soundlessly a few times before he could form the words he needed.

'I need to know more about Ann's death.'

Falconer waved his arms at the bunch of students who hovered behind his visitor, agog at what might now be said. Reluctantly, they retired into the cubicles at the rear of the hall which formed their sleeping quarters. The fire did not heat these small boxes so well, and they would be cold. But Falconer sensed that the conversation he was to have with Segrim would best be in private. His clerks would have to get their warmth from hiding under the coverings on their truckle beds. He invited Segrim to sit on one of the rickety chairs beside the open hearth, but the old man chose to pace restlessly around the room. Falconer sat anyway, and asked Segrim what more did he want to know about the matter.

'I know what was said about the man who it is believed murdered my wife, but I cannot put out of my head that damned Templar.'

Falconer sighed. So that was what all this was about. The Templar – Odo de Reppes. Segrim had travelled to the Holy Lands recently with a Templar, who the old man thought had been involved in an intricate plot to murder members of King Henry's family. Odo de Reppes had indeed shared in the crazy murder a year or so earlier of Henry, son of Richard, King of Germany, and nephew to the old King of England, while he was at prayer in Viterbo. On the infamous day, Sir Humphrey had found himself at the back of the church, packed out with noblemen who were seeking to speak to Henry. So all Segrim got to see was the back of a distant figure, kneeling before the altar. Then all Hell had broken loose.

A group of armed men had stormed up the aisle, swords in hand. They had hacked Henry to pieces. Three of the men were later identified as Simon and Guy de Montfort and Count Rosso, father-in-law to Guy. It was assumed then that the deed was revenge for the death of the de Monforts' father, Simon de Montfort, at the Battle of Evesham, seven years before. But as the murderers left the church, running out the way they had come, one of them turned to briefly stare at Sir Humphrey. A pair of cold green eyes shone from behind the full-face helm. Segrim had been convinced it was the Templar. Now he embellished his story.

'On my return journey from the Holy Lands, the Templar pursued me by sea and land for months on end, until I thought I had eluded him at Honfleur.'

The mention of the French port hit a nerve with Falconer. It was there he assumed Saphira Le Veske still resided. She had gone there on business and had not returned. It had been some months now, and Falconer hoped to be able to track her down once he was in France. If Roger Bacon gave him the time to do so. He tried to get his mind back on Segrim's story, as the old man went on.

'Then, after crossing the Channel, I next saw him in Berkhamsted the very day young Henry's father – Richard, King of Germany – died. And the Templar saw *me*. That is why I went into hiding in Oxford town before daring to return home. And why I still think Ann was murdered by or at the behest of the Templar because he was afraid she had been told of the conspiracy by me.'

Segrim's face was ashen, and he groaned.

'It was my fault Ann was killed.'

Falconer stood up and grasped Segrim by his shoulder.

'No, Sir Humphrey, it was not your fault. If anything, it was mine. It was an act of revenge against me.'

Sir Humphrey's dark and troubled eyes gazed into Falconer's. He shook his head.

'No. I cannot rid myself of the idea of the great conspiracy. I have tried to find Odo de Reppes, but the commander at Temple Cowley is tight-lipped about the man. You know how the Templars close ranks and protect their own. It leaves me with a feeling of deep suspicion.'

'But what can I do for you, Sir Humphrey?'

'I have heard that you plan to travel to Paris. Talk to the Grand Master of the order for me. Find out the truth.'

Falconer would have protested that he was unable to carry out this request. He was supposed to be in Paris to learn about the implications for the teaching in Oxford of Bishop Tempier's

Condemnations. And secretly he was to talk to Roger Bacon
– something which would be very difficult to arrange in itself.
On top of all that, he had a personal desire to find Saphira.
Now Segrim was asking him to meet Brother Thomas Bérard,
Grand Master of the Order of the Poor Knights of the Temple
of Solomon. He hesitated, but not for long. Segrim's face
showed a deep yearning for the truth, and Falconer could not
deny it to him. Besides, he might not know the Grand Master,
but he did have a close friendship with Guillaume de Beaujeu,
Templar and Preceptor of the Kingdom of Sicily. If Falconer
could not get the truth from the Grand Master, then he might
from one who was almost as important a man in the order.
As long as Guillaume was in Paris also.

'I will do as you ask, Sir Humphrey. But what I learn may
have no bearing on Ann's death. Nor relieve any sense of guilt
you feel.'

Segrim took Falconer's hand and shook it.

'That will be for me to decide when you tell me what you
have found out. Thank you.'

Falconer watched as the old man stumbled, stoop-shouldered,
out into the snow. He had had precious little sympathy for
the man when Ann had been alive, knowing how badly he
treated her. Now he felt nothing but pity for the lonely figure
returning to an empty manor lost in the snow. But he had no
more time to ponder on Segrim's request, for the ever-
exuberant Thomas Symon burst through the door of Aristotle's.

'Was that Sir Humphrey Segrim I saw? What did he want
here?'

Falconer bent down to pick up his saddlebags.

'Yes, it was Sir Humphrey, and I will tell you what he
wanted as we ride for Dover. We had better make a start before
the weather becomes too bad. We have at least a week of
travel before we reach the coast. Ten days, perhaps, if the
snow gets any worse. And then the crossing will depend on
the state of the weather. We may have to wait a long time,
but you can use it to learn some Dutch, which you will need
in Calais. And from there to Paris could take as much as
another month.'

Thomas made a quick calculation in his head.

'Then we may get to Paris by the Feast Day of St Albinus
of Brittany. That would be appropriate.'

'Hmm. The beginning of March. Perhaps, if we are lucky. If not, it may even be the Feast of St Hugh. All Fools' Day.'

The two travellers laughed, hoisted their bags on their shoulders and began their long pilgrimage.

FOUR

Paris, May 1273

Edward finally reached Paris, where he came to do homage to the French King Philip for the lands he held in Gascony. He stood at the window of his guest apartments in the Royal Palace on the island that sat in the middle of the River Seine. He watched as the waters were split by the end of the Ile de la Cité. It felt like standing in the prow of an enormous ship barging its way downstream to the English Channel. He sighed deeply. The burdens of kingship were beginning to feel heavier on his shoulders the closer he came to England. Which might begin to explain why his progress from the Holy Lands had been so slow. He had spent some carefree and pleasure-filled months in Sicily and Italy, and had taken joy in fostering the myth of Eleanor's part in his rescue from the Assassin in Acre. It had begun at the banquet laid on by Charles of Anjou in Sicily.

After sampling some of the crane bird meat suggested by his wife, Edward had turned to her and whispered in her delicate ear.

'Why do we have to sit with this man? He was diverted by a mere storm from continuing the Crusade after Louis' death. He left me to campaign on my own.'

Eleanor stroked his hand.

'You should feel sorry for him. Look at his wife.'

She inclined her head to Charles's rather plump and sour-faced spouse, who was sitting further down the table. Edward laughed.

'You are right. But, if I had a wife like that, I would not have hurried back from combat so quickly.'

Eleanor joined in his laughter, rousing the curiosity of Charles, who sat the other side of Edward.

'What amuses you, Edward?'

Edward grinned mischievously.

'I was reminding Eleanor of her prompt action when the

Assassin stabbed me in Acre. She did not hesitate to lay her pretty lips on the wounds and suck the poison from me.'

He looked at the smiling face of his wife, admiring the full red lips to which he referred. She, meanwhile, put on a solemn look. In fact, she had been carried weeping from the room when she saw him covered in blood after the attack, the wounds already beginning to turn black with poison. But Edward was into his stride, and embellished the story, which later was to precede them across Europe.

'Yes, she sucked it from my many wounds, and spat it on the floor, not caring for her own safety. Would you not like your wife to have done similar?'

Charles looked down the table at his wife's thin lips, topped with the suspicion of a moustache. He smiled wanly and turned back to his other guests. Edward cheerfully shovelled more crane meat into his mouth.

The next time he heard the story retold had been in Burgundy. The Count of Châlons had challenged him to a tourney while he was still in Italy. As a responsible king and crusader, he should have declined. As a man still in his prime, and mindful of the burden he was facing back in England, he accepted. Making sure he called many barons and earls to be at his side when he reached Châlons, he was ready. It had been just as well. There had been a feast the night before the tourney at which the count asked if it was true what he had heard about the attempt on Edward's life.

'And what was that?' asked Edward with a faint smile on his lips.

'That your wife struck the assailant down with the tripod stand of a table.'

Edward maintained a straight face at the obvious and extreme exaggeration of the story he himself had begun. The very thought that the slender Eleanor could have lifted the heavy metal tripod off the ground at all was to him ridiculous. But he was happy to allow the myth to grow.

'Oh, indeed. She may appear a small and weak woman, but childbearing has strengthened her beyond imagination. She lifted the tripod and brained the man.'

The count's eyes widened, and he looked at Eleanor with fresh admiration. Soon Edward could see that the story was being repeated along the table among the count's guests.

He felt a sudden sharp pain in his ankle, and he turned to look at his wife.

'My dear, why did you kick me?'

Eleanor made a moue with her lips.

'Because you are beginning to make me sound like a muscly Amazon from the legends.'

Edward leaned towards her.

'That is because you are a legend, my dear. And don't forget the tales say the Amazons bared their breasts in battle.'

He felt the sharp pain in his ankle again.

The next day the count had singled him out during the fray and had tried to drag him from his horse. The fighting, which was supposed to have been a display of chivalry, became serious. It was only the fact that Edward had his barons by his side in numbers that had saved the day. Edward miraculously escaped with hardly a scratch.

Now, in Paris, he began to wonder if there had been a more sinister motive to the affray. He thought back over the recent attempt on his own life in Acre. And the members of his own family who had died in the last few years, beginning with his eldest son, John. Too many deaths to let things lie. There were matters here to resolve, but he didn't yet know how to begin.

William Falconer hurried through the Porte St-Victor and made his way through the narrow streets of Paris towards the Franciscan friary near Porte St-Germain. He had news that at last permission had been given for Roger to see him. It was about time. He and Thomas Symon had been in Paris for almost two months now, and Falconer was tired of endless debates with the French masters about Aristotle and Bishop Tempier's rulings. Just before learning of Roger, his latest encounter had been with Girard d'Angers in the cloister of the Abbey of St Victor that very morning. The tall, etiolated master had bristled at Falconer's accusation of his succumbing to conservative oppression over his teaching of Aristotle.

'How dare you! Do you not agree with Bishop Tempier that Aristotle must be wrong to assert that the world is eternal, when we know God created the world? Or that God does not know things other than Himself.'

Falconer had snorted and turned away from the skinny cleric. In truth, he could not deny that it was an insidious pressure

that the Church was putting the teachers at Paris under. If any
of them were found to have knowingly taught any one of the
thirteen propositions that Tempier had banned, the master could
suffer automatic excommunication. And the threat of the
Inquisition if he persisted. But Falconer's intellectual rigour
was offended by the craven nature of such as Master d'Angers
at the university. He came back at the man like a ravenous
dog savaging a bone.

'Your bishop also denies Aristotle's proposition that human
acts are not ruled by the providence of God. Do you agree
with him?'

D'Angers, with a face like thunder, stood his ground.

'Naturally.'

Falconer smiled sweetly at the springing of his trap.

'Then tell me if the death of that young student yesterday
was an act to be found within God's providence.'

It was fortunate that, at that very moment, Thomas Symon
came scurrying along the covered cloister of the abbey. Or
Falconer may have said something that got him further into
trouble. D'Angers wasn't above passing on this conversation
to those who would be less tolerant of this English master's
intemperance. Even though Thomas Symon, as scribe to
Falconer's meetings with the Paris masters, had not been
present at this informal dispute, its content could still be
reported. But now it seemed that Thomas had news for his
master, and he drew Falconer away from d'Angers. As they
retreated along the cloister, the French master tossed his head
and stormed off in the opposite direction. For his part, Falconer
did not regret the intervention.

'Tell me. What have you learned about the dead student?'

He had been unable to resist finding out about the incident
as soon as he had been told of it. Though he was in a foreign
country, and had no authority at the University of Paris, a
suspicious death aroused all the usual instincts in him. He had
required Thomas to ask around, and to listen to the gossip
that no doubt already filled the narrow alleys of the university quarter. But Thomas was now waving away his enquiry.

'William, it is not the murder that I have come to tell you
about. It's Friar Bacon. He has sent a message. He can see
you now.'

'Roger? Then let us go to him'

The streets of the university quarter, which took up most of the city south of the river, were narrow. And the houses' upper floors hung out either side, making the streets like tunnels. Falconer was reminded of the back lanes to the south and east of the main thoroughfares of his home town, Oxford. Except for one specific difference. The streets of Oxford could be muddy and clinging when it had rained. In Paris, the streets had been paved with stones at the order of the old king, Philip Augustus. It made getting about so much easier. The same monarch had built the city walls that loomed over them right now. Once through the gates at Porte St-Victor, Falconer turned towards the Place Maubert with Thomas Symon in hot pursuit of his gangling gait.

The Franciscan friary was across the other side of the quarter that housed the schools and lodgings that made up the university. Paris was more or less split in two by the River Seine, which ran east to west. To the north of the river the commercial city huddled within Philip Augustus's walls. On the south bank sprawled the tentacles of the university. And in the centre of the river lay the beating heart of the city, dominated by the Royal Palace and the great cathedral of Notre-Dame. It was from the top of the cathedral that the boy – Paul Hebborn – had plummeted yesterday.

As Falconer reached the square and turned west towards the convent of the Mathurins, he asked Thomas about the incident.

'The English boy – Hebborn – what do the rumours say about his fall?'

Rendered breathless by the pace of their walk, Thomas did his best to summarize what the students he had spoken to had said.

'For many it is just an accident, though why he came to be at the top of the tower no one could say. But there are some who say he was lured there and pushed off.'

'And did they give any justification for his murder?'

Thomas stopped and shrugged even though it was a pointless gesture as Falconer wasn't looking at him. He was way ahead of Thomas and already crossing the Rue de la Harpe towards St-Cosmé. Thomas lifted the hem of his black robe and scurried on. He had to shout to make himself heard over the bustle and noise of the great avenue.

'Now as for the cause of the murder, you can have as many theories as there are stars in the firmament. Some of them quite gory.'

He had to shoulder his way through a knot of men standing around a game of knuckle bones being played out at their feet. Money was changing hands, and one ruffian elbowed Thomas away, cursing him in such coarse French that the educated clerk hardly understood a word. Thomas held his hands up to the red-faced gambler in a palm-out gesture of peace, and hurried on. Falconer, meanwhile, had reached their destination – the great edifice of the house of the Friars Minor, wherein Friar Roger Bacon was incarcerated. It stood hard by the western wall of the city and was as severe and stark a building as the order could build. The church stood on the road, but it was down the side lane that Falconer went, followed by Thomas Symon, to knock on the door of the friary itself. They were admitted by a solemn-faced friar in a brown robe, who had barred their passage before. Now he did not seem at all surprised that they had come to see Roger Bacon. He simply led them through the cloister to where the friars' individual cells were arrayed. It seemed that, after being stonewalled for two months, the door was to be opened with no explanation for the delay. The friar did indeed indicate a door that already stood ajar on the far side of the cloister, and simply walked away. Falconer walked over, his heart in his mouth, pushed on the door and called out.

'Roger?'

FIVE

Sir John Appleby, fresh from England, was ushered into the presence of his new king. He had not seen Edward for nearly four years, and he was pleased by the manly bearing his monarch seemed to have acquired. Edward had always been tall – hence his nickname 'Longshanks' – but to Appleby's eyes he now had that intangible attribute: presence. The king was standing when Appleby entered the chamber he occupied in the French king's palace on the Ile de la Cité. And his wife Eleanor stood by his side. She too looked every inch a queen – long and slender, but with the shapeliness of a woman who had borne children. He lingered for a moment on her full lips, and thought of the story of them sucking the poison from her husband's wounds. Almost reluctantly, Appleby's eyes turned back on the king. His black hair hung in full swathes either side of his tanned face. The sign of a crusader, who had spent time under the blazing sun in the Holy Lands. His symmetrical features were marred only by that droopy eyelid, which was the mark of his family. The old king had had the same feature also. Edward held his muscular and long right arm out towards Sir John, and when he spoke Appleby detected a slight lisp that he had been unaware of before. But then he had not been this close to the new king when he had been prince.

'Welcome, Sir John. I understand the Archbishop of York and Robert Burnell are anxious to see my return.'

'Indeed, sire, they are keen to shuffle off the responsibilities they have so readily assumed.'

The two men Edward mentioned had assumed the regency of England on the death of Henry of Winchester, and were ensuring a smooth transition of monarchy to his son. In the past, there might have been a power struggle with the one who was to inherit out of the country. Edward had felt confident, though, that all would be well, and he was in no hurry to return. Philip of France had hinted that there was trouble in Edward's holdings in Gascony, and he meant to sort it

out first. The king sat, and indicated that Sir John could do
so too. He was growing in confidence in his new role.

'I am sure they do. But first, tell me of the court and the
goings-on in England. Four years is a very long time.' As
Eleanor poured Sir John some Rhenish wine, Edward leaned
closer to the knight. 'Tell me about my father's death.'

Appleby put on a suitably solemn face and talked of Henry's
last days.

'He bore his illness nobly, sire, and was much distracted
by an Oxford master, who had your father play the part of a
coroner. His late majesty discovered, in the most marvellous
manner, who it was had murdered his wardroper. Of course,
he was guided by this master, who it is said is clever at solving
that most heinous of crimes.'

Thoughtful, Edward leaned back in his chair.

'I would know this man. I may have some business for him,
if he is still at court when I return to England.'

'Oh, you may speak to him sooner than that, sire. The new
chancellor of Oxford University sought leave of the archbishop to send him to the university here. It was on matters
of philosophy that I cannot begin to understand. But what I
do know is that Master William Falconer has been here these
two months already.'

The cell that Falconer and Symon entered was dimly lit by
a single candle, and made even gloomier by the lack of a
window. As Thomas's eyes adjusted to the low light, he
slowly became aware of what was around him. He gasped
in astonishment. The tiny cell was filled with books and
parchments stacked floor to ceiling, and every surface was
covered with the same clutter. Thomas had never seen so
many books outside of one of the monastic libraries in
Oxford. In the centre of this chaos, at a small table where
the solitary candle flickered, sat a tonsured man hunched
over a manuscript. He was busily scribbling and seemed to
be ignorant of their presence. Falconer was less surprised
than his young scribe at such a scene.

'Roger, have you no time to greet an old friend?'

The Franciscan friar paused in his feverish scribbling, laid
down his quill and turned on his stool.

'William, they told me you were in Paris. What took you

so long to come and visit? Did I not make it clear to Pecham how urgent the matter in hand was?'

Falconer looked at his old friend, whom he had not seen for some years. Time has been less kind to Roger Bacon than it has been to me, he thought. The friar's hair was completely white, and his features were drawn and of a pasty hue. He had clearly spent too much time locked in a windowless cell. But behind the pallor, Bacon's eyes sparkled with intelligence. It was the Roger of old, as driven and opinionated as ever. Falconer strode across the small room and hugged Bacon, who had risen stiffly from his stool. Falconer saw that the friar had added a stoop to his catalogue of ageing, but his demeanour was as bright and lively as before. He pushed Falconer out to arm's length and surveyed his friend.

'You have aged, William. I hope your brain has not suffered as much as your face over the years.'

He laughed, and shook Falconer's hand vigorously. Then he saw Thomas hovering in the doorway.

'Who is this? Do you have an acolyte now? He is too young to be anything other than a fresh student.'

Falconer laughed.

'This is Thomas Symon, and he is old enough to be a master of Oxford University. Do not let his boyish looks deceive you. He is well versed in the Quadrivium and Trivium. And he is now broadening his knowledge of medicine here in Paris.'

Thomas blushed as the famous Roger Bacon – Doctor Mirabilis to those who admired his works – examined him closely.

'So William has you dissecting bodies, does he?'

Thomas gasped. His pursuit of understanding how the body worked by means of cutting it open had to be a well-kept secret. Dissecting corpses was strictly forbidden by the Church, except in very specific circumstances.

'How did you . . . ?'

Falconer waved a dismissive hand.

'Roger is prone to wild guesses and speculation in his hunt for knowledge. Tell him nothing, and he will only construct a life history about you from looking deep into your soul.'

Bacon grinned at Thomas.

'If what William says is true, then you might as well tell me the truth in the first place.'

Falconer patted the friar on his shoulder, helping Symon out of his dilemma.

'Thomas is here to help me carry out the task you set me through Pecham. So, to answer your earlier questions, yes, I have been here two months and was despairing of carrying out what you wanted of me. I have been bored stiff having circular debates with scholars too scared to listen to the truth, and Thomas has whiled away his time in one medical school or another. They stopped me seeing you until today, and now they act as if there was no impediment in the first place. What is going on, Roger?'

Bacon grimaced.

'This has been going on since my old comrade, Guy de Foulques, died. When they made him Pope Clement, he took an interest in my work. Eight years ago he asked to see my writings. This was the result.'

He pointed at a cupboard with openwork doors. Inside, Falconer could just make out stacks of parchments that had been roughly stitched together to form three books.

'The first is the *Opus Maius*, covering causes of error, Christian philosophy, languages, mathematics, perspective, experimental science and moral philosophy.'

Bacon pulled a face and indicated the thickness of this first tome.

'It became rather a large work, and I then thought that Clement would not have the time or the patience to read it. So I wrote the *Opus Minus*. A sort of summary.'

Thomas stared at the second tome, which seemed to him almost as thick as the first. Falconer simply laughed out loud.

'You haven't changed, Roger. You could never sift out the essential from the merely interesting.' He then pointed to the last weighty tome. 'And the third book?'

'The *Opus Tertium*.'

'Let me guess. There was so much you omitted from the first and second books, you just had to write it all down in this third volume.'

Bacon looked rueful.

'You are exactly right, as ever, William. I sent them all to the Papal Curia through the agency of one of my students. But hardly had John got there, when Guy went and died. So here they lie, gathering dust.'

He rattled the cupboard doors, showing they were locked.

'I was allowed to keep them, but they are safely locked away beyond my reach. And I was hidden away to gather dust too.' He shuddered. 'William, they forced me with unspeakable violence to obey their will.'

Falconer was alarmed by the change in Roger's voice. Now it was unusually uncertain, his tone wavering. He grasped his friend by both shoulders, as an embarrassed Thomas Symon looked away.

'But now you are free to do as you please again. See – we are here.'

Bacon shrugged.

'But I'm still spied on and suspected of heresy.' He turned back to the table and sat down on the stool again. 'Now, when I set down my thoughts, I am reduced to using cipher.'

Both Falconer and Symon looked over his shoulder at the parchment he indicated. It was the one he had been scribbling on when they arrived. Neither could immediately fathom the orthography, which was made up of simple strokes and curls. The text was dense, and as Bacon had been writing it like a normal language, and not ciphering every letter as he went along, Falconer assumed it was a language of his own creation. But before either visitor could look too closely, the friar nervously covered the text with a blank sheet of parchment. Then he stared at the two men with a serious look on his face.

'But that is not why I asked Pecham to get a message to you, William. I am minded to compile a new compendium of knowledge. And I need a safe way of getting it from inside these walls.'

Falconer frowned at the problem Roger had presented to him. But it was Thomas who immediately saw the means of securing safe passage for Bacon's compendium. And in a way that would give him a task that would please him greatly. He spoke up boldly.

'Have you permission to leave the friary from time to time, Brother Roger?'

Bacon frowned, wondering what the young man intended by the question.

'Yes, of course I may. As long as it is only for a few hours each day.'

Falconer immediately saw what Thomas Symon was proposing. He punched the young man's shoulder with joy.

'Thomas, I think, is suggesting that your own head is the very vessel which can carry your ideas unseen past the portals of this friary.'

Symon nodded eagerly.

'Yes. I have visited a number of the medical schools already, and I could arrange for you to teach at one. Every day, you could come to the school ostensibly to teach, and could dictate what is in your head to me. I have a good, clear hand, and can take down what you say at a reasonable speed.'

Bacon laughed out loud.

'I will be smuggling my encyclopedia out piecemeal.' He shook the young Thomas by the hand, but had a warning for him. 'It will take up much of your time for many months.'

'I have not much else to do. And I will be learning as I write.'

Bacon turned to his old friend Falconer.

'And you, William, what do you propose to do all this time?'

Falconer smiled easily.

'I have tired of my official task – that of understanding Bishop Tempier's Condemnations. I will look into the death of this student who fell from the Notre-Dame tower. After that, I am sure something will come along to keep me busy.'

He was not to know that Sir John Appleby already had orders from King Edward to track down this Oxford master who was adept at solving cases of mysterious death. And so was blissfully unaware that he would soon be embroiled in a labyrinth of mysteries that would tax him to the limits of his brain.

SIX

The streets on the south bank of Paris were almost empty of people. A heavy downpour had driven everyone indoors, and the wet pavements gleamed like pewter, reflecting the dark grey clouds that scudded over the city. Falconer kept under the overhanging eaves for shelter from the rain as he retraced his steps towards St-Cosmé church. He was going in search of the body of Paul Hebborn, the student who had fallen from the top of Notre-Dame Cathedral. He would have preferred to have Thomas with him as he didn't like looking too closely at corpses. But Symon's skills as a scribe were sorely needed by Roger Bacon, so he had left the young man planning his task with the friar. Falconer was short-sighted, and to see anything of significance on the body he would have to don his eye-lenses. He had had these fashioned a number of years ago now, refining the armature that held them on his nose and ears himself. But they were still a cumbersome appurtenance, and he was embarrassed about wearing the device in the presence of strangers. He hoped that the signs on the body would be so obvious that he would have no need of lenses.

Crossing the broad Rue de la Harpe, he turned abruptly down the narrow lane almost opposite the one from which he had emerged. His target was the convent of the Mathurins, an order of monks dedicated to the task of the redemption of captives, particularly those in the Holy Lands. The monks were derisively known as the 'Friars of the Ass', as their rule forbade the monks to travel on horseback. But the Order of the Trinitarians, to give them their proper name, was much favoured by popes and kings. The convent in Paris had eventually become their headquarters, and, as their founder had been a doctor of the university, Paris's medical schools – and corpses – gravitated towards the convent. If the body was to be found anywhere, it would be in the hall of the Convent of St Mathurin. Just before Falconer reached the convent entrance, the heavens opened again, soaking his sturdy black robe thoroughly. He stood in the rounded archway of the main door, shaking the rainwater off his grizzled curls.

'You had better come in and dry off, sir.'

Though Falconer was more used to English vernacular, enough French was spoken in higher circles in England that he could still comprehend the invitation. He peered through the gloomy doorway at the figure silhouetted in the open entrance to the convent. The man was tall and wore the habit of a Trinitarian – a white robe emblazoned with a cross of which the upright was red and the crossbar blue. He ducked through the archway out of the rain.

'Many thanks, Brother. It seems that Paris is as wet as Oxford, though I am thankful for the lack of mud in the streets.'

The monk closed the door behind him.

'Ah, you are a master at Oxford, then, that other hotbed of Averroism.'

He made reference to an interpretation of Aristotle's theories now disapproved of but close to Falconer's own heart. He was about to argue with the monk when he spotted the hint of a smile on the man's lips. He was being teased and refrained from rising to the bait, returning the jibe.

'Not if your bishop has his way.'

The monk laughed and waved his hand dismissively, stepping through a small door set in the thickness of the convent's wall. He quickly re-emerged with a coarse cloth in his hand.

'Here, take this and dry yourself.' He handed the cloth to Falconer, who began to dry himself as the monk carried on talking. 'There are many serious false assertions made by Aristotle, but they will matter little to you if you catch a chill and die.'

Falconer vigorously towelled off his wet hair and face, and replied.

'I could debate with you long and hard about the doctrine of souls and monopsychism, but I fear my errand is more mundane. And not a little melancholy.'

'You have come about the boy.'

It was a statement, not a question, from the monk, who took the wet cloth back from Falconer. William quickly saw that the monk had assumed he had some official status as he was of the same nation as Paul Hebborn. He didn't bother to correct the mistake. It would make seeing the body all the easier, and, after all, he was not lying. He had come to see the boy.

He nodded sadly.

'Yes, I have.'

'He is in the side chapel. Follow me.'

Falconer followed the white-robed monk into the church, his wet boots squelching on the tiled floor. The interior rose high above his head in a series of round arches set on sturdy pillars. Nothing disturbed the silence except the sound of their respective footsteps. They entered one of the side chapels, an ill-lit chamber where the cold made it quite suitable for the storage of a dead body. When the monk stepped aside, Falconer saw the corpse on a bier before the altar. The greyish shaft of light – heavy with dust motes – that filtered through the small circular window above only added to the melancholy scene. The body was shrouded in a white sheet that bore ominous dark stains on it. Reluctantly, Falconer drew the sheet aside. The sight made his gorge rise.

The poor boy's skull had been smashed and his face was distorted by the impact with the ground. But even so, Falconer could discern a look of horror in the bulging eyes, the pupils nothing but dark pools. Mercifully, the broken body was still clad in a particoloured surcoat over a white tunic, held tight by a belt from which hung the boy's purse. The brightness of the surcoat and the red woollen hose that were on Hebborn's legs suggested he was of noble birth. In Paris, as in Oxford, wealthy clerks were at pains to show off their station in life. But still, all his family's wealth had not saved him from a terrible death.

The patient monk whispered something that Falconer did not catch.

'I'm sorry. What did you say?'

'I was asking if you had seen enough. Only it will soon be nones, and I must go and pray for his soul.'

'Indeed.' Falconer paused for a moment, as if moved by the sight of the boy who in fact he had never met. 'I wonder if I may have a moment alone with . . . Paul.'

The white-clad monk bowed his head in acquiescence and silently glided from the chapel. A short while later, Falconer followed him out. In response to the monk's enquiry about the disposition of the body, he hesitated. The Trinitarian monk clearly still imagined he was somehow related to the boy, or acting on behalf of the family.

'I am sure his family will be in touch very soon. Thank you for your time, Brother.'

He hustled out of the convent before any more embarrassing questions could be asked of him. Hidden in his sleeve was the purse that had hung at Paul Hebborn's waist.

'You stole a dead person's scrip?'

Thomas, back from his long session noting down Roger Bacon's thoughts, was sitting opposite Falconer at the long refectory table in St Victor's Abbey. They were taking a modest supper, and though no one else sat close to them his tones were low. But he could still hardly believe what William had said that had caused his outburst. Falconer, for his part, soaked his crust in some ale and shovelled the sweet softness into his mouth. He smiled and swallowed before replying.

'He no longer had any use for it, and it may yet tell us something about his death. I have not yet had chance to look inside it, but we can do that after vespers.'

Symon paled.

'We? So I am to be involved in this sacrilege, am I?'

Falconer leaned across the scarred oak table and took the stale bread that his former student had left in front of him. He held it up questioningly. And when Thomas, with a sigh, ceded the scrap to him, Falconer repeated his previous manoeuvre, and chewed on another ale-soaked crust.

'You know you are as curious as I am about this. You just don't have the nerve to do what I did.'

Thomas shook his head wearily and watched as Falconer rose from the table, wiping his fingers down the front of his shabby black robe.

'Come. Let us return to the abbey guest house and see what we have recovered.'

They left the refectory and walked along the south side of the cloister to the passage that gave out on to the separate buildings that made up the abbey's infirmary and guest quarters. The two of them shared a room there, which in barely two months Falconer had cluttered with all sorts of curiosities and texts. Indeed, it had begun to resemble his own solar back in

Aristotle's Hall in Oxford. Thomas, who preferred tidiness
around him, guessed that it made the regent master feel more
at home in his temporary sojourn in Paris. As for himself, he
felt like an interloper. But he fancied he was such an ascetic
that it shouldn't matter. He could make his home wherever
he could lay his head. And now he was so fired up with his
new task of recording Doctor Mirabilis's thoughts that any
discomfort seemed to pale into insignificance. But he would
have liked to have discussed what the friar had said to him
today after Falconer had left.

'Listen, young Thomas,' said Bacon, 'and I will tell you
about the boundless corruption everywhere. Even the Court
of Rome is torn by the deceit and fraud of unjust men. The
whole Papal Court is defamed of lechery, and gluttony is lord
of all.'

Thomas had gone pale at such words being spoken out loud,
and he was not surprised that the Franciscan order had kept
Bacon under lock and key so long. He had been anxious to
test Falconer with his friend's words. But William was more
intent on examining Paul Hebborn's scrip. He was already
pulling the drawstring and tipping the contents out on to a
space he had cleared on the small table in the centre of the
room.

'Hmm.'

Falconer rummaged in his own purse, extracted his eye-
lenses and put them on. Peering down at the tabletop, he poked
at the scattering of items with a bony finger. There was a horn
spoon, three small coins, a broken comb and a tattered copy
of Priscian's grammar book.

'Not much to go on, is there?'

Thomas agreed.

'It was not worth stealing, after all.'

'I wish you would stop referring to it as stealing. I merely
borrowed the scrip in order to help trace what happened to
the boy.'

'Yes, but it hasn't helped, has it?'

Reluctantly, Falconer had to agree, and he shovelled the
items back into the leather purse.

'I shall have to talk to his master and fellow students
somehow. Though without any authority here, I am not sure
how they will receive me.'

'He was studying medicine, under an Englishman called Adam Morrish near the Petit Pont.' Thomas named the bridge that linked the Ile de la Cité to the university quarter on the south bank of the river. 'I could talk to the students, if you wish. The faculty of medicine has what they call here a dean as its head. He is called Gérard de Osterwiic. I have met him, and he is a most amenable man. He will know all about the individual schools of medicine. And if we are to set up this subterfuge of Friar Bacon teaching at a faculty outside the order's building, it might as well be at the Petit Pont.'

Falconer frowned, seeing that this might cut him out of the process altogether.

'Will you have time to do that, and act as scribe for Roger? That will be your primary task, after all. Perhaps I should speak to this dean.'

But Thomas would not have it. He felt for the first time that he was at the centre of things in Paris, where before he was scurrying at Falconer's shabby boot-heels. And, though neither man knew it then, Falconer would soon find his burden greater than Thomas's. Sir John Appleby was already reckoning to be at the Abbey of St Victor soon after prime on the very next day. Edward was chafing at the bit to speak to the regent master who had served his father in his last days. And to present him with a complex puzzle that he had been thinking about all day. He knew he could make use of this Falconer to serve his own ends. It was just a matter of how he would arrange to have Falconer do his bidding.

SEVEN

William Falconer was never an early riser, and at Aristotle's Hall in Oxford he relied on the students lodging in the hall to have drawn him a bowl of water in the morning. With it he would refresh his face and wake himself up. In the abbey in Paris where he and Thomas were staying, the seemingly incessant chant of the monks at prayer woke him early and kept him awake. It seemed that, no sooner had they completed nocturnes, they were intoning lauds. And hard on the heels of lauds came prime. By then the abbey was already buzzing with activity, and Falconer could not blank out the sound by burying his head. What made it worse was that young Thomas fitted into the routine of the monks so easily. Dawn had barely sneaked its way into their chamber, and Symon was already up and dressed. He cheerfully called out that he was on his way to see Dean Osterwiic, and would then ask around Paul Hebborn's former fellows for information.

'And then I will start my work for Friar Bacon. What do you intend to do with your time, William?'

Falconer groaned.

'I did intend to dissect open a young master of Oxford University. But unfortunately he is still alive.' He grabbed the nearest object to throw at Thomas Symon. He launched it before realizing it was Hebborn's purse. 'Get out of here, and leave me in peace.'

From under his bedclothes, Falconer heard the muffled laughter of his young companion and the slamming of the door. He couldn't sleep, however, because he could think only of the flame-headed Saphira Le Veske. His lover had plagued his thoughts ever since he had arrived in Paris. Even though they were no longer separated by the Channel, he felt as far away from her as ever. Their final disagreement returned again and again in his head. Right from the moment he expressed his concern about her travelling alone, and her indignant retort. She had said he was overbearing, and he had knowingly walked right into the trap.

'And I am just a celibate teacher in holy orders who has no rights over you, I suppose.'

That had made Saphira see red and come up with a heated reply.

'Of course you have no rights over me, William.'

His next thoughtless sentence had sealed his fate. Repeating it over and over in his head did not alleviate the stupidity of it. Nor could it cause it to be retracted.

'Why can't you just do as I say for once?'

For Falconer, the words fell to the ground with just as leaden a weight this morning as they had done months before. He groaned again, understanding at last just what he had done, and swung his bare legs out of the bed. Reaching for his black robe, he pulled it on over his linen undershirt and scrubbed his unshaven face with his calloused hands. Just as he bent down to pick up the purse he had tossed at Thomas, there was a knock at the door. He stuffed the scrip in his own purse and opened the door.

Before him stood a stocky man in his middle years, accoutred in the dress of the English court. He wore a dark-blue cloak over his deep-red surcoat, which was slit up the front to reveal yellow cross-garters over the man's red hose. His greying hair was topped with a blue sugarloaf hat, the brim being turned up in the latest fashion. Falconer smiled at the sight. The man was dressed more gaudily than any of his rich students back in Oxford, but he was far too old to be so garbed. The peacock smiled, and spoke with a West Country accent.

'Regent Master William Falconer? My name is Sir John Appleby, and I am the servant of King Edward. May I speak?'

'Well, sir, it seems you already have.'

The man ignored Falconer's terse rejoinder, and the master could see that this vision in red and blue was not going to be put off by his manner. He stepped aside and beckoned the man in to his cluttered quarters. He was glad that he had at least risen and had not been caught abed. King Edward's messenger entered the cell and cast a judicious eye around the interior. His gaze, when it returned to Falconer, did not betray anything but a bland pleasantness. Falconer asked him his business.

'Why, the king's business, of course. I have a message from His Majesty.'

Appleby gazed around again, looking for somewhere to sit. But discerning no place that was not piled high with books and papers other than the dishevelled bed, he remained standing. He began the speech that Edward had taxed him with learning that very morning.

Edward, as it turned out, was an earlier riser than even Sir John. A result no doubt of his time as a warrior for Christ in the Holy Lands. He had insisted that his messenger should frame his call for Falconer in the form of a request, not a command.

'He must come of his own free will, Sir John, and feel there is no compulsion. He must do what I ask as if he himself wishes it.'

Appleby bowed low.

'Yes, Your Majesty.'

He conned his part in the deception, and was about to leave and carry out his task. But Edward grasped his arm in a vice-like grip. He stared Appleby hard in the eyes, his drooped eyelid appearing to wink.

'But be in no doubt, Sir John, that you must ensure he comes.'

Now Appleby stood before the regent master whom Edward so wanted to see, and wondered why. He saw a tall, powerful-looking man who had gone a little to seed. His broad shoulders, hidden under the loose black robe of an academic, hinted at a past involving the swinging of a broadsword. And his face still had strength in its lined features. But the hair was thinning and grey, and he detected a little rounding to his backbone. Besides, this Falconer looked as though he had just dragged himself out of bed, though it was already terce. Not a man Sir John would employ. But the king knew best, and Appleby had a message to deliver. He did so to the best of his ability, weaving a tale of Edward's desire to know of the last days of his father. But he finished with the words that Edward specifically told him to say.

'Between you and me, Master Falconer, the king has double cause to mourn, what with the death of his father following on from that of his son in somewhat suspicious circumstances. He is troubled in mind and needs reassurance. You can do that for him.'

He rose to leave at that point, but he had already seen the

flicker in Falconer's eyes at the mention of suspicious death. He allowed a small smile to play across his face. He felt he had hooked the man for the king. When he reached the door of the miserable chamber, Falconer spoke up.

'Tell the king I am his servant and will attend him at his pleasure.'

Appleby turned back to the academic.

'Come to the palace this afternoon, and be at the gate close by Ste-Chapelle. I will meet you there.' He extended a hand. 'And thank you, Master Falconer. You will not regret this.'

Falconer inclined his head non-committally and closed the door behind the gaudy courtier. After the man had gone, a big smile lit up his face.

Thomas Symon only found the medical school after a little difficulty. He had first asked one of the monks in the abbey where the school of Adam Morrish the Englishman might be found. Solemnly, the monk had told him in his native French that it was in one of the streets running out from the Petit Pont.

'You cannot miss it, for it is appropriately named for a medical school. The butchery.'

Thomas had thanked him, but didn't see the monk's mischievous smile when he turned his back on him. He made his way up the winding lane that led through the Place Maubert towards the bridge that linked the south bank of Paris with the island on the River Seine. Close by, and not certain which way to turn, he had stopped a passer-by and asked for Butchery Street. The man, carrying a bundle of sticks on his back, took one look at Thomas and spat on the ground at his feet. Puzzled, Thomas found the bridge before he dared ask again. This time he enquired of a rich-looking merchant who was hurrying to cross the bridge on his way north.

'Excuse me, sir. Do you know where Butchery Street is?'

Once again he was waved away with a peremptory gesture. Not sure what he had done wrong, he stopped on the end of the bridge, gazing down at the muddy waters that flowed swiftly beneath. Further along, houses clustered on both sides of the bridge, obscuring the view. A shabbily dressed young man was seated on the parapet, swinging his legs idly over the void. He grinned at Thomas.

'I couldn't help overhear your question, friend. Why do you seek a street that doesn't exist in Paris?'

Thomas frowned, sure that the monk could not have deliberately misled him.

'No, it surely exists. A man called Adam teaches medicine there.'

The shabby youth tilted his head back and roared with laughter, threatening to fall off the parapet with the violence of his seizure. He flicked his long hair out of his eyes and, swivelling round, dropped to the safety of the bridge's floor. He stuck his hand out for Thomas to take.

'You Englishmen may be part Norman, but you mangle our language something awful. My name is Jacques Hellequin. But you may call me Jack.'

He made a great show of speaking the last sentence in what he fancied was courtly English. Thomas took his hand and squeezed it firmly. It was good to meet someone in Paris who did not turn his nose up at the sight of an Englishman.

'It is good to meet you, Jack. I am Thomas Symon from Oxford. But what do you mean about mangling your language?'

Jack's eyes twinkled.

'There is a world of difference between *boucherie* and *bûcherie*. One is indeed an abattoir, but the other is a wood-cutter's shed. Master Adam's medical school is in the street named after the latter. Though, come to think about it, it would be more appropriate if it were in the other. In fact, I can't wait to tell my fellow students of your unintentional pun.'

Thomas silently vowed he would have his revenge in some way on the monk who had set him up to appear a fool.

'You are a student at the school?'

'Yes, I am. You have fallen on your feet with me, Master Symon. I will show you where the school is. But first you must know of the difficult situation that exists there.'

Thomas feigned ignorance of any problem, hoping that his new friend was referring to the very death that he wished to investigate. His young and innocent face, usually an embarrassment to him when he wished to appear wise and knowing, sometimes was an advantage.

'What is that, Jack?'

Jack Hellequin grimaced.

'One of our numbers died the day before yesterday.'

Thomas expressed horror at what might have caused death in a medical school.

'He did not contract some deadly disease that I might catch too?'

'No, indeed.' Jack squeezed Thomas's arm reassuringly. 'You could not die of the same cause. Unless you too threw yourself off the tower of Notre-Dame.'

'Ah, yes. I heard tell of that poor unfortunate. Threw himself off, you say? I heard it said he was pushed.'

Jack's brow clouded over, and he seemed to stumble a little in his progress down Rue de la Bûcherie.

'Who told you that? That is a foul thing to say. No, the truth was that Paul was a tortured soul who did not fit in well with the rest of us. He was English, and the rest of us are either French, Norman or Picard. And though our master is English too, Paul kept to himself a lot. He was a misfit.'

Thomas was about to question this analysis of the dead youth's behaviour while alive, but his guide stopped in the street in front of a nondescript house in the row of tenements that made up Rue de la Bûcherie, each with its back to the river. Jack Hellequin made an extravagant gesture towards the crumbling façade.

'And here is that great seat of learning – Master Adam Morrish's medical school.'

Thomas held back his eagerness for more information and followed Jack through the portal.

EIGHT

The gateway giving access to Ste-Chapelle and the Royal Palace was closely guarded. And the Frenchman in his royal livery stared suspiciously at William Falconer when he presented himself. He was even more surly when he heard the master's English accent. But finally he was persuaded to send a message to the English court sojourning in the guest quarters of King Philip's palace. From the fixed stare he got from the guard, Falconer could only imagine the man disbelieved such a shabby individual as himself had any business with the glittering courts of the two kings. However, he had to allow Falconer through the gate when the gaudily clad Appleby came to meet him. Though the guard's puzzlement was only increased by the apparently friendly exchange between such opposites. Who could fathom the English and their wardrobes?

Falconer was led into the palace by Sir John Appleby and through a maze of rooms and corridors. All the time, Sir John prattled on about how remarkable the king was, and how he admired his maturity and good sense. Falconer nodded politely, only half listening to the courtier. He had met his sort before, when he had been summoned into the presence of the old king, Henry, who had died last year. The ailing monarch had been surrounded by men who jumped at his every whim, and doctors who were afraid to tell him he was dying. The powerful very rarely heard the truth from those in their presence. Falconer had been an exception, and Henry had seemed to relish the cut and thrust of their arguments over who had killed the king's wardroper, and why. The Oxford master resolved he would behave exactly the same when he met Henry's son, the new king. Then he realized Appleby had asked him a question.

'I'm sorry, Sir John, my hearing must be getting as bad as my eyesight. What did you say?'

'I was saying that you should show respect in the king's presence and refer to him as Your Majesty. He is only just growing into his new role, and he is not as secure in it as his father was. After all, Henry of Winchester ruled for more than fifty-six years, and . . .'

Falconer abruptly interrupted.

'And saw off a rebellion of his barons. Yes, I know. But Edward himself was a canny operator. He was clever enough to switch sides back and forth in the Barons' War. I doubt he is as vulnerable as you think.'

Appleby pulled a face.

'Hmm. Be that as it may. He is your monarch, so don't remind him of his switching of allegiance. He now professes to love his father.' He stopped to eye up Falconer's appearance. 'What a pity you could not bring yourself to dress more appropriately. Still, he may appreciate your humble garb for what it is.'

Though making the best of Falconer's one and only outer garment, the courtier could not resist flicking away some of the grime on his shoulder. He then pulled the jaunty sugar-loaf hat off his own head, straightened his surcoat and knocked on the studded oak door that they stood before. A voice ushered them in, and Sir John opened the door, leading Falconer into the room.

Falconer's first impression of Edward was of his height. But he was broad-shouldered too. His time in the Holy Lands had developed him as a fighter, and even Falconer had heard the tale of his recent exploits at the tourney in Châlons. Having stared at the king for some time, while Sir John announced him, Falconer realized Edward was assessing him too. He felt embarrassed, knowing his age was beginning to tell and that he was more than a little ragged around the edges. But when Edward spoke, he was reassured.

'I can see there is a fighting man under that dowdy scholar's robe, Master Falconer. Your shoulders tell me that you once wielded a sword, and you have not allowed the years to deprive you of your strength.'

Falconer felt childishly pleased by Edward's recognition of his former life as a mercenary soldier. He had indeed spent his youth fighting wars across Europe. Until he had become sickened by the carnage. A horror that had grown to be greater than he had revelled in the chance being a mercenary had given him to see the world. The University

of Bologna had been the turning point in his life, where he
had begun again to devote himself to the world of scholarship.
But the king was correct in his second surmise. He had tried
to keep himself fit, considering it important to keep his body
as sharp as his brain. However, he shook his head in regret.

'Sadly, Majesty, the years are beginning to take their toll,
and I am not as vigorous as I was.'

'And yet your mind is not affected. Sir John tells me you
have solved many intractable cases of murder in and around
Oxford. Please sit.'

Falconer had the presence of mind to allow the king to sit
before taking up the invitation to be seated himself. Sir John
snapped his fingers, and a servant materialized with a jug of
the best Rhenish, which he proceeded to pour into two goblets.
Falconer thought of Saphira Le Veske, and her task in Honfleur
of sorting out the family wine business. But his distracted
thought was only fleeting, as the king was already embarking
on a story of strange and terrible deaths that drew Falconer
in. As he drank the red wine, Falconer listened closely to the
tale. Then he had some questions to ask.

'You say the attempt on your life was in June of 1272?'

'Yes, by a servant called Anzazim, who was a local man
but one who had proved himself loyal to me until that moment.'

'And your uncle Richard, King of Germany, died in the
April of the same year.' Edward nodded, and Falconer
continued. 'But it could not have been the same person
involved, as the two incidents were thousands of miles apart.'

'I understand that. But I was not thinking of the person
carrying out the deed when I asked you to investigate. Anzazim
and whoever else it was were merely weapons wielded by
someone in the shadows.'

'But was Richard's death murder? He had had a stroke and
had been suffering from the half-dead disease for months.
Could his demise not have been entirely natural?'

'Yet all the reports I had later said he was recovering. Why
did he suddenly die at that particular time, and so close to
the attempt on my life? And as both were only a year since
the outrage in Viterbo that involved the de Montforts, it leaves
me deeply suspicious.'

'Yes. I agree that the death of Henry of Almain, Richard's son,
was clearly a case of murder, and one where the perpetrators are

known. Everyone in the Church of St Silvester witnessed it. Guy and Simon de Montfort are known to be the killers. So what can I add to that case?'

Edward sighed.

'Nothing more, I suppose. But isn't it an indication of who might have been involved in the other murders? Including that of my eldest son?'

'Ah, yes. John, who died in Berkhamsted in the August of the same year, 1271.'

Falconer detected a wavering in Edward's voice as he mentioned his one-time son and heir, John. Though he had no children of his own, Falconer could guess how cruel the death of a child could be. Even in a time when death was the natural bedfellow of birth. It was known that Edward and Eleanor had lost three daughters before John had been born. But they had all died either stillborn or as tiny infants. Life was precarious in the first years of any child's existence. John had lived to a robust five years before his untimely death. And while in the care of his uncle Richard too. Could all these cases have a common thread? Falconer chose his next words carefully.

'Majesty, I know this is hard for you, but you must realize in each of these cases the corpse is a long time cold in the ground.' He heard Sir John wince at his apparent harshness, but he pressed on. 'And the threads of truth that will need to be picked out are equally cold and buried deep. Where do you think I could possibly start?'

Edward sat upright in his chair, drawing on a mantle of majesty.

'You can dig wherever you wish, Master Falconer. Sir John has a letter signed by me that gives you authority to question who you will from the highest to the lowest. Many of the men who surround me will have been present during at least one of these . . . incidents. And you may have as long as it takes to uncover the truth. Do it for John's sake, if no one else's.'

The king clicked his fingers, and Appleby gave Falconer a folded parchment that was to be his pass to all areas of the king's life. Edward then rose from his chair and held out his hand. Falconer too got up and took his king's hand, before retiring from the room. After the regent master had gone, Edward looked at Appleby, a big grin on his face.

'I think that went well, don't you, Sir John?'

Appleby nodded eagerly.

'Indeed, sire. I think you pointed him in the right direction.'

Thomas was making good progress in his search for information about Paul Hebborn. While the students of Adam
Morrish sat in the gloomy schoolroom waiting for their master,
they chatted idly with him. Three of them had known Hebborn
quite well, even though the boy had been quite stand-offish.
Geoffrey Malpoivre, a stocky but elegantly dressed individual,
suggested that Hebborn had been encumbered by his stammer.

'He could hardly get a single word out without tripping
over it. It made him awkward and reluctant to mix with the
rest of us. I tried to draw him into our circle, but to no avail.'

'So you are of the opinion that he took his own life.'

Malpoivre shrugged his shoulders and spread his hands in
a Gallic gesture Thomas was beginning to recognize. It
suggested a fatal resignation.

'What other conclusion could you come to?'

A lively youth called Peter de la Casteigne could not resist
chipping in.

'The story is that he was pushed, though. You all know how
John Fusoris teased him. He made Paul's life a misery.'

Jack Hellequin raised a cautionary hand.

'You can't go around saying things like that. Fusoris is not
here to defend himself, and to all intents and purposes you
are accusing him of murder.'

'Who is being accused of murder?'

The tone of the voice was commanding, and all, including
Thomas, turned to look at who had spoken. In the doorway
of the room stood a slight figure of a man, silhouetted by the
daylight filtering in from outside. Thomas could not make out
his features as only one candle burned in the room itself. But
his guess that this was Master Adam Morrish was confirmed
when Jack Hellequin stepped forward and spoke up.

'Master Adam, we were merely having an exchange of
views about Paul's death. Idle speculation on our part. Nothing
serious.'

Adam Morrish stepped into the room and closed the door
behind him. As he stood in the light cast by the flickering candle,
Thomas was able to make out his features better. His hair was

short and cut in a clerical tonsure, which, added to his thin and boyish features, gave him the appearance of someone no older than his students. But Thomas knew that, if this man had obtained a degree in medicine, he had to be at least in his late twenties. And observing the knowing and curious look that was now cast his way, Thomas guessed Adam was actually older than he seemed. He took a step towards the man, his hand extended.

'Master Adam, I am Thomas Symon from the University of Oxford. If you will allow it, I would like to listen to your lectures on medicine. It is a subject I am most interested in myself.'

The man took Thomas's hand in the lightest of grips, and the contact was so fleeting that Thomas was unsure whether he had grasped a man of flesh or a wraith. A secretive smile crossed Morrish's face.

'It will be good to have another Englishman present.' He turned towards his students. 'Here, I am plagued by Picards, Normans and French.'

The young men in the room sniggered and nudged each other. Morrish clearly held his class in the palm of his hand. While the mood was still genial, Thomas decided to test out Morrish's opinion on his late student's demise.

'Do you think it was idle speculation . . . to suggest Paul Hebborn's death was murder?'

The smile on Morrish's lips froze for a moment, and Thomas was aware of an icy look in the other man's deep-set eyes. Then, as suddenly as it came, the cold look disappeared. Morrish was all geniality again.

'Master Symon, you must know how students like to gossip. I dare say it is not long since you were a student yourself.'

Thomas Symon blushed at the truth of Morrish's veiled rebuke, but he held his tongue. Morrish filled the silence with his opinion on the matter.

'I regret not seeing that Paul was unhappy here. I was so absorbed in my teaching that I did not see he had not fitted in with this crowd of reprobates.' He waved his arm at the still-grinning group of youths. 'There was no doubt some gentle ribbing taking place. Perhaps it got too hurtful for him to bear. I blame myself for not being aware of that. Paul was a terrible stammerer, which I put down to his shyness. I tried to cure him of it, but to no avail.'

'But to throw himself off the top of Notre-Dame . . . Wasn't that a little extreme?'

Morrish smiled at Thomas, who felt he was now being treated as a child. A nuisance who was to be indulged only so far and no further.

'He found solace in the cathedral, and could be found there most evenings. It is no surprise to me that it was the site of his death. Now, if you will permit me, it is time to begin my lectures.'

Morrish abruptly turned his back on Thomas and left him to slide like a naughty child into a place on the back row of benches set out for his students. Soon they were immersed in the *Isagoge of Johannitius*.

NINE

'Ah, the *Isagoge of Johannitius*, who was known in the Arab world as Husain al-Ibadi.'

'He was a Muslim, then?'

'No, he was Christian, but he was the director of the caliph's House of Wisdom in the ninth century. His knowledge is all based on Galen, mind you. And I bet you can't wait until you progress to the Byzantine text on urines by Theophilus.'

Thomas smiled broadly at Falconer over the refectory table. Conversation was not forbidden in the abbey, but the content of their discourse was a little eccentric. One of the monks seated next to them was staring at them with distaste written large on his features. Thomas endured Falconer's teasing.

'You can mock us medical people and our obsessions with the waste products of the body. But be careful. When next you want a corpse examined for a cause of death, I shall leave it up to you to delve inside the carcass.'

Falconer shuddered at the thought, as did the monk who was following their banter with horror.

'You are right, Thomas. You butchers do have your uses.'

Falconer's reference to Thomas's facility with knives reminded him of the monk who had set him on the wrong track that morning. He still owed the man a trick in return for his misleading guidance to Butchery Street. The medical school could have been easily found with the right directions, but at least Thomas's confusion had resulted in his striking up a friendship with Jack Hellequin.

After Adam's lectures had finished, he had walked with him down to the bottom of the street. There, the narrow houses, stacked cheek by jowl, ended, and a view opened up of the River Seine. A few small rowing boats were drawn up on the muddy bank, and he and Jack sat on an upturned one. It was the first time that Thomas had realized that right across on the opposite bank was the massive bulk of Notre-Dame Cathedral. From the back of the school, it was clearly possible to see the towers, from one of which Paul Hebborn had fallen to his death.

'You are thinking of Paul.'

Jack's observation startled Thomas for a moment. Was he that obvious? If he was to be anywhere as good as William in winkling out truths relating to murder, he would have to wear a more veiled visage. Still, he could use the situation to find out more about the dead youth.

'Yes, I was. Was it true what Geoffrey Malpoivre said, that Paul was a misfit?'

Jack looked at the muddy earth at their feet, poking it with a stick he had picked up.

'Don't believe everything that Geoffrey tells you. He likes to think of himself as the leader of our little group. And, God knows, he has the money to permit him the right. Most of the others fawn over him in the hope of a free drink at the tavern every night.'

'But you don't.'

Jack shook his head sadly.

'Don't imagine I'm a paragon of virtue, either. I am poor enough to be grateful for Geoffrey's beneficence too. And I can fawn with the best of them to gain that. But I don't blind myself to his overbearing manner. As for Paul, he didn't fall under Geoffrey's spell, either. And it's true that he was outside the magical circle somewhat. You must understand that the university is divided into four nations. The French Nation predominates, but those from Rouen make up the Norman Nation, while those in the north who speak Flemish and some French are the Picard Nation.'

'And the fourth is the English Nation?'

'Yes, including German and Slavic speakers. They are very much in the minority, and I suppose that is how Paul felt. One among many. But to get back to my original point, don't imagine that Geoffrey Malpoivre is all generosity and under-standing. He was just as capable as any of us of teasing Hebborn unmercifully for his stammer. Only Master Adam seemed to sympathize with his difficulties.'

Thomas looked at Jack, who was still scratching the mud into random shapes with his stick. The young man sometimes seemed very old to him.

'Your master is a generous man, then?'

'Adam? Oh, yes, he is generous. If he takes to you.'

Thomas had wanted to tell Falconer all that he had learned.

But after dinner William seemed distracted and full of his own concerns. Thomas lit a candle in their shared room and sat on the end of his bed.

'I could tell you something about Paul Hebborn, but you look as if you are bursting to tell a story of your own, master.'

Falconer sat on one of the low stools and looked at Thomas with surprise.

'Either I am getting more obvious with age, or you are becoming more perspicacious, Thomas Symon. I will allow that it is your greater wisdom, if only because it then does not mean I am weakening as I grow older. And less of the master, if you please. You are Master Thomas in your own right now, and an equal. Almost.'

'Then, William, tell me what is on your mind.'

Falconer pulled his stool closer to Thomas, causing the legs to screech on the stone flags.

'You will not believe who I spoke to today. But our conversation was an uncanny echo of a tale told us last year in Oxford.'

Thomas was lost already, and his puzzled look pleased Falconer no end. He could still perplex his young and eager companion, despite his apparent mental decline over the years. He decided to stretch out the agony a little more first.

'But you are right. Your investigations into the death of Paul Hebborn take precedence. Tell me what you have found out. Oh, and did you arrange for Roger Bacon to meet you at the school of Adam Morrish?'

'I did speak to Master Adam about using a room in his school, and that in return I could arrange for a very great scholar to teach there. He was curious as to who it could be, but said I could use the room anyway. There is a downstairs room at the back that is too small to teach in, but I could use it. I looked it over. It was dirty and damp – the house backs on to the river. But it will serve.' Thomas paused enough from his outpouring to say what was really on his mind. 'Now for God's sake tell me who you have been speaking to, and what your reference to a tale from last year is all about before I burst with curiosity.'

Falconer burst out laughing.

'Then I will tell you. Do you remember the strange story Sir Humphrey Segrim told us?'

'About the Templar knight who pursued him across the world to the Holy Lands and back?'

'That is it. He thought the death of Ann, his wife, was because he knew of a complex conspiracy to murder. And the Templar was trying to make sure Segrim and his wife, whom he might have told, never revealed the truth.'

'But we found that to be a fantasy when we uncovered who really killed Mistress Segrim.' Thomas paused uncertainly. 'Didn't we?'

'We revealed that it had nothing to do with Ann's death, yes. But we didn't prove either way that what Segrim believed as true was not the case. It simply became irrelevant.'

Falconer pulled the flagon of beer that stood on the table towards him. He poured two generous servings in pewter jugs and drank deep from one before continuing. Thomas took the other jug, sipped, and returned it to the table as Falconer spoke again.

'Strangely enough, Sir Humphrey came to me before we left Oxford and begged me to find out if there was any truth in the tale. And to find out about the fate of the Templar.'

'Odo de Reppes? He just disappeared, didn't he? The Templars are good at that. Dealing with their own.'

Falconer nodded and drank from his jug again.

'You are right. He did disappear. But we do not know the reason why he did. After all, we do not know if he committed any crime or not.'

Thomas pushed his tankard around the table and wiped the wet circle the base had left on the bare oak with the sleeve of his robe.

'What has this to do with what is happening now? Surely you do not intend to pursue the matter on Segrim's behalf? It was a crazy idea then, and it remains so.'

Thomas was more vehement than he needed to be, partly because it was he who had been taken in by Segrim's story in the first place. It had diverted him from the trail that led to Ann Segrim's real killer. The gleam in Falconer's eyes told him, however, that his former teacher was not going to leave the matter alone. Falconer began to explain why.

'Today I spoke to someone who cast doubt on our assessment of Sir Humphrey's tale. He suggested that there might be a link between several deaths over the last three years, including those that Segrim mentioned.'

Thomas was still unconvinced.

'But how can that be? We know who killed his wife and why, and it bore no relation to any of the deaths he witnessed. It was just coincidence that he was present when Earl Richard of Cornwall died, and when Henry of Almain was slaughtered in Viterbo. And we know who did that. It was down to the de Montfort brothers, Guy and Simon. And they paid for it. Didn't Simon die soon after?'

'Yes, and Guy was excommunicated and his lands confiscated. But it was the Templar who Segrim reckoned he saw in both locations.'

'Odo de Reppes? What happened to him anyway?'

'He just disappeared. But if I am to follow up these old cases, I shall have to find out where he is now. And by the way, that will serve also the promise I made to Segrim before I left England.'

'That you would find the Templar?'

'And ask him if he had intended to kill Segrim or his wife.'

'And if he was really involved in this mad conspiracy. That is a question he will no doubt answer honestly.'

The contempt in Thomas's voice was palpable. But Falconer remained calm.

'Even if he lies, what he says and how he says it can provide evidence for me.'

'Of this great conspiracy? Who in his right mind thinks such a plot exists?'

Falconer smiled.

'Only the madman who has just inherited the throne of England.'

Thomas gasped, and his face turned red in embarrassment.

'King Edward believes it? You have spoken to the king?'

'He has his suspicions, let us say. And he wants me to examine these cases, and two more he imagines may be connected.'

'What cases are these?' Thomas wanted to express his deep doubts about the whole affair. 'More deaths of kings?'

'In a way, yes. Richard was King of Germany, and his son could have acceded to the throne. In the same way that the young Prince John was heir to the throne of England before he too died.'

'John was five years old, and died . . . oh . . . three years ago, as I recall. How are you going to investigate such an old, cold affair?'

'As I always do, by talking to witnesses and people who knew him. But that is for much later. And we may have to leave it until we return to England. What interests me more at the moment is the attempt on Edward's own life in the Holy Lands.'

Thomas groaned in exasperation. How could William expect to examine a crime that took place thousands of miles away? And one where again the perpetrator was known and had been punished already? Falconer read the disbelief on his young companion's face well.

'You think I am wasting my time. But even those cases where we think we know what happened can tell us a lot. Remember Aristotle's principles from *Prior Analytics*. The syllogism states one supposition can be inferred from two other premises. For example, suppose all men are mortal, and all Athenians are men. Therefore . . .'

'Yes, yes. Therefore all Athenians are mortal. William, this is me, Thomas Symon. I know this. You taught me. Besides, the youngest clerk knows this.'

Falconer waved his arms by way of apology.

'You must forgive me, Thomas. But I often find I need to convince others of the deductive methods I use to solve murders. And there is no harm in being reminded of principles now and again. Assemble the truths and compare one with the other until . . .'

Thomas broke in on the lecture, trying to suppress his laughter. He added his own conclusion.

'Until you are overpowered with a plethora of facts, and use your intuition instead.'

Falconer threw a playful slap at the younger man and rocked precariously on his low stool.

'Until the greater truth appears,' he stated firmly, then paused dramatically. 'It's then that you use your intuition.'

Both men now laughed, and Falconer urged Thomas to finish his beer so he could pour another one.

TEN

The candle was now burning low, soon to be no more than a stump in a heap of congealed wax. The ale mugs were empty – Falconer's sitting in a pool of spilled beer. But still the two men talked deep into the night. It was now Thomas's turn to put before his mentor what he had learned about the death of Paul Hebborn. It was precious little so far.

'Though he had no particular friends, there are four students with whom he associated most. All centred on Geoffrey Malpoivre.'

'The rich one.'

'Yes. He is the one with money, and he makes use of the power it gives him. He denigrated Paul and made fun of his stammer. He can be cruel, but cruel enough to kill is another matter.'

'And the other three?'

'Peter de la Casteigne is a joker, always ready with a jest. I can imagine him hurting Paul's feelings without realizing it. But as for having a reason for killing him? Who knows? Then we have Jack Hellequin. I like him, and I can't see him having killed. He seemed so concerned about Paul's death, but for now he must remain on the list.'

'And the fourth one?'

'That is John Fusoris. He is a Picard, but I have not yet spoken to him as he has not returned to the medical school since Paul died.'

'Do you know why?'

Thomas picked up on the suspicion in Falconer's tones.

'Not yet. The others say he had been drinking heavily the night Paul fell – or was pushed – from the tower.' Thomas automatically corrected himself as he saw Falconer lift a warning finger. 'He may be recovering from a hangover . . . or . . .'

'From a deep sense of guilt.'

'Yes. But let us not jump to conclusions too rapidly. Guilt is not yet an axiom – a self-evident truth – in his case.'

Falconer peered closely at Thomas in the gloom caused by the guttering of the single candle that stood on the table beside them.

'I am glad you explained the meaning of an axiom for me, Master Symon.'

Thomas blushed, but he held his own.

'In the same way you explained a syllogism earlier.'

'I think we are both tired and fractious, Thomas. The impending doom of our solitary candle suggests it is time to retire. I shall bid you a good night.'

'Goodnight, William.'

Both men retreated to their respective beds, pulled off their outer robes and lay back on the narrow pallets provided for them at the Abbey of St Victor. Falconer could soon hear the regular breathing of his young companion, but his mind still spun, going over the events of the day. He recalled Thomas's derisory remark about the death of kings and, smiling, murmured to himself.

'How appropriate.'

Falling asleep himself, he dreamed of corruption – both of the body, with a vision of maggots crawling out of eye sockets, and of the soul.

'You can't see the king. He is busy.'

Falconer was being frustrated by Sir John Appleby, who today had changed into a pale-blue surcoat, slit up the sides to reveal red leggings. He was bareheaded, being indoors, but his favoured sugarloaf hat sat conspicuously on the table between the two men. As he turned his head away from Falconer, the master noted that he was balding and his locks had been artfully arranged to cover the growing patch of bare skin. No wonder he wore his hat more often than not. When he turned back to face Falconer, he did have a suggestion.

'I can take you to see the men-at-arms who served Edward all the time he was in Outremer. They were in Acre at the time of the attack, and they could tell you what happened.'

Falconer raised a hand.

'That is all I ask. That someone who knew this . . . Assassin can speak to me.'

The mention of this word – Assassin – brought a sneer to Appleby's lips.

'Ah, yes. The hashish eaters of the Old Man of the Mountain. Who could have known that Anzazim was one of them? They were supposed to have been wiped out years ago by those other demons from the East, the Tartars.'

'So I understood. But then it is said these agents lived normal lives and remained incognito for years only to be awoken for a special task. What would be interesting is to discover who woke Anzazim up.'

Appleby shook his head, suggesting he had no idea and cared even less. So Falconer merely asked to be taken to see these men-at-arms. He refrained from pointing out that they had served Edward so well that they had failed to protect him from a poisoned dagger. Sir John led him out of the royal apartments and down a winding stone staircase that led into the lower levels of the palace. Here was the functional heart of the king's court, or more accurately and literally its bowels. The stone chambers that made up the armoury and soldiers' quarters were partially below river level, as could be seen by the damp on the walls. The stonework was made up of heavy blocks that bore the weight of the palace above. And its every surface was home to a green slime that covered it like some plaguey growth. In this unsavoury atmosphere was a large crypt of a space with criss-crossing arches supported by hefty stubs of pillars. At one end a fire burned, but its heat barely penetrated the long room. Bed pallets lined the chamber either side, and at the rough table beside the fire lounged two equally rough-looking soldiers with bushy beards and shaggy manes of hair. They looked at first like two peas in a pod to Falconer. As Sir John and Falconer approached them, one nudged the other, and they both sat up, alert and wary as if on a battlefield.

'Here we are, Master Falconer. This is John Clisby and Thomas Cloughe.'

As Appleby announced each man, he stood up, both of them almost having to remain stooped because of the low ceiling. They wore stained white surcoats over sturdy chain mail, the hooded part of which hung over their backs. Their swords remained buckled around their waists, and each man's left hand rested easily on the pommel. Falconer recognized the stance of a warrior, ready for anything. They were not relaxed in his presence. Though it might have been Appleby's effete and courtly manner that had made them wary of these intruders on their private space. Falconer looked Appleby in the eye.

'Thank you, Sir John. You may leave us now. I am sure I can find my own way back.'

The courtier began to demur but, catching Falconer's steely blue gaze, gave up. With a flap of his hand, he dismissed himself from the other three and retreated into the far gloom of the crypt. Falconer turned his gaze on the two men-at-arms and sighed.

'What a popinjay.'

The men grinned and one, perhaps Thomas Cloughe – Falconer could not remember – spat on the earthen floor. He ground the phlegm in with a heavy boot and returned Falconer's stare. There was a moment's silence while Falconer and the two men assessed each other, then Falconer spoke.

'Shall we take the weight off our feet? I see you have a flagon there. Is there some ale left in it?'

The other man – presumably Clisby – grunted and pushed the flagon over to their unwelcome guest. Falconer was beginning to tell them apart now, for he could see a scar under this man's left eye. So, he was scarface John. And one of Cloughe's eyes was turned slightly inwards, making him boss-eyed Thomas. Grudgingly, Cloughe wiped the rim of a goblet on his surcoat and passed it to Falconer. It must have been the one he had been drinking from, for there were only two goblets in evidence on the table, but even so Falconer took it and poured some beer into it. He let the silence hang for a while more, until he could see the wariness in the soldiers' eyes turn to worry. Falconer was an adversary they could not figure out, and as soldiers that was a life-threatening situation.

Having got them nervous, he flung out a question.

'Tell me about Anzazim.'

Relieved to be given a lifeline, both men began speaking at the same time. They stopped, looked at each other and, with a small nod of the head from the boss-eyed man, Clisby took the lead. Falconer put down Cloughe as the follower then.

'That was a surprise to us all. I mean, even the king himself trusted the bastard. He was in and out of the prince's . . . king's . . . well, still prince then . . .'

'Just call him Edward,' offered Falconer.

'Yes, master. As I was saying, he was in and out of Edward's quarters like a rat up a hole. And a rat he turned out to be – a murderous rat.'

'Did you know him well?'

It was Cloughe who spoke now. He leaned forward, and his sword tip dug a scar in the earth as he pushed it back. Forming his words, he clasped his hands together almost as if he was at prayer. He didn't look Falconer in the eye, but kept his cross-eyed gaze on the ground between his knees.

'I spoke to him more than once. He was bringing letters from a Saracen lord who had taken a shine to Edward. He passed himself off as a Christian convert, so despite his black face and heathen robes eventually he had almost free passage of the castle at Acre. He was just another familiar face, who came and went. Harmless.' He raised his gaze to Falconer. 'How were we to know he was a Hassatut?'

He was using a name Falconer had heard little of before, but he knew it to mean a secret agent of the Nizari sect. An Assassin, in other words. He looked the troubled man in his good eye.

'The day he tried to kill Edward, did you see a change in him?'

Cloughe looked puzzled, exchanging glances with Clisby.

'What do you mean – a change? What sort of change?'

Falconer shrugged.

'A wild look in his eye, perhaps. A nervousness about his movements. They do say these agents – these Hassatuts – eat opium. He would have a wide, staring look.'

Clisby leaned over his companion's shoulder and took up the story.

'You could be right there, master. I saw him that day, and he had eyes like deep pools. Dark and evil.'

Falconer realized he had fed these men too much information, and they were giving him what they thought he wanted to hear. Besides, how reliable was their information after all this time? He tried another tack.

'Who else was present when you showed the . . . man into Edward's chamber?'

Clisby frowned and glanced at Cloughe. An unspoken exchange took place between them, then Cloughe answered for them both.

'Why, no one, sir. Though the Lady Eleanor arrived soon after the commotion. She was there as we dragged that cursed Anzazim away, bleeding his life away like a pig.'

While Falconer was struggling to extract information from illiterate soldiers, Thomas Symon was having the same problems with the altogether smarter students of medicine. Even Jack Hellequin seemed to have clammed up on him. Only the youthful Adam Morrish was free with his information. But then he was the teacher. In the morning, Thomas patiently sat through Morrish's lecture on the humours, and how each element was related to bodily fluids – fire to yellow bile, earth to black bile and so on. He had nothing to learn about these standard approaches to curing illness in men. But he squirmed a little when Morrish began to expound the Greek physician Galen's views on blood carrying the pneuma, or life spirit.

'It is this which gives the blood its red colour. And the blood passes through a porous wall in the chambers of the heart to reach all parts of the body.'

Thomas knew this to be erroneous. He had opened up enough hearts – perhaps five in the last two years – to know there was no porous wall inside but a clever muscly set of openings. But he could say nothing in the presence of these young students. Anatomy was forbidden except in the case of the bodies of murderers. He stoically sat through the rest of Morrish's lecture, his stomach rumbling through lack of sustenance. At the end, he decided to try his luck again with the taciturn students, grabbing a bite to eat in the process, before he met Friar Bacon in the dank rear room of the school. It would be the first time they would sit down together to begin the mammoth task of recording Bacon's compendium of all things. But before Thomas could escape the school, Morrish took his arm and, smiling, asked to speak to him. Reluctantly, Symon watched the other young men leave for the nearby tavern, where no doubt Geoffrey Malpoivre would stump up for wine or ale. When the last student had left, and peace had descended once again on the schoolroom, Morrish guided him to one of the benches and sat down beside him.

The man had the look of someone who was relaxed and confident, something that seemed to elude Thomas. Though Morrish's face was youthful, his eyes were deep pools that spoke of knowledge and wisdom. He stared into Thomas's eyes, and he had to look away. Morrish's voice was mellifluous and confident too.

'You did not agree with me – or should I say, Galen – about the movement of blood around the body.'

Thomas shrugged, uncertain what to say. Morrish patted him on the knee and invited his response.

'You can speak openly. I am not a follower of Bishop Tempier and his thirteen Condemnations.'

Thomas looked up, and Morrish nodded encouragingly.

'You have some experience of anatomy, don't you? Please, tell me. I should like to know.'

Thomas felt he could trust the man and began to explain what he had learned from anatomizing several bodies. He became so enthusiastic about his subject, and in impressing Adam Morrish, that he almost forgot the time. It was only when he saw Morrish look away towards the door to the schoolroom that Thomas realized they were being listened to by someone else. His heart lurched, imagining what might happen if the Church got to hear of his illicit forays into the inner workings of the human body. It was only when the person at the door spoke that he breathed a sigh of relief. It was Roger Bacon, come for their appointment.

'Ah, Friar, it's you. I was just . . . I was . . .'

Bacon raised a hand to stop Thomas's uncertain flow of evasions.

'You have no need to explain to me, Thomas Symon. I have indulged in similar adventures, and equally have no desire for anyone in authority to know.' He stepped forward and held a hand out to the other man in the room. 'You must be Master Adam Morrish.'

Morrish, his eager face beaming, took the friar's hand and shook it vigorously.

'And you, sir, are Roger Bacon, if I am not mistaken. It is a privilege to meet you.'

Bacon lowered his eyes modestly to the ground.

'Well, I do not know about that. I admit I have a certain reputation, but you, sir, though new to Paris, are carving out a reputation too.'

For a moment Thomas thought he saw a look of alarm cross Morrish's face. But then it was gone, to be replaced by a wide grin. Perhaps he had imagined the reaction. The two men were exchanging compliments, and he was excluded from their circle. Until Bacon broke off and beckoned to him to come forward.

'Thomas, we forget our manners. You are a busy young man, and I must not waste any more of your time than I must in order to carry out our task. You must excuse us, Master Morrish, but Thomas and I have an appointment with some parchment and ink.'

Morrish's brow furrowed with a look of curiosity, but he contented himself with one question only.

'You will find time, will you not, to speak to my students? They are a bunch of dunderheads, but you may be able to knock some sense into them.'

Bacon seemed disconcerted by Morrish's easy charm, but he nodded briefly.

'Yes, I will gladly do as you say. I must, after all, earn my keep in your school. Payment in kind is all I can offer for the use of your back room. Now, come Thomas, we shall begin.'

Soon the two of them were settled in the damp back room, Thomas with a quill in his hand and a fresh piece of parchment staring blankly up at him on the table. He had ruled the sheet with lines, but there was nothing else on it for now. Soon, it was to be covered with black marks that would capture the ideas of Doctor Mirabilis in some miraculous way. Thomas stared nervously at the page, while Bacon gazed out across the river to the two looming towers of Notre-Dame Cathedral.

The friar took a deep breath and sighed.

'I have the stink of corruption in my nostrils, so that is where we will begin. Write this down, Thomas.'

ELEVEN

alconer's attempt to speak to Queen Eleanor might have
failed dismally, if she hadn't walked in on his conversation with Sir John Appleby. He had sought out the
dandified courtier soon after nones in the afternoon. The knight
appeared to have dined well and looked soporific. But when
Falconer asked to see Eleanor, he immediately bristled.

'You may have been asked by the king to investigate some
unexplained deaths. But that does not give you the right to
come here demanding to see the queen.'

Falconer's attempt to point out that he had 'demanded' no
such thing was brushed aside.

'Did not your interview with Clisby and Cloughe satisfy
you? Did they not tell you the truth?'

'Yes and no, Sir John. I have no doubt that they were entirely
truthful in so far as they knew the facts. But they could not
help on the crucial issue of who told the Assassin to act.'

'And why do you think the queen can answer that?' He
snorted derisively. 'The lady can have no idea what caused
Anzazim to betray the trust placed in him. Besides, she cannot
speak to you as she has left the palace and is already on the
way to visit her family in Castile.'

'That is a pity. I was told she was present immediately after
the murder attempt. I thought she may be able to recall something that was said by Anzazim. I dare say that no one has
asked her such a question before.'

Falconer looked at Appleby, and was suddenly aware of a
look of surprise in Sir John's eyes. He realized the man's gaze
was fixed, however, not at Falconer but over his shoulder. But
before he could turn around, there was the sound of silk rustling
and a pleasant voice spoke out.

'What question might that be, sir?'

Falconer had heard tell that Eleanor was beautiful, but he
was not prepared for the person who now stood in the doorway
of the chamber. Her figure was well shaped, made more attrac-
tive by the swell of pregnancy. Her thick mane of loose hair

reminded him of Saphira's tresses. But Eleanor's locks were dark and glossy where Saphira's were flame-red. Her face was pleasant and well proportioned, no more. But what made it exceptional were the eyes. They were bright and intense, showing Eleanor to be a very confident and intelligent woman. It was her eyes that raised her above the common crowd, as well as her breeding. Falconer replied to her query, taking his chance before Sir John could intervene.

'Your Majesty, I am William Falconer, taxed by the king to investigate the attempt on his life. I merely wished to talk to you about the unpleasant incident with your husband in Acre.'

Eleanor shivered and crossed her arms around herself, as though trying to protect herself from the evil memory of that day. Falconer immediately regretted his blunt approach.

'Of course, if it is too painful a memory, I will understand.'

Eleanor pulled herself upright, lifting her chin high. She was visibly growing into her role as the Queen of England.

'No, Master Falconer, I can speak of it, and tell you all I know. But it will be little, I'm afraid.'

She waved a hand, and Appleby hurried out of the room, no doubt on his way to inform Edward of this turn of events. Eleanor, meanwhile, crossed to the large and comfortable chair that stood beside the empty hearth and sat down, smoothing her gravid belly. Falconer remained standing and formed his first question carefully.

'Did Your Majesty think that Anzazim was a reliable servant before this incident?'

Eleanor paused, making clear that she was giving the question fair and full consideration.

'I saw him several times, bringing communications from the Emir of Joppa to my husband, and I even spoke to him once or twice. He appeared to be a very courteous and charming young man. My husband trusted him, so I see no reason why I should not have. Oh, and before we continue, Master Falconer, please no more Your Majesties, or this will be a very long and tedious conversation.'

Falconer nodded politely and went on.

'Thank you, Your . . . My Lady, what caused you to enter the chamber just after the attempt on your husband's life?'

Eleanor frowned and sat a little forward in the chair, clasping her hands around her right knee. For a moment she looked like a young girl eager to please her old uncle.

'I heard a commotion. A cry from my husband, I think. My instinct was to go to him, so I did.'

'Not to run and hide in fear of your life?'

Eleanor smiled, and involuntarily Falconer found himself captivated by this pretty woman. He had to remind himself she was the queen, a mother several times over and fast approaching her thirtieth birthday.

'I am not a shrinking violet, Master Falconer. Nor do I live in fear for my life. Besides, if there had been any danger, I am sure the men-at-arms surrounding my husband would have held me back.'

Worldy-wise as well as beautiful, then.

'I am sure they would have. Please, tell me what you saw and heard when you entered the king's chamber. Any fact, no matter how small, could be of significance.'

'I am not sure I registered much. My eyes were mainly for my husband. He was standing by the window on the other side of the room, clutching his hand into a fist. The room was in a mess. A table had been tipped over and the marble top shattered. Two guards were dragging a body out of the room. I did not see at the time who it was. All I could see was blood everywhere. I did not know if it was that of my husband or the other man's. I just ran to Edward's side. He tried to convince me he was all right, but then he collapsed at my feet.'

By now, Eleanor's grip on her knee was so tight that her knuckles were white. Her voice suddenly sounded strained.

'Of course, you must dismiss from your mind the romantic myth of my sucking the poison from his wounds.' She smiled fleetingly. 'That was made up as a jest by Edward much later. You know, I only found out the next day that the man being dragged away was Anzazim. The trusted Anzazim, whom I had quite liked. So despite what he did to Edward, I still prayed they did not hurt him too much before he died.'

Falconer's heart lurched in his chest.

'He was not already dead when he was taken from the chamber?'

'No. He must have been alive, because I was told that he cursed Edward before he succumbed. They fed his body to the dogs, you know.'

The fact that Anzazim had still been alive after the attack

was just the sort of information Falconer had hoped for by interviewing Eleanor. He now knew he would have to speak to Clisby and Cloughe again. Before he could take his leave, though, Eleanor asked him something.

'Have I answered the question you were proposing to ask just before I came in?'

'I don't know, My Lady. Can you think of any reason why Anzazim should have acted as he did? It is said the Assassins are motivated not by principles but by money. That they will perform their deeds at the behest of those who can pay. Can you think of anyone who would have paid Anzazim or his masters to try to kill your husband?'

Eleanor didn't hesitate this time, her answer coming pat.

'Many people had reason to hate Edward, Master Falconer. As a result of the Barons' War several families were dispossessed and enmities created. The Earl of Derby hated Edward for breaking the terms of a truce during the conflict. And of course the de Montfort family had more reason than most to seek revenge for the defeat of Earl Simon.'

Falconer refrained from suggesting that 'defeat' was more than a polite euphemism for what Simon de Montfort had suffered. At the Battle of Evesham, the earl went down under a relentless attack. But it did not stop there. His body was mutilated and his head cut off and displayed on a lance. His own son, Simon, witnessed the grisly sight. Falconer thanked Eleanor for her patience and bowed out of the now cold and gloomy chamber. He did not therefore see Edward entering by another door, which had been kept ajar so that he could hear Falconer's entire conversation with his wife. Eleanor looked up at him and smiled.

'Did I do well, Edward?'

The king nodded.

'Perfectly. You have set him on the right track, my dearest.'

Falconer found his own way back to the subterranean world that was the soldiers' quarters. With any luck, Clisby and Cloughe would still be off duty, as little must be required of them in the French king's palace. If not, he was determined to find them at their post, wherever that may be. But as he entered the crypt-like chamber, he saw he was in luck. There was a gaggle of men-at-arms lounging on their pallets. Most had their heavy chain mail off and were relaxing in their undershirts and breeches. There was a smell of stale sweat in the air that reminded Falconer of any number of billets he had experienced from Bologna to Vienna. His own past rose up in his mind and reminded him that, even though these men looked at ease, they would still be alert to intrusion or impending danger. Predictably, several sharp eyes turned his way. One grey-haired old veteran, his hands clasped behind his head, called out pleasantly.

'Are you lost, master? This den of iniquity is surely not where you aimed to be.'

Falconer smiled easily, casting his eyes around the room for the two men he sought. He cursed his poor eyesight, but did not wish to show his weakness by putting on his eye-lenses.

'Indeed it is, my friend. I am looking for John Clisby and Thomas Cloughe. Can you tell me if they are here?'

There was a brief lull in the general chatter that had filled the room before it began again, though in a more tense, artificial manner. Everyone seemed to be covering up something they would rather hide from this intruder. Falconer felt a cold shiver of apprehension run down his spine. Only the old soldier appeared unperturbed by his question.

'I am afraid you are too late, master. They have gone.'

'Well, if they are on duty somewhere, can you tell me where that is? I spoke to them earlier today and would like to ask them for some more information.'

The old man eased himself up from his prone position, turning to lean on one elbow.

'You misunderstand me, friend. Thomas and John have left. They have been sent on ahead to Gascony to prepare the ground for the king when he travels there to see to his holdings. It is said Gaston de Béarn is in revolt again and needs his arse tanning.'

The soldiers near to the man burst out in coarse laughter at his jest. They were obviously absorbing every word that was said between him and Falconer despite their apparent lassitude. Falconer felt sorry for this Gaston de Béarn, if these rough English soldiers were to be set on him. Even so, he was suspicious at the sudden departure of the main witnesses to Edward's attempted assassination. Firstly, he had almost missed speaking to Eleanor, who no doubt by now was on her way to Castile. And now the two soldiers had been spir-

ited away. He wondered if Sir John Appleby was interfering
for some reason in his investigations. Was he envious of
Falconer's private access to the king? He could not be sure.
He threw out a question to the room generally anyway, more
in hope than expectation.

'Is there anyone else here who was present in Acre when
Anzazim was interrogated?'

His enquiry brought forth another roar of laughter, and
Falconer stood still, puzzled by the reaction. It was the old
soldier who set him to rights.

'Everyone here was present when the bastard was *interrogated* as you put it. Though I am not sure I would call it such.
Everyone wanted a piece of him, so we all crowded into the
cell where he had been thrown by John Clisby, and we all gave
him a good kicking.' He waggled the heavy, studded boots that
he still had on his feet. 'He didn't say much before he died.'

Falconer sighed. Another dead end, then. Almost literally.
As he turned to go, though, the old man called after him.

'He did beg a lot, mind you. And cursed both the king and
those who had put him up to it.'

Falconer paused, hardly daring to ask the question that he
burned to know the answer to.

'And who did he say had put him up to it?'

The old man winked.

'One of us lot, he said. A Latin, he said. Though those
infidel bastards don't know one Latin from another. As far as
they are concerned, we all look alike. So he could have meant
an Englishman, he could have meant a Frenchie, a Hungarian
or a Slav. Who knows? Anyway, I stopped his foul mouth
with my boot, and that was that.'

The rest of the soldiers cheered in approval of their
comrade's actions. Falconer was simply sad that Anzazim did
not have the easy end that Eleanor had hoped for. But now
the mood of the men around him had changed, and Falconer
saw he had learned all he would be able to from them. But
he was not that discontented. He now had some inkling of
who might have paid the Assassin to act. That was more than
he had had at the start of his day. He had a positive trail to
follow, and tomorrow he would take it further. He already
knew where he had to go.

TWELVE

Darkness had fallen on Paris, but the streets still bustled with life. A few wealthy merchants had servants rushing ahead of them with blazing torches, but most people strode boldly out in the centre of the main thorough-fares. They took care to keep away from the shadows of the overhanging buildings. Not only because they feared robbers might lurk in them, but to avoid tripping over the beggars who sat, often with starving curs curled at their feet, along the edges of the streets. Starvation was an ever-present curse that drove poor families off the land and into the city in hope of feeding themselves. Their plight made Thomas shiver, because it could so easily have been his own. If a benevolent local priest had not paid for his journey to Oxford and the university, he might have dragged his own family into penury. He was the fourth child that Peggy and Jack Symon had produced, and they could barely support three. Of course, Thomas could have worked on the land when he grew up and helped in that way. But the priest saw in the bright and eager child something worth fostering. He had gambled his stipend on Thomas and had been proved right. The eager farm boy was now Master Thomas Symon of Oxford with prospects before him.

As Thomas strode into the open space of the Place Maubert, he clutched the satchel he had slung over his shoulder. It contained the first part of Roger Bacon's proposed compendium, and he needed to keep it safe. He couldn't help thinking of what the friar had dictated. His hand had trembled at Roger Bacon's words, and he had been half afraid to write them down. Even Pope Gregory had been criticized by the fearless Franciscan in words that still shone clearly in Thomas's mind.

'Everywhere we shall find boundless corruption, and first of all in the Head. The Holy See is torn by the deceit and fraud of unjust men. The whole Papal Court is defamed of lechery . . . the prelates run after money, neglect the cure of souls and promote their nephews and other carnal friends . . .'

He had tried to temper Bacon's outpourings.

'Master, do you think it is proper to condemn the Pope in such terms? It is not surely safe.'

Bacon had turned on him with a look of scorn on his face.

'We are scholars, Thomas. *Proper* and *safe* are not scientific terms I understand. Facts and truth are what we seek, and when we find them we must proclaim their shining brightness. Shall we carry on?'

Thomas lowered his head in embarrassment. He had thought Falconer a hard taskmaster. He was beginning to think that Friar Bacon was going to be infinitely worse.

'Yes, master. I am ready.'

He had buried his head in the work of a scribe and tried not to think of the meaning of the words.

'Master Symon. Thomas.'

He realized someone was calling him from across the big open space that was the Place Maubert. Looking back, he saw Jack Hellequin beckoning him from the doorway of a down-at-heel building on the corner. It looked as though it had been squeezed unceremoniously between the two sturdier structures either side of it. Both of which probably wished they could elbow it out of the way. A withered branch with drooping leaves hung over the door. It was a tavern, and a poor one by the look of it. Thomas wasn't sure what to do, but Hellequin gesticulated urgently again, and he walked over to him.

'What is it, Jack? I am tired and I must speak to my fellow master before he retires.'

'No, you must drink with us. Geoffrey is buying.'

Thomas hesitated, but he wasn't sure if Falconer would even be at the Abbey of St Victor to listen to his tales of Bacon's madness. William had been preoccupied by the task the king had set him and would surely no longer be interested in Thomas. He made a quick decision. After all, he needed to learn more, if he could, about Paul Hebborn. Then perhaps Falconer would listen to him. He smiled, and let Jack take him by the arm and guide him into the noisy tavern.

Inside was a scene of debauchery to Thomas's eyes. He was used to drunken behaviour from his time as a student in Oxford. Though he rarely got involved with them himself, as he felt too strongly his duty to the village priest who had funded his tuition. He sometimes wished he could have bent a little, but his conscience always pricked him. So he had been a somewhat sober observer of the excesses of his fellows. In this low, mean tavern on the south bank of the river, sobriety had not dared enter. The predominance of young men, some in garish garb, suggested it was a place frequented by students of the university. But there were solid knots of simply clad artisans drinking hard amid the swirl and eddies of the more agitated student imbibers. Thomas swallowed hard and followed Hellequin to a group of young men, some of whom he recognized as Adam Morrish's students. A goblet was thrust in his hand, and someone filled it from a jug of red wine, splashing the contents over his neat black robe in the process. He made an ineffectual effort to wipe the stain away.

'Is there no ale?'

Thomas would have preferred weak beer to this French wine that always went to his head. But Jack chastised him for his caution.

'Drink up. You are in Paris now. None of your English ways here.'

Thomas took a deep breath and gulped the wine down. As he spluttered and coughed, his goblet was filled again. And the group of young men cheered. Jack clapped him on the back, encouraging him to take another draught. He did so, and prayed he would stay sober enough to remember anything he was told about Hebborn. He looked around.

'Where is John Fusoris? Is he still not recovered yet?'

Geoffrey Malpoivre, who had been the man filling Thomas's goblet, snorted in derision.

'John is weak-willed, and a namby-pamby. He could not stand the thought of Hebborn squashed on the pavement at the foot of Notre-Dame's tower. When I described the mess to him, he threw up. He will never make a doctor, if he can't stand the sight of a dead body. What about you, Master Thomas? Do you have a strong stomach?'

By now, Thomas's stomach felt quite queasy, but not from any thoughts of a broken body. The wine was having its effect. He swallowed hard and spoke with unaccustomed bravado.

'I have seen the insides of plenty of broken bodies, Geoffrey. Some of them murderers whose internal organs I could legally dissect. But I have carved up others too. Perhaps I could explain to you the texture and feel of a man's bowels when they are still hot and steaming. They are quite slippery,

in fact, and when they spill out of the body cavity they are
very hard to restrain.'

Malpoivre went a nasty shade of green and thrust the half-
empty jug of wine at Thomas before rushing towards the door
of the tavern. When the sound of his heaving penetrated the
din, the bunch of roughly dressed labourers by the door cheered
and slapped each other on the back. Thomas looked at the
wide eyes of the students around him and smiled. He lifted
up the jug.

'Anyone else for wine?'

Hellequin held out his goblet.

'I will take what's left. I applaud your taking Geoffrey down
a peg or two. But I wish you had done it some other time.
He was the only one of us with money for drink, and now he
won't dare show his face in here again for a while.'

The other students groaned at the loss of their purse-holder,
and a couple began to drift away from the group. Hellequin
drank the wine carefully that Thomas had poured, not wishing
to swallow the lees at the bottom of the jug. He cast a quizzical
look at his new companion.

'Have you really cut open human bodies, Thomas?'

Despite the wine clouding his brain, Thomas still had his
wits about him. The Church condemned anatomy, even of
hanged murderers. He was aware also that the remaining
students were agog to hear his every word. He decided to tell
a partial lie and crossed his fingers.

'To tell the truth, I am a farmer's son. What I know of
anatomy and the feel of entrails is based on killing beasts of
the field. Slippery stuff – cows' innards.'

The other youths looked disappointed by his confession,
but Jack Hellequin squinted at Thomas, evidently disbelieving
him. He sat back in his seat and toyed with his empty goblet,
twirling it in his fingers. Thomas, a little dizzy with the wine
and the noise of the tavern, looked around him. He ought to
leave now, but he wanted to find out about John Fusoris and
his mysterious illness. Had the boy simply been upset by
Malpoivre's boasting? Or had he either seen Hebborn's body
after the fall from Notre-Dame, or caused it to fall in the first
place? Thomas did not know that, or if he was allowing
himself to be misled by his own fancy. The only way to find
out was to talk to Fusoris, and for that to happen he needed

someone to tell him where he lodged. He decided to ask Hellequin.

As he turned to do so, he saw across the gloomy room the two students who had sloped off sitting on their own in a corner. One was Peter de la Casteigne, the other one a sandy-haired and freckled youth he did not know. They were chewing on something, though how they had afforded food he did not know. They looked even more soporific than before, when they had been drinking wine. Peter lifted a lazy gaze to Thomas and sniggered sleepily. But before he could think any more of the incident, Hellequin rose up, cutting off his view of the youths, and offered to help him home. Arm in arm they made their way to the door. The cold air of evening hit Thomas, but he stood still and took a deep breath of it.

'I can find my own way back, Jack. Thank you all the same. But what you can help me with is to guide me to John Fusoris' lodgings.'

'Why would you want to go there?'

'I am concerned for him, even if none of you are.'

'You have never met him.'

'That's as may be. Think of me as the good Samaritan, then. I will cross this road for a stranger.'

He waved his hand at the broad, triangular-shaped space before them, a little embarrassed at his effusive speech. But if Hellequin was only half as drunk as he felt, then he wouldn't have noticed. The Frenchman shrugged and took Thomas's arm again.

'Whatever you wish. It's this way.'

It was not far to a ramshackle row of tall tenements that, like the medical school, backed on to the River Seine. Even in the dark, Thomas was aware that the bulk of Notre-Dame loomed menacingly over this quarter of the city. Were none of the students free of the shadow of Hebborn's death? Hellequin pointed at a narrow house, which had a flicker of light evident in one of the upper windows.

'That's John's room. As you can see, he can't stand the dark any more. What he will do when he runs out of candles I don't know.'

'Thank you for your help, Jack. You can go now.'

Thomas stepped up to the door, leaving Hellequin in the lane. But the student still called after him.

'He won't let you in. He thinks the Devil is after him.'

Thomas felt an icy chill as he listened to Hellequin's laughter drifting eerily down the lane as he walked off. The dullness in his brain was wearing off, and he checked that Fusoris' window still showed a light. Then he knocked on the door. No one came. He stepped back into the lane and called nervously up to the window.

'John Fusoris. John? It is a friend. Come down and let me in.'

There was no reply. Pressing his ear to the door, he could hear nothing inside. But he felt the door give. It was not locked, and gingerly he pushed it open. It was dark inside and, when he poked his head over the portal, smelled damp. Just like the room he was using to take down Bacon's words. The river seemed to be seeping into everything along its bank. He clutched the satchel to his side reflexively and thought of Bacon's warning of corruption in the air. He stepped over the threshold.

'John?'

A rustling noise startled him, causing his heart to beat fast in his chest. Then he saw a rat scurrying away into the darkness at the back of the house. He swallowed and called louder.

'John Fusoris? Are you there?'

A shape appeared at the top of the staircase that clung to the side of the chamber where Thomas stood. The figure of a man was outlined by yellowish candlelight behind it. The flickering flame cast long shadows that wavered on the steps below the figure. A high-pitched voice, cracked and fearful, piped up.

'Go away. Don't come for me now. I am not ready.'

Thomas frowned. If this was John Fusoris, what had scared the youth so?

'I have not come to harm you, John. My name is Thomas Symon. I am a master of Oxford University, come to study in Paris. Can I talk to you about Paul Hebborn?'

A thin, almost inhuman wail split the air, and the figure on the stairs retreated. Thomas heard a door slam, and cursed his insensitive words. He was always rushing into things without considering. Now he had no other option but to blunder on. He ran up the stairs and turned to the right, where the upper room overlooking the street had to be located. The door was closed firmly against him.

THIRTEEN

Thomas pressed gently against the door, and it gave slightly before slamming closed again in its frame. He pushed harder, and again it gave a little before closing. He heard a whimper from behind the door. The scared youth must have been putting all his weight behind the door, resisting Thomas's efforts. He tried to persuade Fusoris to let go, but to no avail. It became a trial of strength, which the more resilient Thomas eventually won. His final push opened the door wide, as the pressure behind it gave way. In the half-light of the room he was aware of a low shape scrabbling across the floor. Thomas was reminded of the rat that had scuttled away from him in the deserted room downstairs. But this was a human being, not a rat, even if he was frightened of his presence. He let his eyes adjust to the poor light from the flickering stub of a candle before stepping fully into the room. When he did move, his nostrils were assailed with the stench of an unwashed body and human excrement. John Fusoris had besmirched himself. Stifling his disgust, he knelt down close to where the sad figure of the student huddled.

Fusoris had squeezed himself into a dark corner, making himself smaller than Thomas could have imagined a human being could have done. He was naturally quite slight, but his body looked emaciated. Thomas wondered when he had last eaten. Not since Hebborn's plunge from the tower? He reached out to touch Fusoris, but the youth squealed, and Thomas drew his hand back.

'John, look at me, John. I am not here to harm you.'

Slowly, the youth turned his face from the wall and looked sideways at Thomas. His face was thin, and so his eyes looked unusually large in his gaunt skull. They looked like deep, dark pools of horror to Thomas. Black pools reflecting the yellow flame of the candle. Fusoris flinched and looked away again. He spoke in a broken voice.

'Go away. You are the Devil come for me. You are his agent.'

'Why should you think I am the Devil, John?'

'You have come for me like you came for Paul.'

'Did Paul get taken by the Devil, John? How do you know?'

Fusoris shivered and clutched his arms closer around his thin body.

'Because Paul is dead. The Devil killed him . . . threw him off the tower of Notre-Dame.'

Thomas was troubled. Was this just an insane fantasy or a twisted version of the truth? Either way, he had to help John in order to find out more. But what was wrong with the boy? Was he possessed by demons, which had caused his insanity? And if so, could he be saved and brought back to reality? John might have actually witnessed the death of Paul Hebborn. If it were possible to get him to talk about it rationally, Thomas might learn who killed Paul Hebborn. But his fear was that the boy might be telling the truth now, and that the Devil may come for Thomas too.

Suddenly, the room felt very cold, and Thomas wished Falconer were here. William was so much more rational than he was, and more sceptical when it came to the realities of Satan and Hell. Thomas was yet to be convinced that such punishments did not await the sinner. He looked into the youth's eyes, and what he saw made his mind up. Gently, he touched the tense figure of John Fusoris and began to coax him out of his corner.

Falconer blew out the candle and lay in the darkness, his mind spinning fantasies. He had been expecting to talk to Thomas Symon about what he had uncovered during the day. Without Saphira to test his ideas on, he had become reliant on the young man. The thought of Saphira sidetracked him for a while, and he dreamed up fanciful encounters with her. He would travel to Honfleur and find her in the first tavern he entered. Or he would be walking through Paris, and there she would be in the street. Of course, whatever he imagined always resulted in the happiest of meetings. There would be no awkwardness or necessity to apologize on either side. When he had come back to his senses, he realized that it was late and that he had dozed off. Something had roused him. Looking across at the other bed, he also saw that there was still no sign of Thomas Symon. He thought he heard a sound in the abbey cloisters that was not like the sound of

monks going to pray. That was more a soporific slapping of
sandals on stone. He had heard the sound of voices. Raised
voices.

He got up from his bed and crossed the room in the dark.
He cursed as he bumped his shin against a stool that stood in
an unexpected place, and grabbed the door handle. Looking
out, he could see lights flickering from inside the cloisters, with
big shadows sliding down the walls and across the floor. He
walked barefoot down the corridor from the guest quarters
towards the disturbance, the slabs striking cold on the soles of
his feet. As he got closer, he was surprised to hear Thomas's
voice raised in anger. The young man was usually so measured
and temperate that he wondered what was agitating him so.
The candlelight and voices were now coming from one of the
small cells that lined that side of the cloister. Falconer peered
in through the open doorway.

Lit by two candles, the scene was confusing. Two monks
were restraining a skinny youth on a bed. The youth, with his
lank, dark hair plastered across his skull, was wriggling under
the monks' grasp. His wail was in counterpoint to Thomas's
staccato call for calm and understanding. One monk turned
his head from his task and replied breathlessly.

'He has the Devil in him and should be restrained. We shall
have to drive the demons from him, but in the meantime he
must be tied down.'

Thomas tugged at the monk's arm.

'He is merely overexcited. If you left him alone, he would
recover. That is why I brought him here. For some calm and
reflection. With you here that is not possible.'

The monk turned away from Thomas and uncharitably
punched the boy in the face. He slumped into silence. His
assailant stood up, a look of triumph on his face.

'This is our abbey, and you are merely a guest here. You
should not have brought this filthy creature to us. But seeing
as you have, then we will deal with him. Now if you will
please go, I will lock him in.'

Thomas groaned and, seeing Falconer for the first time,
rushed over to him.

'Thank God. William, you must help me. This is John
Fusoris – he can help us with Hebborn's murder.'

Looking back into the room, where the youth lay prostrate

on the bed, and the two monks stood over him menacingly, Falconer drew Thomas aside.

'Let them get on with it, Thomas.'

'But . . .'

'The boy is in no fit state to answer any questions now. If it is peace you want for him, then it will do no harm for him to be locked in the room for a while. Come away and tell me what you have found out. Anyway, my feet are freezing on these slabs and I could do with warming them up. Bring one of those candles.'

They left the monks to their task and retreated to the privacy of their chamber. Falconer tucked his legs under his bedclothes to warm his feet, while Thomas slumped down exhausted on his bed. The wine and his encounter with the mad youth suddenly began to tell on him. He felt drained of all energy. But Falconer wanted to know what he had learned while it was still fresh in his mind.

'If you go to sleep now, you will forget something, or you will embellish the facts to fit your opinion of what did happen.'

Thomas groaned but sat up. This is what he had wanted, wasn't it? William's attention? He began to tell Falconer all about the medical school and the students who gathered themselves around Geoffrey Malpoivre and his groaning purse. About their drinking, and regular teasing of Paul Hebborn for being English and having a stammer.

'But not all of them were cruel to Hebborn. I get the impression that Jack Hellequin, whom I know the best, had a regard for the outsider.'

'Hmm. The name of the Devil's horseman.'

'I beg your pardon?'

'You are perhaps not familiar with French passion plays. In them, the hellequin is a black-faced emissary of the Devil. Mind you, his role is to roam the countryside chasing the damned souls of evil people to Hell. So your Jack may be a useful ally.'

Thomas ignored Falconer's jest and carried on.

'Then I was told of John Fusoris, who had befriended Hebborn. But I could not speak to him at the school because, since Hebborn's death, he had locked himself away in his lodgings. That is why I sought him out. He lives close by the river, across from the towers of Notre-Dame.'

'Not a happy presence for the friend of someone who fell from that very spot.'

'Or was pushed.'

Falconer leaned forward, interest etched on his lined face.

'You have new evidence?'

Thomas hesitated.

'I may have.' Hearing Falconer sigh, he pressed on eagerly. 'That is why I brought John Fusoris here. Though his story was confused, he insisted that the Devil came for Hebborn, tempted him and led him to his death.'

'But you only have the words of a mad boy to base your opinions on.'

'No.' Thomas was emphatic, and rummaged in his purse. He drew out some dry leaves of an oval shape. 'I have these. I found them in his room, scattered on the floor. They look to me like bay leaves, which do have magical properties and are said to be emetic. Fusoris had fouled himself.'

Falconer took the leaves, sniffing them and rolling them in his fingers. He was assailed by a half-forgotten memory of involuntarily eating these leaves himself. He had descended into a mental Hell due to them. He shook his head.

'No. These are not bay leaves. They are *Catha edulis*, known as khat in Arabia, where they are eaten to produce feelings of euphoria. It is said the ancient Egyptians used them to release human divinity. If Fusoris ate these, it is no surprise he is unstable and fearful. They can affect you in that way.' He shuddered at his own experience of descending into a cellar that became a hallucinatory Hell due to the leaf. 'Were his pupils dilated?'

'Yes, they were.' Thomas was excited, forgetting his exhaustion. 'I knew he wasn't possessed. There had to be another explanation for his behaviour.'

He remembered the thoughts he had had about Fusoris being mad or owned by the Devil, and blushed at his naivety. It was something he would not admit to the sceptical Falconer. Instead, he brought one of the leaves to his lips and sucked it. Falconer pulled his hand away, though, before he could experiment further.

'Don't. It is not easy to stop once you have started. I know I recommend practical experimentation. But take it from me, in this case leave it to second-hand knowledge to inform you.

If Fusoris has been eating these leaves, then I suggest we leave him to recover from their effect. Get some sleep and you can tackle him in the morning, when his mind will be a little sounder.'

Thomas gladly lay back on his bed.

'You are right, William. I will sleep well tonight.' He closed his eyes as Falconer snuffed the candle out. 'Oh, and remind me never to drink unwatered French wine again.'

FOURTEEN

'I wish you wouldn't journey to Castile, darling. You are, after all, heavy with child.'

Edward was holding his wife's hand and gazing anxiously into her beautiful eyes. She patted his hand and reassured him, a pert smile playing across her lips.

'My dear husband. As you well know – for you were responsible for them all – this will be my ninth child. He or she will slip out hardly without me knowing.'

Edward ignored her sauciness this time. He so loved their sexual banter, but this was important to him.

'Yes, and of the eight you have brought into the world, only three are still alive. So many have died so soon after their birth that I wonder if it is wise for you to be travelling at such a time.'

'You have no cause to be worried so. Oh, I know you were downcast by the death of little Johnny. It is natural to mourn the loss of your firstborn son and heir. But you have Henry now, and he is five already . . .'

She faltered in her reassurances, recalling that young Henry was at the very same age at which John had died. Edward was always convinced that there was some mystery surrounding his death. And she knew that was part of the reasoning behind his appointing the Oxford master to look into the deaths that had come thick and fast in his family recently. She also knew who Edward suspected of being behind those deaths.

'Do you think Master Falconer is on the right track?'

Edward smiled quietly.

'Oh, yes. We have pointed him in the right direction, and he will winkle the bastard out. He will run from cover soon like a startled stag, I am sure of it. And when he does, I shall be ready with my bow and arrow.'

Not knowing his actions were being discussed at that moment, Falconer had risen early in order to make time to get across

Paris. He was bound for the Marais – the northern marshes outside the city wall – where the Templars had established their great commandery. But before he left the abbey he roused a sleepy Thomas. The young man groaned and held his head.

'Leave me alone, I am dying.'

Falconer laughed.

'Of thirst, no doubt. When I recall my early days of excessive wine drinking, I can sympathize with how you are feeling. I recommend that you find a barrel of water, dunk your head in it and then try to drink your way out of it.'

'What hour of the day is it?'

'The monks have already held the prime service, so I would suggest you think about checking on John Fusoris before you have to be at Master Adam's medical school for your tryst with Roger. You have a busy day ahead of you. And so do I.'

Thomas raised his head gingerly, holding it in his hands to make sure it did not spin off his shoulders. He could not believe what he saw. William was already up and dressed, and it was not yet terce.

'Where are you bound that has dragged you out of bed so early?'

Thomas had hoped that Falconer would assist him to get the truth from the young student. He was still inexperienced in interviewing witnesses to crimes, much preferring the inert form of a dead body. Truth could be extracted from that at his own pace, and without protest from the victim. Falconer shrugged his shoulders.

'I have to follow up the trail of this Latin connection with the attempt on Edward's life. I believe he thinks the de Montforts were responsible for it. In the same way they were of course responsible for the murder of his nephew. And the only real source I have for that is Odo de Reppes.'

'But he has been missing for almost two years.'

'And if he is to be found again, the Grand Master of the Templars should know how and where. But Thomas Bérard, the last Grand Master, has been dead these last four months. So the Paris Temple and the Province Master is my best hope of finding anyone who can help, and it's not far to the north, just outside the city walls. You will do fine with Fusoris, as long as you can keep the monks from punching him on the nose again.'

Thomas grinned from under his bedlinen, recalling the way the youth had been subdued yesterday.

'Yes. I have heard of robust Christianity, but never seen it in action until yesterday. Good luck with your search, William.'

Falconer waved a hand in farewell and left Thomas to rouse himself. He had a fair idea how to find the Temple, though he had never crossed the Seine to the north bank since arriving in Paris. But once across the Petit Pont, he found it easy to cross the island in the middle of the river by the wide road that divided the Royal Palace from the cathedral of Notre-Dame. Straight ahead was a narrow plank bridge that barely allowed one person to pass another once on it. Wary of its dizzying setting high above the river, he set about negotiating it with some care. On more than one occasion he stepped cautiously to one side to allow others coming in the opposite direction to pass him. They seemed unconcerned by the narrowness of the crossing, however. Safely on the north bank of the river, which locals called the Right Bank, he walked eastwards along the strand to a big open square that shelved down to the river. Here, there were scores of labourers in rough clothes, some carrying farm implements, others with sacks draped over their shoulders against the weather. Prosperous-looking merchants strode boldly from one group to another, and on inspecting each individual critically would tip one man on the shoulder and walk away. It was some sort of hiring fair, and Falconer felt sorry for the scrawny, ill-favoured ones who were left from this cull of workmen. They would be hard-pressed to find other work in Paris.

Having made his way through a maze of narrow streets, aiming always in what he hoped was a northerly direction, he emerged on another broad avenue. To make sure he was still going towards the Temple, he asked a passer-by if this was the Rue du Temple. The man nodded briefly without breaking his stride, hardly even looking at his questioner. Falconer threw an ironic thank you to his disappearing back, annoyed by the apparent curtness of the denizens of this great city. He had a passing thought that perhaps London felt the same to foreigners too. Once through the narrow and well-fortified Temple gate in the city walls, he could see his goal. Not far away there reared the high and forbidding walls of the Paris Temple of the Order of the Poor Knights of the Temple of Solomon, the order more simply known as the Templars. Above the crenellated wall, he could see the roofs of several substantial buildings. But the most impressive, climbing higher even than the spires of the church, was the louring, multi-turreted presence of the Temple tower – at once a meeting place, treasury and donjon. The entire complex of buildings was set somewhat apart from the rest of Paris on what had once been barren marshes, and gave the impression of aloofness. It was an example of the Templar order setting itself apart from the rest of the world, and a little above the common herd. Falconer walked along the causeway built up to cross the marshland that the Temple stood on and onwards up to the closely guarded entrance to the complex.

When he asked to speak with the Province Master of the order, he was met by a rebuff. Apparently, the last Paris Master had been Amaury de la Roche, but no one had been appointed since his departure.

'Then I will speak to anyone in authority.'

The sergeant-at-arms to whom he was speaking looked him up and down and made no move to find anyone. Falconer realized that he was not the most impressive of arrivals at this portal. Coming on foot from Paris had covered his boots in mud. And dressed as he was in his usual drab black academic robe, he did not present the most powerful or authoritative of images. He sighed and produced Edward's letter from his purse.

'Tell whoever is in charge here that I am on the business of Edward, King of England.'

The stocky sergeant raised a sceptical eyebrow but apparently recognized the wax seal on the letter. It would have been no use his looking at the letter, as he could not read. He turned away and walked across the inner courtyard. Falconer called after him.

'Tell him my name is William Falconer, Regent Master of Oxford.'

Whatever he had said must have had its effect, for it was not long before the sergeant came scurrying back, a grim look on his red face. He cocked a thumb over his shoulder and spoke through gritted teeth.

'Come with me. Sir.'

He had obviously been reprimanded over delaying the man

from Oxford in his task for the English king. Grinning, Falconer followed the soldier back across the courtyard and past a high wall. He faltered only a little when he saw they were approaching the dreaded donjon tower. But before they reached it, the sergeant turned to the right and entered an imposing building next to the tower. It looked like private quarters and was presumably where the Province Master normally lodged. Falconer wondered who was living there now, and who he was being brought to see. He entered a grand hall with arching beams high above his head spanning the vast space. Slit-like windows afforded little light, the only glow coming from the blazing fire at the far end of the hall. He could just make out the silhouette of a tall, well-built man standing before the fire. Even if he squinted, his short-sightedness would allow him no better image. He looked enquiringly towards the sergeant, but the man, having led him into the hall, had retreated, his task complete. The figure by the fire turned around and raised his hand, beckoning Falconer. His resonant voice carried down the hall.

'Come, Master William Falconer.'

There was something familiar about the voice, but Falconer could not place it. He started to walk down the long room, his boots thudding on the stone slabs. It was only when he was close to the man that he could make out his features. His hair was a little greyer than when he had last seen it, and his face a little more lined. But it was him.

'Guillaume. Guillaume de Beaujeu, by God!'

Thomas sat at the back of the schoolroom and listened in silence as Adam Morrish elucidated a text from Theophilus on urines. He was familiar with the text, and so his mind was wandering. Back at the abbey where he and Falconer were staying, he had looked in on John Fusoris after breaking his fast. The cell holding him was still locked, but Thomas could peer through the grille set in the door. The youth was huddled in one corner of his pallet, his knees pulled up to his chest. But he appeared to be sleeping, so Thomas decided Falconer's advice had been wise. He should leave Fusoris to allow the toxins of the khat leaves to exit his body before making any attempt to question him. In a way, it struck him that he had not been so far wrong to think of the youth as possessed by

the Devil. In this case, the possession had been by the medium
of the drug, and time would exorcize it from his body. Now,
as Adam's voice droned on, he felt himself dozing off.

'He learned his medicine in Padua.'

For a moment Thomas thought the voice was inside his
head. But then he realized it was in the form of a whisper,
close to his ear. He glanced to one side, and saw that Friar
Bacon had slipped into the back of the room and was listening
to the exposition of Theophilus. Bacon leaned over to him
again.

'There, they reply heavily on the *articella* – the little art –
and not so much on Johannitius. They are in error, of course.'

As though he heard Bacon's criticism, the teacher out front
gave the two other Englishmen a hard stare, hardly pausing in
his textual analysis. Bacon and Symon grinned at each other
like naughty children and sat quietly through the rest of the
lecture. Afterwards, as the rest of the class made their way out,
calling out jibes and barging into each other, Morrish walked
over to the two of them, his face now glowing with pleasure.
It seemed he had forgotten, or at least forgiven, their whispered
asides. He took Bacon's hand and shook it vigorously.

'Friar Roger, welcome again to my school. I hope you have
not forgotten your promise to lecture to my students at some
point. I myself would value your erudition. On any subject
you care to expound upon.' He threw a glance at Thomas.
'You are very lucky to be involved with such a celebrated
scholar, Thomas. Are you recording his ideas for the benefit
of us all?'

Before Thomas could reply, Bacon cut in.

'Just some notes on the present state of teaching in Paris.
Nothing exceptional. My order prevents me from being . . .
controversial.'

Thomas almost burst out laughing at the pious and humble
expression on Bacon's face. Only he knew how controversial
the text he had begun to scribe really was. Yet in the presence of a master of the University of Paris, and with Bishop
Tempier winkling out those who he thought carried heretical
ideas in their heads, it was wise to be moderate and modest.
He spoke up to support Bacon's deception.

'Indeed, Master Morrish, it will be a contribution to the bishop's
clearance of all suspicious concepts from the university.'

Morrish stared at him closely, unsure if he was being mocked or not. But he took Thomas at his word.

'And your fellow master from Oxford, Master . . .'

'Falconer.'

'Yes, Falconer. How fares his task of collecting information on Bishop Tempier's Condemnations and their effect on teaching?'

Thomas was a little taken aback by Morrish's question.

'I did not know you were aware of that.'

Morrish smiled, pleased at having disconcerted the young Englishman.

'Oh, the university is a small world to itself. Word travels fast, especially of visiting scholars. I am sure Oxford is the same, is it not?'

Thomas shrugged his shoulders, knowing the man was correct. The academic world in Oxford was parochial and prone to gossip more than a small English village.

'I think you are right. But to answer your question, Master Falconer has gathered all he needs. He is now on another task, set him by our new king, Edward.' Foolishly, he revelled in impressing Morrish with his association with Falconer, wanting to surprise him much as Morrish had done to him. 'He moves in elevated circles now. Today he is on his way to the Paris Temple to speak to the Grand Master.'

As soon as he spoke, he knew he was exaggerating merely for effect like some child. He knew William had told him the Grand Master was dead. But he liked the pallor that came to Morrish's face at his pronouncement, and he smiled sweetly.

'Now the friar and I must get on.'

They went through to the back room and sat down together across the table. While Thomas got out his clean parchments and ink, Roger Bacon sat looking pensive before he spoke.

'I don't care if you link my name and that cursed Tempier in one breath. It all adds to the mist of obscurity and conformism I would like to hide inside for the time being. But I don't think you should discuss William's affairs so openly. This town, even more so than Oxford, is a mare's nest of rumour, gossip and envy. Particularly envy.'

Thomas hung his head in shame at his boastfulness. He hoped it wouldn't get Falconer into trouble. Bacon patted his hand consolingly.

'Now take this down.' He took a deep breath. 'As all may read in the works of Aristotle, Seneca, Alfarabius, Plato, Socrates . . . and others, the ancient philosophers attained to the secrets of wisdom, and found out all knowledge. But we Christians have discovered nothing worthy of them, for our morals are worse than theirs.'

Thomas sighed and began to scratch away on the virgin surface of the parchment.

FIFTEEN

The two men sat either side of the fire grinning at each other, each with a goblet of wine in their hand. One was well built, with a neat white tunic covering his broad shoulders and slim waist. He exuded power and self-confidence even though his greying hair betrayed his advancing years. The other was somewhat older still, and a little more down at heel, his dowdy black robe hiding a shape that had once been that of a fighter but was now softer, more generous around the waist. The second man stared at the other in mock astonishment.

'*You* are the new Grand Master, Guillaume?'

De Beaujeu laughed, raising his glass to toast his own success.

'Yes, William. Who would have thought it when we met all those years ago?'

Falconer cast his mind back some dozen years to a time when the Papal Legate was in Oxford. An attempt had been made on Bishop Otho's life, and someone else had got killed. Falconer had at first suspected de Beaujeu, who had appeared in the town just at the right time. His shadowy presence had attracted both Falconer's attention and that of the town constable, Peter Bullock. In fact, the Templar had been on a mission on behalf of the former Grand Master, Thomas Bérard, concerning the appointment of the next Pope to succeed Alexander. He was a killer of men in wars, but not a murderer. Once Falconer's mistake had been rectified, the two men had struck up a friendship based on mutual respect. It had lasted the years, even though they rarely encountered each other. Each had gone his own way and pursued different goals. It seemed that de Beaujeu had achieved his, and Falconer was not surprised.

'Actually, I had no doubt you would be the Grand Master eventually. Even if you had had to eliminate all the opposition on the way, you would have got there.'

He remembered the Templar's extraordinary skill in silent

death. De Beaujeu was more like a Muslim Assassin than he probably dared to admit to himself. Now the Templar saluted his companion and old friend.

'And you, Master William Falconer, you come before me as emissary of King Edward of England, no less. Or was that merely a ruse to gain admittance to the Temple?'

Falconer's face took on a more serious look, as he recalled the task that had led him here.

'Indeed it was not. I can show you a letter from the king, if you don't believe me.'

De Beaujeu held up his hand.

'That is not necessary between old friends. What is it you seek?'

'Something you can help me with, actually. It concerns a Templar who got himself into trouble in England a couple of years ago. He then disappeared from view, and I don't know if he is alive still. But I would dearly like to talk to him, if he is.'

De Beaujeu frowned. He may be the Grand Master of the Templar Knights and could wield great power. But the order took seriously the protection of its own. It would be a dangerous game to expose another Templar to the scrutiny of an outsider. Even one as respected as William Falconer. And he had a good idea who it was whom Falconer was hunting. He had to play the game through, however.

'Who is this man you are seeking?'

'He is called Odo de Reppes.'

It was as de Beaujeu thought. He knew all about de Reppes – had been advised by Thomas Bérard on his deathbed what deadly affair the Templar had been involved in. What he did not know was why his friend needed to talk to de Reppes. And so he now wanted some time to consider his options. He played dumb, though he did not like doing so with Falconer.

'I am the new man, you understand. There is much for me to find out concerning the affairs of the order. Matters that only each Grand Master would know about, and some facts die with him. Let me ask around and see if de Reppes can be unearthed. Only then can I consider your request – whether I can allow you to see him or not.'

'I understand that, Guillaume. I know your allegiance always has been and always will be to the order. I can expect nothing less of you, especially now. I can assure you of one thing, though. If what I have heard of de Reppes' actions is true, then I can do him no more harm than he has already done to himself. And if they are untrue, then it is as well to set the facts right. How much time do you need?'

He was so relieved at Falconer's retreat that de Beaujeu spoke without thought.

'A day or two will suffice, I am sure. Come back the day after tomorrow, and I will hope to have news for you.'

Falconer nodded and took his leave of his old friend. He was escorted back to the gateway of the Temple by the same sergeant-at-arms, who must have waited patiently outside the great hall until the Grand Master's visitor left. Walking across the marshy land between the Temple and Paris's city walls, Falconer glanced back at the Temple tower. Its many turrets jutted up into the cloudy sky like arrows aimed at the very heavens. He grimaced, as a few drops of rain fell.

'What sort of game are you playing now, Guillaume? What do you know about Odo de Reppes that you would hide from me?'

Falconer had seen through de Beaujeu's hasty assessment of his ability to trace Odo de Reppes. If he had truly not known where he was, it would surely have been impossible to say he could tell Falconer in only a day or two. He had expected to be delayed by weeks while the man was sought. And even then he might have been dead already, or far away in Outremer. But the new Grand Master had promised a response much more quickly than that. Nor had he directly said he did not know where de Reppes was located, choosing the words of his reply with care. Falconer therefore knew that the Templar's location was almost certainly already known to Guillaume. He had just needed time to work out what his friend wanted him for. Well, Falconer would let de Beaujeu have the time, if in the end he let him speak to the man. In the meantime, he would see how Thomas Symon was doing with his hunt for the murderer of Paul Hebborn.

Reaching the banks of the Seine, Falconer stepped cautiously on to the narrow plank bridge called the Planche Milbray that he had crossed on his way to the Temple. The wooden surface was now made even more slippery by the drizzle. He trod carefully, and was halfway across when he heard a cry from

behind him. Looking back, he saw that an old man was
clutching on to the handrail. He was clearly complaining about
someone who had pushed past him in his haste to cross the
bridge. The figure, now approaching Falconer, was enveloped
in a black cloak with its hood pulled up over his head. Nothing
unusual in that, thought Falconer; it was raining, after all.
Which also probably explained the person's need to hurry. He
turned back and walked on, planting his feet firmly on the
planks. Suddenly, the speeding figure was upon him, having
closed the gap between them extremely quickly. Falconer
turned aside to let him pass, but the figure hit him hard with
his shoulder, deliberately barging into him. As Falconer lost
his balance, he was aware of a pale, youthful face staring at
him from under the hood. Then he slid between the handrail
and the planks and could see only the swift-flowing river
looming up below him.

SIXTEEN

Thomas Symon was in a hurry to return to the Abbey of St Victor and John Fusoris, but Roger Bacon had detained him long past the time when he should have left. The friar had been in full flow and reluctant to finish, even though he could see that his scribe was itching to go. He had concluded on a flourish that still rang in Thomas's head.

'Many wise men – considering the predictions of the Sibyls and Merlin and Aquila and Festo – have reckoned that the times of Antichrist are at hand in these days of ours.'

As he strode through the streets of Paris, he shivered again at the words and clutched the satchel that contained them. The bag was stuffed once more with parchment pages, and Thomas's collection at the abbey was growing. He thought the material so inflammatory that he wondered if the building might be struck by the hand of God and destroyed. It was as though the freeing of his words from the confines of the Franciscan friary had released Bacon from his holy shackles. But the outpouring was not the friar's only way of recording the truth as he saw it. Thomas knew Bacon was still writing in a private book using his peculiar ciphered hand. He always carried it with him when he left the friary for fear of its being confiscated. Thomas had sneaked a look once when Bacon had gone to piss out of the back of the school building into the river. As he flicked through the pages, his eye was caught by a vivid illustration of a woman, naked save for a head-dress, standing in a bath shaped like a flower. Each of her arms was extended into a tube with junctions off it. The tubes made Thomas think of the veins he had seen in anatomized bodies, or perhaps the pipework of the female generative organ. He had blushed at the explicit nature of the drawing, and then quickly closed the book as he heard Bacon returning. He had not had time to consider what the mysterious book meant as Bacon had continued his discourse immediately.

Moreover, he now had other pressing business to pursue.

Before he spoke to John Fusoris, he wanted to speak to Hellequin. He was sure the young man knew more about Morrish's students, and their behaviour, than he was letting on. He was determined to confront him with it. Entering the Place Maubert, he sought out the inn with the withered vine hanging over the door and entered. Looking around the bustling interior of the tavern for any sign of Hellequin, de la Casteigne or the other students, he was shocked to see Falconer seated at a table drinking deeply from a large goblet. He pushed through a crowd of revellers, who behaved as though they had been drinking all afternoon, to stand before Falconer.

'William. What are you doing here?'

Falconer looked up at Thomas wearily.

'Recovering my equilibrium, Thomas.'

Before he could ask what Falconer meant, Thomas felt a hand on his shoulder. It was Jack Hellequin with a fresh flagon of wine in his fist.

'Stand aside, Master Symon. Your friend is in need of further refreshment. He almost fell from the plank bridge.'

'Fell from the bridge?'

Falconer held out his empty goblet for Hellequin to fill.

'Yes. And if it wasn't for this young man here, I would have landed up in the Seine and got carried away downstream. I would no doubt have ended up crossing the English Channel sooner than I had expected.'

Falconer shivered at the thought and took another deep draught of the wine. Hellequin sat beside him and took up the story.

'I was crossing to the Right Bank and saw someone in difficulties. A woman was screaming, and I ran. The man, whom I now know as your friend Master Falconer, was hanging on to the planks of the footway with his fingernails. I managed to grab his wrists and haul him back, or he would have been lost.'

'But how . . . ?'

Thomas was so shocked that he couldn't even frame his question. Falconer quickly explained.

'It was raining, and the planks of the bridge were slippery. I was careless, that's all.'

Thomas dropped down on to the bench opposite Hellequin and dragged a goblet towards him. Forgetting his resolve of that very morning, he poured some wine from the flagon and drank it off. Falconer laughed and rested his hand on Thomas's.

'You look more scared than I was as young Hellequin pulled me to safety, Thomas. But take it steady with the wine. We do have other matters to attend to back at the abbey.'

Thomas took the hint and put his goblet down. In truth, the wine was rough, and its acid nature reminded him of his sore head from that morning. He belched.

'You are right. But I am glad you are safe, and I thank you, Jack, for plucking William from a certain death.'

He stuck his hand out and Hellequin took it, even though he scoffed at his words.

'You exaggerate. I am sure I just saved the master from a dunking. Are you sure you will not stay? It is Master Falconer's coin that has purchased this flagon, and it is only half empty.'

Falconer rose from the table, shaking his head.

'Share it with your friends, Jack. Thomas and I have much to talk about. And I am in need of some rest. This day has been altogether too exciting.'

He made for the door. Thomas began to follow him before remembering why he had come to the Withered Vine. He had wanted to ask Jack about the khat that Fusoris had taken. And where he thought he might have got it from. But Falconer was already out of the door, and a couple of the other students had appeared as if from nowhere. They had a good nose for free supplies and were ready to partake of Falconer's wine. He left them to it and followed Falconer out into the busy square.

As they walked towards the Porte St-Victor, Falconer said something that shook Thomas to the core.

'It was no accident on the bridge. I was deliberately pushed off the planks by someone who didn't want me to know who he was. He was hooded, and I got only a glimpse of his face. And then I was over the edge.'

'Why would someone do that?'

'Perhaps because I had been asking the wrong questions. Or maybe the right questions of the wrong people.'

Thomas glanced nervously over his shoulder, fearing that whoever had been Falconer's assailant might still be lurking. If he knew he had failed, he would surely try again. He also was reminded of Bacon's admonition over telling Adam

Morrish too much of Falconer's affairs. Could his indiscretion have resulted in the attack on his friend? He sincerely hoped not. Then a thought occurred to him.

'If Jack Hellequin saved you, did he not see the attacker? If the attacker came at you from behind – from the Right Bank – and ran past, and Jack was coming from the Left Bank, he should have seen him. Or did the man run in the opposite direction?'

As they passed under the arch of the gateway, Falconer smiled.

'I see I have taught you well. He could have seen him, for he said he was crossing towards the Right Bank when he saw the commotion. The attacker came up behind me, and barged me over. But I was rather too busy hanging on to know what he did then. The next thing I knew, Hellequin was pulling on my wrists, and I was lying down on the bridge and giving thanks for my luck. When I asked him about the incident, he said he saw no one suspicious, though several people passed him walking towards the Left Bank. My attacker may have thrown his hood back and slowed his pace, of course, in order to appear inconspicuous.'

By now they had entered the cloisters of the abbey, and the sound of vespers could be heard from within the chapel. The calm of their surroundings was in sharp contrast to the turmoil of both their days. And though it was unlikely that they would be overheard, they retreated to the sanctuary of their shared room before continuing their conversation. Falconer slumped on his bed, unwilling to admit even to himself that the experience had shaken him. He took a few deep breaths before daring to speak to Thomas. He was afraid that a tremor in his voice might betray his state, and scare Thomas more than he already had been.

'And did your day go well, Thomas?'

The younger man nodded from where he stood, arranging the stack of parchments on the table.

'The friar is as scathing as ever concerning the Church, and yet we have hardly begun to record his store of knowledge.' He sighed, patting the newly written texts. 'I had hoped to learn more.'

'Have patience. Roger has always moved at his own pace, but he will get to the point. You will learn from him.' He sat

up, having cleared his head a little. 'Now shall we see if we
can get some food from the kitchens? Then we can talk to
John Fusoris without our stomachs rumbling.'

They were in luck. The cook, a lay servant who did not care
for the fourth pillar of the Rule of St Benedict – diet – gave
them each a bowl of stew that had been prepared for the sick
in the infirmary. It had been flavoured with garlic, and pepper
and cumin, and was delicious. A crust of bread wiped around
the wooden bowl ensured that none of the stew was wasted.
Falconer would have lingered by the fire, but Thomas was now
anxious to speak to John Fusoris. Grumbling, Falconer rose
and brushed the breadcrumbs off his robe.

'Come, then, let's get on with it.'

They returned to the cloister and walked around its perimeter
to where the cell holding the student was located. When they
got there, they found the door ajar. Thomas, his newly filled
stomach churning with apprehension, called out.

'John, are you there?'

There was no reply, and he pushed the door wide open.
The cell was newly cleaned, with fresh rushes on the floor,
and it was quite empty. Thomas groaned.

'Oh, John, what has happened to you?'

Grim-faced, Falconer spun around and marched off towards
the chapel. Thomas, fearing William might burst into the
church and cause mayhem in the middle of the service, raced
after him and grabbed his arm.

'William, stop. Think what you are doing.'

'I know what I am doing, Thomas. There is a stink of
corruption here, and I mean to winkle it out.'

He pulled away from Thomas's grip and carried on his
purposeful march to the chapel doors. Fortunately, the service
had just ended, and the monks were emerging. Falconer caught
sight of one of the monks who had subdued Fusoris when
Thomas had brought him in last night. He stuck out an accu-
satory finger.

'You. I want a word with you.'

The other monks who surrounded the one accused shied
away in fear of this angry figure. The monk himself stopped
in his tracks, struck dumb by the verbal onslaught. Then, as
his companions scuttled away, he saw who it was had shouted
at him, and he put on a truculent face.

'If you want the boy, you are too late. He has gone of his own volition.'

Falconer stepped up close, thrusting his face into the other man's.

'I don't believe you. He was afraid for his own soul, so why would he choose to leave the sanctuary of the abbey?'

The monk backed off, no longer sure of himself. He glanced around to see if anyone would come to his rescue. But the three men were alone. Everyone else had disappeared. He broke down.

'Someone came for him. A friend, he said. And the boy was calmer this morning. It was as though the demon that possessed him had been driven out, thank the Lord.'

He made to sidle past Falconer, but William grabbed the long, pointed hood that hung down his back. Choking, the monk begged him to let go.

'You can go when you have told me what this friend looked like.'

'He was young. Well, young-looking, and of average height. Normal. And dressed in a dark cloak with a hood. He had the hood up, so I could not see his face properly. It was raining.'

Falconer let the hood go, and the monk hurried off into the darkness of the cloister aisle clutching his throat. Falconer looked at Thomas, concern brewing in his heart.

'I have a bad feeling about this, Thomas. If I were more religious than I am, I would think the Devil was stalking Paris in the shape of a young man in a black cloak. First he pushes me off the bridge, then he comes to collect poor John Fusoris and carry him off to hell.'

Thomas frowned.

'Do you believe the two incidents are connected in some way? And what about Paul Hebborn? Perhaps this same person pushed him off Notre-Dame.'

'I am afraid you may be right. I think we had better try to find John before some harm comes to him. Though I don't know where we can start.'

'We can try his lodgings. He may have gone back there.'

'Show me the way.'

In the end they found John Fusoris quite quickly. Leading Falconer directly towards the river bank, Thomas took the narrow lane to the right past the convent of the Bernardins.

Emerging from the other end of the lane, they saw lanterns bobbing about further along the river bank. Getting closer, they could hear the sound of men's voices calling out to each other. One rough accent carried the loudest.

'Over here. He's here.'

The lanterns converged on the outflow into the Seine of a stinking, turgid stream. Falconer got there ahead of Thomas, his long legs eating up the ground.

'What have you found, friends?'

A ring of coarse-looking faces, half-lit by the yellow lamps the men were holding high, stared at him. The man with the rough accent spoke up.

'Another drunk drowned in the river, master. It needn't bother you. We can take care of him.'

The men's faces betrayed nervousness, and the swinging lamps cast eerie shadows over them. Thomas guessed that they were scavengers, living off the misery of others. A dead body would be good pickings for them. For it was a body he could see at their feet. Whoever it was lay face down in the mud of the river bank, the clothes soaked from being immersed in the river. Thomas was fearful that his and Falconer's lives were at risk in such company. But his companion seemed unconcerned. He leaned over the body, discerning that the clothes were too stained with mud to be sure if they were those of a labourer or a man of quality.

'Shine your light over here, friend. Let me get a good look.'

The leader of the scavengers was so surprised at Falconer's taking charge that he obeyed instinctively. He held the lantern closer to the body. Falconer hefted it by the shoulders and turned the body over. Thomas groaned. It was John Fusoris, and there could be no doubt that he was dead.

SEVENTEEN

Much later, they were leaning on the parapet of the Petit Pont watching the reddish light of dawn creep along the river towards them. It had taken the rest of the night to arrange the proper disposition of John Fusoris. Falconer had guarded Fusoris' remains, while Thomas had made arrangements for the Mathurin convent, which had housed the body of Paul Hebborn, to take the new corpse. Mud from the river bank stained the slab on which Fusoris was laid. But the same self-effacing monk who had spoken to Falconer about Hebborn had gently cleansed his features and straightened his hair. The dead youth still looked fearful, however. His eyelids were now closed, but before the monk had dealt with them he had had a wide-eyed look about him. His stare reminded Falconer of Hebborn's look when he had come to see the first dead youth.

Now, breathing in the freshness of the new day as the river flowed below them, Falconer passed this information on to his young companion.

'I remember Hebborn's eyes were wide when I examined him. Just like Fusoris.'

Thomas frowned in concentration, squinting into the dawning light. The sun was beginning to flood the river's surface with gold.

'You mean his stare, or his pupils?'

'His pupils, I suppose. I recall thinking Hebborn's eyes were like deep dark pools. Does that signify something?'

Falconer knew Thomas's knowledge of anatomy and the physical reactions of the body to poisons or drink already far outstretched his own. Thomas could not say for sure, though.

'If you saw his eyes when he was alive, there could be some significance. Some drugs make the pupils dilate. But after death the pupils relax and open wide anyway.'

Falconer grunted in frustration. It seemed his observations on Paul Hebborn's body were useless.

'Then the fact that Fusoris' pupils were wide open when I

spoke to him only serves to confirm he was eating khat leaves. But then we knew that.'

Thomas paused, a little confused by Falconer's statement.

'When you spoke to him? When did you do that? You didn't speak to him when he was incarcerated in the first place. I remember that because I was there.'

'Oh, didn't I say? Last night I couldn't sleep. Kept tossing and turning on that infernal pallet they call a bed at the abbey. So I got up and walked around the cloister. There was a candle burning in one of the cells. When I looked through the grille, I saw that Fusoris was awake too and kneeling in prayer. I asked him how he felt.'

Thomas couldn't believe that William had not already told him this.

'And what did he say?'

Falconer shrugged his shoulders and squinted into the rising sun.

'He was still a little incoherent. Still talking of the Devil and temptation. What he did say, though, was that Paul had been weak and had given in to temptation. He said that Hebborn had eaten of the forbidden fruit. He used those exact words – eating forbidden fruit – and said the Devil had tempted them all.'

'Who do you think he meant?'

Falconer thought about Thomas's question, picking through what Fusoris had said with more care. At the time, he had been tired and inclined to be dismissive of the boy's garbled message. Now he wondered if there was not some truth in it. He cursed himself for ignoring what had been placed in front of him.

'I think he was referring to all the other students. Do you think they have been up to something as a group, something that caused Hebborn and Fusoris to be killed?'

Thomas thought Falconer was on to something. He recalled the two students of medicine eating something and giggling together in the tavern the night he got drunk on coarse red wine. One of them he didn't know the name of, but the other one had been de la Casteigne. He could get the truth out of him easily enough. Or from Jack Hellequin. He was suddenly hesitant in case he found out an unpleasant truth about Hellequin, whom he had grown to like.

'Shall I speak to them? Find out what has been happening?'

'Not yet. We don't know who is the one who has caused all this. Who the person is whom Fusoris saw as the Devil tempting him and others. To show your hand too soon may endanger your life. Fusoris talked to you, and he died. Perhaps Hebborn was killed for the same reason. Damn it all, we don't know enough about him to come to any sensible conclusion. And his body will have been buried by now. We have nothing.'

Suddenly, he snapped his fingers and delved into the scrip tied to his waist. Thomas was puzzled, until Falconer pulled something from his purse. It was Paul Hebborn's scrip that Falconer had stuffed into his own purse and forgotten about. He pulled open the drawstrings and carefully tipped the contents on to the level stone parapet of the bridge. The horn spoon, three small coins, a broken comb and the book still did not say much of the dead boy's life. Thomas pushed them around with his finger.

'Is there nothing else?'

Falconer shook his head but felt the purse to make sure. Running his fingers along one of the stitched seams, he felt a hard lump. Excitedly, he turned the scrip inside out, and a small object fell out on to the parapet's surface. He was disappointed.

'It's just a stone.'

But Thomas eagerly picked up the object and began to examine it. It was the size and shape of a pebble, and sandy in colour. He sniffed it and then cautiously held it to his mouth and licked it. Falconer was intrigued by the look of triumph in Thomas's eyes.

'What is it, Thomas?'

'It is a resin produced from a plant. In the East men rub the plant buds until the resin accumulates on their hands. Then they scrape it off. Eating it causes euphoria, which is why it is taken. But it can also cause fear and anxiety. If Hebborn ate some of this, he could have feared for his life and imagined any sort of phantasmagoria – demons, Devils pursuing him or the fires of hell.'

Falconer shuddered. He recalled his involuntary experience with khat, which was bad enough. This sounded infinitely worse. If the students had been fed this, no wonder they

behaved strangely. Then Thomas said something that struck
a chord with him.

'There is a rumour that the Eastern sect of Assassins is
associated with eating it, and that is why they are so crazy.
But it is just a rumour – a slur on their beliefs, perhaps.'

'You are talking about opium, aren't you? That in the East
they call hashish.'

Thomas nodded, and Falconer thought of King Edward's
account of Anzazim's attack. The mad appearance of the
Assassin's eyes. He looked at the pale stone Thomas held in
his fingers, marvelling at what it could cause to happen.

'Throw it in the river.'

'What?' Falconer's reaction surprised Thomas. 'Is it not
evidence of wrongdoing? Why get rid of it?'

'Because it is too dangerous to leave lying around. Throw
it in the water.'

Thomas did so, and the small stone plopped into the river
to settle among the mud and other stones on the river bed.
Falconer squared his shoulders, gathered up Hebborn's sad
possessions and patted his companion on the back.

'Come. Let us break our fast and work out what we are to
do next.'

'You go ahead. There is something I want to do before I
return to the abbey.'

Falconer watched as Thomas hurried off then walked along
the streets of Paris towards the abbey. His sombre mood was
not lightened by the brightness of the rising sun.

Guillaume de Beaujeu was glad of the day's grace he had
given himself to consider Falconer's request to see Odo de
Reppes. As his friend had no doubt divined from his ill-
considered delaying tactic, Guillaume knew exactly where the
disgraced Templar knight was to be found. He should have
told Falconer that it might take weeks to find out the truth.
To tell him it would take only a day or two gave away the
fact that he already knew. He was normally more canny than
that. Perhaps seeing Falconer again after so long had lulled
him into the slip. He had even considered recovering the situation by saying he could not trace the man. But that would
have implied he was incompetent as Grand Master.

And then that very morning he had received an unusual

request. In any other circumstances it would have been a summons, for it was to attend the King of England in King Philip's palace. But Guillaume was now a man in a powerful position himself and had met Edward before in Outremer. The invitation had been presented by a curious popinjay of a man. He had doffed his sugarloaf hat and bowed low.

'Grand Master, Edward, King of England and Gascony, begs the pleasure of your presence in the French king's Royal Palace at your earliest convenience.'

Filled with curiosity, Guillaume agreed to attend as soon as he and his escort could saddle up. Sir John Appleby bowed most obsequiously yet again and left to take the Grand Master's reply to his master. It was not long before Guillaume and four knights of the order were clattering over the Pont aux Changeurs towards the Royal Palace set on the Ile de la Cité. Once he had dismounted inside the palace grounds, Guillaume was confronted again by the gaudily dressed Appleby, who took him with no further ado to Edward's chambers. There, the tall, well-built king greeted Guillaume like an old friend, shaking him firmly by the hand.

'Welcome, Grand Master. Welcome, Guillaume. It is good to see you again. We must have last met on that unfortunate sortie to Krak des Moabites.'

Edward was referring to an expedition into OutreJourdain to besiege a Crusader castle in the land of the Moabites, which had been lost many years earlier to Saladin. In fact, the castle had been longer in Muslim hands than it had been in those of the original builders. Guillaume was flattered that Edward should assume a friendship with him on the basis of such an acquaintance. He had been a career Templar on his way up, but still just one of the commanders under Prince Edward's control. He smiled politely and murmured his acknowledgement of the reminder. Edward continued to press on.

'Of course, it was a waste of time. Reinforcing Acre was my primary task, which I am glad to say I achieved before having to return to take up greater responsibilities. But I am sure, like me, you would prefer to be back there fighting, despite the heat and dust. It was such a . . . pure existence.'

Guillaume saw the longing in Edward's eyes and could almost believe the man would rather be on a battlefield than burdened with the cares of state. He had to remind himself that Edward had shown a rare ability for political expediency during the Barons' War in England. He had switched allegiances to suit himself, often enraging his own father in the process. To present himself as a simple soldier was a subterfuge. He wondered what trick the new king was up to now. He did not have long to wait to find out.

Falconer, meanwhile, had a day to wait before his chance came to speak to Odo de Reppes. If such a chance truly existed. He was convinced that Guillaume de Beaujeu knew exactly where the disgraced Templar was to be found. But if that was in England still, then his task would be hampered, and at the very best become a long-drawn-out one. It may be that he would have to return to England before completing his investigations anyway. What had troubled the king most in the series of attacks on his family had been the death of his little son and heir, John. Falconer knew he would have to probe that affair soon. And review what he knew from Sir Humphrey Segrim about the events at Berkhamsted Castle two years earlier.

Unable to sit still in the gloomy and sparsely furnished room in the Abbey of St Victor, he took himself on a walk around the city of Paris. His meandering steps led him through the portal close by the abbey and past the convent of the Bernardins. Almost inevitably, he walked near to where Fusoris' body had been found on the banks of the river, past Adam Morrish's school and over the bridges connecting the Ile to the Left and Right Banks. With a determined tread, he studiously avoided the plank bridge and made for the sturdier stone bridge hard by the Royal Palace. It was the Pont aux Changeurs, and it teemed with hawkers, dealers and money-changers. Many of the last group of people were Jews. Usury – to make money from money – was forbidden to Christians by the Church, which placed it on a par with prostitution. Some Christians bore the burden of disapproval and carried out the trade. But many more Jews resorted to moneylending as it was one of the few businesses allowed them.

Approaching the island end of the bridge, Falconer's thoughts of the Jews reminded him of Saphira Le Veske. He was still desirous of finding her in Honfleur and resolving their differences. He was also thinking of the others in Oxford that he had left behind. Peter Bullock, the town constable, would no doubt be patrolling the university town, keeping a keen eye out for wrongdoing. Then Sir Humphrey Segrim entered his thoughts again as he recalled his promise to the old man. In order to assuage the knight's sense of guilt that he had brought down the wrath of Odo de Reppes on his wife, Falconer needed to hear the truth of the Templar's deeds in England. Segrim had seen him in Berkhamsted when Edward's uncle, Richard, King of Germany, had died. Killed by Odo, Segrim had insisted. It was curious how fate had now drawn Falconer into investigating that very death, along with that of young Prince John while in Richard's care. He could not have imagined that occurring when he had met Segrim months ago in Oxford.

Pushing through the crowds that thronged the buildings perched precariously over the river on either flank of the bridge, he was surprised to catch a glimpse of someone. It was only a fleeting sight, but it was one of a handsome figure in a green dress. The woman's hair was covered by a modest snood, but a couple of errant locks of red hair had escaped the head-dress. He uttered her name.

'Saphira?'

EIGHTEEN

Falconer stopped, and people began to push past him on the bridge, complaining at the obstruction he was causing. He thought the person he had seen had been moving towards one of the buildings to his right, but he had lost sight of her. Could it have been Saphira? Or had his eyes been deceiving him due to him thinking about Oxford and all he had left behind? There was only one way of finding out.

He forced his way across the street towards the place where the red-haired woman had disappeared. The narrow stone building had a small sign over the door in Hebrew, with a name carved below it. It read 'Manser of Calais'. Falconer hesitated for a moment, recalling the terms on which he and Saphira had parted, then pushed open the door and stepped into the darkened room beyond. Two faces, a little startled by his abrupt appearance, looked up at him from where they sat either side of a small table. One was an old man with a hatchet face half hidden by a beard and with deep brown eyes. The other face was that of Saphira Le Veske. Her look of alarm was abruptly replaced by a broad smile on recognizing who it was had entered.

'William! You have saved me a long and tedious hunt. How did you find me so soon?'

She held out her hand, and Falconer's fears about his reception fell away. He clasped her hand in both of his, squeezing a little more powerfully than he needed to.

'Luck, I suppose. I was walking across the bridge thinking of you, and there you were. You are not an apparition, are you?'

'You can feel that I am flesh and blood from the way you are grasping my hand. A mite too tightly, I may say.'

He responded to her teasing and released her fingers.

'I had to be sure. Too many strange things have been happening to me recently. But tell me: how did you know I was in Paris?'

She looked down at her feet, not wishing yet to admit the need she had felt to communicate with William.

'I . . . er . . . sent a message to Rabbi Jacob that I would be longer than I anticipated in Honfleur, and asked him to pay the rent on my house. When I got his reply a few weeks later, he happened to mention he had heard you had left for France too.'

What she did not say was that she had specifically asked the rabbi for some information about Falconer. And that she had been told he was actually in Paris. Oblivious to her hiding these facts, he took a step back and surveyed her. Her shapely figure, clad in one of her familiar green dresses, had not changed. It looked even more enticing, in fact. He pointed to her headgear.

'I see your hair is as unruly as ever.'

Saphira instinctively reached up and tucked an errant curl back under her starched white snood. Then she turned to the money-changer, who still sat at his table, visibly amused by the bantering exchange.

'It seems I do not need your services, Manser. This is the man I came to Paris to seek out. He has fallen right into my lap.'

Manser smiled broadly, nodding his head.

'It is just as well he did. I fear it might have taken me weeks to find one scholar among all those that throng Paris. Even if we could have narrowed it down to Englishmen.' He looked Falconer up and down. 'There are far too many Englishmen in France.'

Saphira laughed and, taking Falconer by the arm, led him from Manser's gloomy counting house. They sauntered along the Right Bank of the Seine towards the hiring square Falconer had seen before. Business there was brisk, and the couple watched in silence for a while, both thinking their own thoughts. When they did speak, it was together.

'I was going to come to Honfleur . . .'

'My business was finished in Honfleur . . .'

They both stopped and laughed. Saphira bowed her head in mock deference.

'Please, master, you must speak first.'

William gave her a serious look that he could not sustain, and they laughed again. Her tinkling laughter wove itself around his low guffaw, and he held his hands up in defeat.

'Saphira, I . . .'

She put a finger to his lips.

'You need say nothing, dear William. Let us call a truce in our battle.'

He nodded his head sagely.

'A truce sounds better for my sense of pride than a complete capitulation. A truce it shall be.'

She took his arm in both hands and clutched it tightly.

'Now, tell me what you have been doing while I have been subjugating the wilfulness of an errant sea captain and setting my wine-shipping business to rights again.'

Thomas's day proved a frustrating one. Despite Falconer's warning of the dangers, he had hoped to question Peter de la Casteigne or Jack Hellequin about his idea that at least some of the students of Adam Morrish had been misusing drugs. But both of them were absent from the lectures. Which was no real surprise, as those students who had come were sorely distracted by the second death in their midst. Most of the clerks could not concentrate on what their master was teaching. And Master Adam himself seemed out of sorts, his lecture on Galen being listless and full of errors. Thomas listened with only half an ear, thinking he might ask Morrish if he kept any preparations on the premises. He knew that hemlock and opium were used as an anaesthetic, and a useful ointment could be made up from opium and lard. Had the students broken in to his supplies themselves? He waited until the end of Adam's lectures in order to be able to question him. But as soon as Adam had finished, the master claimed a headache was plaguing him. He asked Thomas to lock the building after he had finished his meeting with Friar Bacon, and he hurried off before Thomas could speak to him properly. The students dispersed without expressing their usual pleasure at being released for the day.

It was a moment before Thomas realized that the building now stood empty and silent. And that he was alone with the key to the front door in his hand. It was the best chance he would have to search the house. That at least could not place him in any danger. Familiar with the layout on the lower level, he decided to start at the top, and climbed the creaky stairs leading to the upper room, the only one he had never seen inside. He opened the door cautiously, despite the fact that he knew the master had left, feeling he was doing something wrong. The solar was untidy in a way that was unlike Falconer's room in Oxford. His friend's quarters were cluttered with the detritus of his enquiring mind. Esoteric texts were buried under rocks with strange marks on them, and under skulls of animals, and birds' wings were stretched to see how they might support a body in flight. Morrish's room was merely uncared for. He leaned over

the table in one corner of the room to find a battered copy
of the *Isagogue of Johannitius* open and turned on its front,
straining the cords that held it together. Another medical text –
Haly ibn Ridwan's treatise on Galen – lay discarded on the floor.
Thomas was appalled. Did Morrish not know the value of these
works? Letters written on parchment were scattered around as
though of no further use. Thomas knew each one of them could
be scraped clean and reused. Morrish appeared not to need to
care about being penny wise. Searching further, he found nothing
that resembled a pharmacy of drugs, or even a formulary listing
medicines and their uses. Until he looked under the table and
found a small chest. He pulled it out and tried to open the lid.
But it was locked, the hasp deeply scratched and battered. As
he could not open it without the key, he was not able to verify
if it contained opium or any other sorts of herbs and preparations. Idly, he poked the door key he still held in his hand in
the lock and jiggled it. And almost jumped out of his skin when
a voice called out from down below.

'Thomas Symon, are you here?'

He had thought guiltily that it was Morrish and that he
would be caught in the act of prying into the master's affairs.
But it was Doctor Mirabilis come to record more of the information from his compendious mind. Thomas pushed the chest
back under the table and hurried downstairs, his face red with
embarrassment. When he had sat down in their damp, dark
room, quill poised, Bacon had carried on from where he had
left off the previous day.

'Experimental science is at the heart of everything we do,
testing by personal experience all the conclusions of all other
sciences.'

It was as if he had never broken off from yesterday's train
of thought at all.

Sitting in the Grand Master's house in the Paris Temple, the
present incumbent was thinking deeply about his interview with
the English king. Guillaume de Beaujeu was a thoughtful man
as well as a warrior. He was as used to biding his time and
thinking through a problem as he was to making instantaneous
decisions on the battlefield. He had once been captured by the
infidel and had waited months in prison to be ransomed. During
that time he had developed the ability to look at issues from all

sides before coming to a conclusion. He knew too that Edward
was a canny strategist not easily given to revealing his motives
concerning a matter. So it had been no surprise to him that the
English king had spent a while reminiscing about their mutual
past in Outremer. The reminder of their abortive skirmish against
Krak des Moabites castle had only been a preliminary sortie
into that history. He had warmed to his task with more wine.

'Do you remember taking Nazareth?'

Guillaume grimaced to himself. Indeed he did. Edward had
slaughtered all the inhabitants in an orgy of blood.

'Yes, Your Majesty, I do.'

Edward smiled at the recollection of his bloody deed.

'If the Mongols had come down on our side, I believe we
would have taken Jerusalem. Or if Hugh of Cyprus had stirred
his lazy arse and helped.' He looked de Beaujeu in the eye
and quaffed more wine. 'I believe you, like me, supported
Charles of Anjou's claim to the throne of Jerusalem.'

Guillaume, only sipping at his goblet, nodded. Edward knew
very well the Templar stood with Charles and against King
Hugh's claim to Jerusalem. And that both men were close
friends of Tedaldo Visconti, the man who was now Pope
Gregory X. He waited patiently for the next words that he felt
sure would get to the crux of Edward's ramblings. The king
laid his goblet down and leaned forward in his chair.

'So it was a shock to me when I heard rumblings of a plot
from within your order against me and mine.'

Ah, so this was all about Odo de Reppes. How curious that
William Falconer should raise the matter in Edward's name
only the day before. Guillaume put on his solemn face, the
one he used to use when gaming with dice which he knew
was inscrutable. He nodded his head and stroked his beard
with his strong yet elegant fingers.

'A single renegade who has been dealt with already.'

'He is . . . dead, then?'

Guillaume did some quick thinking and reckoned that
Edward already knew that de Reppes was not dead. He was
being tested.

'No. But he is suffering in a way worse than a quick death.
He is imprisoned here in Paris.'

'In the donjon tower.'

It was a flat statement carrying all the horror associated

with the great turreted building that loomed over the northern marshes. The Templar donjon was not a pleasant place to be. Guillaume affirmed the statement.

'He will never emerge alive. Nor will I give him up to any other authority.'

Edward understood the implicit warning. The Templars dealt with their own, and no one else – even a monarch – was allowed to interfere. He raised a hand to ward off the Grand Master's threat.

'I am not seeking to play any part in his punishment. Merely that you allow someone to see him, and to talk to him.'

Guillaume smiled to himself, knowing he had information not even the king was aware of.

'Master Falconer, you mean?'

The king looked startled for a moment, but he recovered well, hiding his confusion in his wine goblet. After he had drunk another mouthful, he continued.

'Then Falconer has already spoken to you. I must compli-ment him on his tenacity and speed of investigation when I see him next. Yes, it is Falconer I would like to be allowed to speak to de Reppes. He can tell Falconer who was behind the murder of my cousin Henry by the de Montfort brothers. And that may lead the master to uncover something about other matters I have asked him to look into.' He grimaced. 'The de Montforts are like the Hydra, sprouting more heads as each one is cut off.'

Guillaume knew that, of the two brothers implicated with de Reppes in Henry of Almain's murder, Simon had died while holed up somewhere. But Guy was still at large. There was a youngest brother too, called Amaury. But he lived in pious obscurity God knows where, and was reputed not to be involved in the trail of revenge following in his older brothers' wake. Edward's weakness over the de Montfort family was useful infor-mation for a Grand Master in any possible future power struggle between the order and the various monarchs of the West envious of its power. He reassured Edward of his cooperation.

'Master Falconer is an old friend of mine, and he is returning to see me tomorrow. I will allow him access to de Reppes on your behalf.'

Edward grinned broadly and lifted his goblet by way of a toast to their mutual enterprise.

NINETEEN

Friar Roger Bacon took the quill from between Thomas's fingers and laid it down on his desk. Thomas looked startled, then embarrassed at his apparent distraction.

'Forgive me, Master Bacon. I had another matter on my mind. Please continue.'

He made to pick up the quill, but Bacon's slender fingers closed over his own. The friar smiled at him, his deep-set eyes boring into the younger man.

'No. If I cannot hold your attention with my discourse on mathematics, then this other matter must be of great importance.' He suddenly looked rueful. 'Or my teaching skills have diminished considerably during my incarceration.'

Thomas was about to protest, but Bacon shook his head.

'It is surely the latter, for I know from William that you are an eager and receptive pupil. Perhaps I should take up teaching again and hone my skills once more. It was what you suggested to Master Morrish, after all, when we began this task. And from what I saw of his lecture the other day, he is in need of some support.'

Thomas laughed quietly. He too saw flaws in Morrish's teaching but had refrained from saying anything.

'You are right, sir. And there is something else you could do to help me, if you did lecture his students. Master Falconer and I have been discussing it.'

Bacon's eyes widened in curiosity.

'Do tell me. I am sorely bored at present and could do with a little excitement.'

Until now, Thomas had imagined that the friar was a serious fellow with only great thoughts in his brain. Now he could see that he shared with Falconer a playful side to his nature. For the first time since they had met, Bacon's eyes sparkled. Thomas told him all about the two deaths in the ranks of the students, and how he thought they had been dabbling with the demonic nature of some of the powerful drugs at a physician's disposal.

'William has warned me that if I press too hard trying to

find out what has been happening, then maybe my life might be in danger too. But if you were to talk to the students, Master Bacon, perhaps it would not seem so troublesome.'

Pensively, Bacon tapped the leather-bound notebook he always carried with him.

'I have been occupied with those forces myself. That is why I keep this record in cipher. Some of what I have written here is too dangerous for those who cannot control their natures.'

Thomas did not admit that he had peeked inside the covers of Bacon's book and seen some of his diagrams. The sketches of plants certainly tallied with what the friar was now saying. But the stranger drawings more resembled dreams than anatomical renderings. He wondered if Bacon himself tested the effects of such cure-alls as opium on his own body. He shivered at what might have resulted if he had eaten the hashish stone in Paul Hebborn's scrip. Bacon, meanwhile, had made up his mind. He was rubbing his tonsured head and pacing the room with excitement.

'Yes, I will do it. I will help you find out from the students about their . . . extra-curricular habits. I am sure I can be at least as wily as William when it comes to this deductive business he seems to so love. Now, Thomas, gather up those sheets of parchment and be on your way. It is quite dark outside, and we cannot afford to waste any more of this candle today.'

He snuffed the wick with a pinch of his fingers and helped Thomas slide the pile of papers into his capacious satchel. Once outside the building, he watched while Thomas locked the door, then the two conspirators took their leaves of each other and went their separate ways. Thomas, on an impulse, turned aside from the straight route back to the Abbey of St Victor. Instead, he cut through the back alleys to stand before the convent of the Mathurins.

Falconer eased the shutter open and gazed out of the window. Even in the darkness of the night, he could see down the narrow lane opposite as it wound towards the river. He fancied he could just make out the glimmer of moonlight on the water. Leaning out of the window, and looking to his right, he could see the very tops of the towers of Notre-Dame Cathedral. They formed a dark and louring bulk on the skyline.

'Close the shutter, William, I can feel the cold.'

Falconer turned back into the room and looked at Saphira lying on the bed. The moonlight turned her shock of red curls to copper, and her skin to pearl. She slid her bare arm out from under the bedclothes and held out her hand.

'Come and warm me up.'

'I will if you promise not to gut me with that knife you keep secreted up the sleeve of your gown.'

He had noticed when she had undressed earlier. Saphira waggled her arm to show she was free of all weaponry.

'It is well to have a little security in Paris's streets, but I find it is unnecessary in my bed.'

He closed the shutter and returned to the warmth of Saphira's bed. After they had met on the bridge, she had brought him back to the area she called Pletzel. It was the Jewish quarter of Paris, and, despite the many expulsions of Jews over the years, the community had survived. It was a discrete collection of houses in a few narrow lanes huddled under the walls of the city, and not far from the square – La Grève – where they had been watching the hiring of labourers.

'We keep ourselves to ourselves, even more so than in England,' explained Saphira, as they had turned into the most unobtrusive of alleys. 'Here, we are largely overlooked even when times get bad. This is my cousin Melka's house.'

She had opened the door and led him inside. Falconer had never seen such a meticulously well-kept property. Melka had to be more house-proud than Saphira ever was. He held back from saying so, however. He wanted to confirm their newly forged truce before testing its mettle. Saphira had sat him down at a well-scrubbed table and brought him a freshly baked flatbread and some wine. She sat next to him, breaking the bread.

'The wine is mine, but the bread has been baked by my cousin. But then you could have guessed that, knowing how undomesticated I am.'

He tasted the bread. It was delicious compared with the rough, harsh loaves he was used to in Oxford.

'Maybe Melka can teach you to bake. Where is she, by the way?'

Saphira cast him a sidelong glance.

'She is visiting her sister for a few days. That is why I am able to stay here. It is a small house with only one bedroom. Shall I show you?'

Falconer had found the bedroom as neat as the rest of the house. It had not stayed neat for long. Now, in the early hours of the morning, he was glad to have Saphira back at his side. And that was not simply for her obvious charms. He stroked her warm flank pensively, and she turned over to face him. Her thick red locks fell across her face, and she flicked them out of her eyes.

'Tell me what is on your mind, William. Our truce is holding, isn't it?'

Falconer grinned.

'Oh, it surely is, Saphira. But that is not what concerns me. It's what I might learn soon from a certain Templar who figured largely in our recent past.'

Saphira sat up abruptly, the linen falling from her full breasts in a way that disconcerted Falconer.

'I knew you were up to something. You could not be in Paris long without winkling out some murder or other. Do tell.'

He pointed at Saphira's pale breasts.

'I will if you cover those up, or I shall be sorely distracted.'

Saphira did his bidding and listened hard while Falconer rehearsed the facts of his latest investigation. She frowned over his involvement with King Edward. She had been placed in danger when Falconer had taken her innocently to the court of his father, Henry, just before his death. Being a Jew in Europe involved keeping out of trouble, and being around a dying king was not a good idea. Now William was working for the son, about whom there were rumours that he disliked Jews so much he might expel them from England. She shivered at the thought, fleetingly wondering what both of them would do then.

'Are you cold?'

Falconer had noted her involuntary shiver and misinterpreted it.

'Yes, somewhat. Come a little closer.'

She felt some comfort from the closeness of Falconer's large, warm frame. He had some extra flesh on him, but she could still feel the muscles of a fighting man underneath. She would put off facing the problem of expulsion if ever it came. In the meantime, she would enjoy every day with her lover. He continued his story.

'So, tomorrow . . . no . . . today, I am to speak to Odo de Reppes.'

Saphira was startled.

'Is he still alive? I had thought after the events around that farcical trial you had to face, that he had been done away with.'

Falconer shook his head.

'No, merely incarcerated. Segrim's story may have been wild and fanciful, but it appears there were some elements of truth in it. De Reppes was probably involved in the murder of Henry of Almain, and may have killed Edward's uncle, Richard of Cornwall and King of Germany. Edward wants to know who instigated the killings, if anyone. I hope for Guillaume's sake it is no one in the Templar hierarchy.'

He had told Saphira of his friendship with the man who was now elevated to Grand Master of the Order of Poor Knights. She had marvelled at his celebrated acquaintances, but he had merely put it down to chance. She now put the question that had been on Falconer's mind for a while.

'Do you think you will get the truth from de Reppes in that case? Might the Grand Master not have set him up to implicate whoever he wants to suit his own ends?'

Falconer shook his head.

'No, Guillaume would not do that. He is a very clever man, but he is honest. And straight with those he trusts. He was not very adept at trying to conceal from me that he knew where de Reppes was being held. Dissimulation does not come easy to him. I am banking on the fact that de Reppes is being held in the tower at the Temple. I shall know soon enough.'

Daylight was beginning to steal through the shutters, and for the first time Falconer thought of Thomas Symon. He sat up, throwing the bedclothes aside.

'I should go. Thomas will be worried about me, especially as I warned him about the dangers of his own investigations. He will probably think I have been murdered for sure this time.'

He paused, remembering he had taken care not to tell Saphira about his dangerous encounter on the Planche Milbray. But glancing at her now, he saw that she had not picked up on his slip of the tongue. She was too intrigued by his reference to Thomas's affairs, which he had so far refrained from mentioning.

'A double enquiry? How does what he is looking into relate to yours?'

'It doesn't. It is merely coincidental.'

Saphira snorted in derision.

'How many times have I heard you say that two deaths in

close proximity do not make a coincidence but a reason for investigation?'

Falconer began to pull on his undershirt. His voice was muffled for a moment as he pulled it over his head, then he emerged from the folds and explained.

'That is the point. These deaths in Paris are recent, so they are therefore not related to a series of murders or attempted murders on Edward's family. They have happened long ago and in different locations.'

'Even though the student deaths happened when Edward arrived in Paris?'

Falconer shook his head.

'No. Totally unrelated, I can assure you.'

He climbed into his old black robe and sat on the edge of the bed to pull on his boots. A worm of doubt was beginning to enter his brain. Saphira leaned forward, letting the linen drop from her breasts again, and laid her hand on his thigh.

'I believe you, William. Now let me just wish you farewell before you return to your celibate bed in the abbey.'

Falconer groaned but did not resist.

The sun silhouetted a windmill on the hill to the east of the Abbey of St Victor. Its arms were stilled, not yet ready for the work of the day ahead. Thomas, on the other hand, was already up and dressed. He was standing at the main doorway of the abbey, uncertain whether to leave or to wait for Falconer. He had spent a restless night, constantly staring at the empty bed across the room. He had finally dozed off in the early hours but had been abruptly awoken by the sound of the monks passing his lodgings on the way to nocturns. He looked instinctively at Falconer's bed, fully expecting him to be there. But he wasn't, and the bed was untouched. He lay back but could find no rest as lauds came and went, and then prime. At that point he rose and dressed, taking only a quick breakfast before stationing himself at the entrance to the abbey. His satchel with writing materials stowed in it was over his shoulder. But somehow he couldn't make himself leave the abbey without knowing something of what might have happened to Falconer. As he waited, the windmill began to lazily turn its arms.

Finally, just as prime was ending in the chapel behind him, he saw a familiar figure sauntering up the road from the easternmost gateway through the city walls. Slightly stooped and shading his eyes from the low morning sun, Falconer called out.

'Thomas. See, I got up earlier than you today.'

The young man was not in the mood for jests. He hurried towards Falconer.

'Where have you been? I was afraid you had been killed by this maniac who has done for two people already.'

Falconer crushed Thomas in a bear hug of a welcome.

'I have been somewhere quite safe. But anyway, why should our killer want to murder me?'

Thomas extricated himself angrily from Falconer's grasp.

'Well, someone tried to push you off the bridge. Have you already forgotten?'

'No. But I reckon that had more to do with what I am trying to uncover for the king rather than the deaths you are pursuing.'

'Either way, you could have ended up dead.'

Falconer grasped Thomas firmly by the shoulders, almost shaking him.

'But I have not done so.' He smiled a little ruefully. 'I can look after myself, you know. But forgive me for causing you worry.'

Thomas shook his head in disbelief. His friend was oblivious to the dangers that stalked Paris, it seems.

'Where were you, anyway, that was so safe? And why did you not return last night?'

Falconer now looked embarrassed, and even somewhat shifty.

'I . . . er . . . met someone. We got talking, and it was too late to return. The city gates would have been closed. And the abbey gates too. They gave me a bed for the night. Now, let's work out what we are doing today.'

Falconer made to walk back towards the abbey. But Thomas would not give up.

'Who do you know in Paris who would give you a bed? The only people you know are ones you have argued with over the Condemnations. None of those would willingly spend the evening debating with you and then offer you hospitality. There is no one else you know in the whole of France apart from Friar Bacon. And I can't see you being accommodated in the Franciscan friary. You would be too afraid you might be locked in like Roger was.'

Falconer shrugged his shoulders and was on the verge of blushing. Thomas suddenly had an inkling as to why.

'No one except Mistress Le Veske, that is. But she is in Honfleur. Isn't she?'

Falconer was now red-faced and embarrassed, and he didn't know why. The boy knew how things were with him and Saphira from way back in Oxford. Why did he always feel like a naughty boy in the presence of one who had been no more than a child himself when they had first met?

'Well, she was in Honfleur. But no longer. Not since yesterday.'

It was now Thomas's turn to blush and to stumble over his words. He disapproved of his mentor breaking his vow of celibacy. Not once, but with regularity. But he equally knew his disapproval was tinged with a hint of jealousy. He had never had a woman, except for a brief encounter with one of the girls working on his father's farm before he went to Oxford. And even that was losing clarity in his memory.

'I . . . didn't mean to . . .'

Falconer smiled and patted his shoulder.

'Thomas. We must all find our own way in this world. And it would be a better place if we did not censure others who do not match up to our own standards. Now tell me, did Roger bite on the tempting worm you offered him?'

Thomas nodded, eager to forget their disagreement over Falconer's absence all night.

'Yes, he has agreed to do some teaching at the medical school and find out what he can about the habits of some of the students there. Master Morrish took ill yesterday, so he should have the opportunity to do so. I will . . . pursue my own lines of enquiry.'

For some reason, he did not want to tell Falconer that he intended to try to open the chest in Morrish's upper room. His friend might say it was too precipitate and risky. Fortunately, Falconer's mind seemed to be more on his stomach than on what Thomas might be doing during the day. He stretched and yawned.

'Now I shall have to beg for some food to break my fast, as the normal mealtime is long past. And then I must go to the Temple.'

They shook hands, and Thomas strode off towards the city, while Falconer ambled towards the abbey kitchens. The monotonous creak of the windmill's arms began its daily call across the valley.

TWENTY

Falconer's second visit to the Paris Temple gate produced a quicker response than his first. It was the same sergeant who stood under the archway as Falconer crossed the drawbridge from the road. This time, however, it appeared that he knew the Oxford man was expected, for he merely cocked his head and turned around. Falconer followed him into the Temple complex and towards the Paris Master's house. His eyes were drawn to the huge Temple tower, its bulk looming over the order's enclave much as the cathedral towers of Notre-Dame did over the Ile de la Cité. Secular and spiritual power expressed in separate buildings imposing themselves on the surroundings. Falconer had an uneasy feeling about the tower and paused to look up at it. He had an idea that Odo de Reppes was incarcerated in one of the four turrets of the donjon. If so, he was held in the same place the order was reputed to store its treasures. Was there a pair of sad eyes staring down at him even now?

'Master.'

The sergeant was impatient to bring Falconer into the presence of his Grand Master. He did not want to appear foolish again the way he had done the first time this Englishman had arrived. Who could have imagined then that such a shabby figure was not only an emissary of King Edward but a close friend of the new Grand Master? Falconer tore his gaze away from the tower and followed the stocky man into the great hall of the Province Master's house, temporary home of Guillaume de Beaujeu, Grand Master of the order. Guillaume was on his feet, pacing the width of the hearth, in which there was a blazing fire. He looked nervous, and that shocked Falconer. His old friend was normally so self-contained and confident. He took the hand that was offered him and felt the strength in Guillaume's grasp.

'Have you any news for me, Guillaume?'

'Yes. Good news. The one you seek is in this very Temple – has been here for over a year. He was brought here from Oxford after the events with which you are familiar.'

Falconer forbore from suggesting that de Beaujeu must have
known that already. He did not want to embarrass his friend,
the Grand Master.

'And can I speak to him?'

Guillaume still could not look him squarely in the eye, but
he nodded his head.

'Of course you may. The order has nothing to hide. Odo
de Reppes has committed a grievous crime, no one is denying
that. But we do reserve the right to deal with our own in our
own way.'

Falconer raised his hands in acknowledgement.

'I merely wish to talk – to ask him some questions about
how he got involved in the death of Henry of Almain.'

De Beaujeu did finally look at Falconer, giving him a hard
stare.

'And that is all you wish to examine him about?'

Falconer frowned, wondering what was behind Guillaume's
question. Did he know more?

'That should be all, I think . . . though it may lead on to
other matters.'

'Other matters?'

De Beaujeu was clearly groping around in the dark for
information that might serve his own purpose in the future.
Falconer guessed Guillaume didn't yet fully know the extent
of de Reppes' perversity any more than he did. He didn't care
about sharing what he learned, but would Edward want him
to? Suddenly, he felt uncomfortable too, and didn't like the
feeling of being pressed like cider apples between these two
great men. He prevaricated.

'There's nothing specific that I know of. But if there were,
I don't want to be limited to that issue alone. I have your
permission to dig deeper?'

Guillaume shrugged his broad shoulders, as if suggesting
there could be nothing that had not already been unearthed
by the Templars themselves.

'Feel free. If there is more iniquity in de Reppes' frame,
then you may extract it. He cannot sink lower than he has
already.' He clapped his hands together by way of ending the
conversation. 'Shall we go?'

Falconer nodded, and Guillaume led him out of the Master's
house and towards the dark and depressing tower close by it

with its four turrets, one set on each corner of the square building. Once again, Falconer imagined a set of eyes following him across the courtyard and up to the very doors of the donjon. Access was by way of a portal in the north side of the tower. From there, de Beaujeu led him to one of the turrets, inside which was a spiral staircase. They climbed upwards.

At the very top of the turret, under what Falconer realized was one of the cone-shaped roofs, stood a sturdy, metal-studded door with a large iron locking mechanism embedded in it. De Beaujeu produced a key from his purse and turned it in the lock. As he swung the door open inwards, a noxious stench assailed Falconer's nostrils and he reeled backwards, almost plunging back down the steep spiral staircase he had just come up. Guillaume grasped his arm and steadied him.

'I should have warned you.'

He stepped into the room ahead of Falconer, his boots crunching on the straw scattered on the floor. Falconer held his nose and followed. It was a dark and stinking cell, the only light piercing it through a tiny slit set high in the curved wall. So much for de Reppes spying on him as he approached. The man would have to be seven feet tall to even get his eye to the slit. And though the Templar had been a big man when Falconer had last seen him, he was not that tall. In fact, as Falconer's eyes adjusted to the gloom, he didn't think he could see de Reppes in the room at all. What was Guillaume playing at? Then he saw him.

Huddled against the far wall was a shape that was no more than a bag of bones. Odo de Reppes had shrunk from a tall and powerful fighting man to a bent and broken skeleton wrapped in chains. Only the eyes that looked up at Falconer blazed with something approaching their original ferocity. They peered out from a face scabbed and hairy and gaunt beyond measure. Falconer would hardly have recognized him. He turned to stare at de Beaujeu. The Grand Master tilted his head to one side in a gesture of defeat.

'It is not of my doing. Bérard, my predecessor, had him tortured to extract what confession he could out of the man. This is what is left. That is why I said you were free to question him but should not expect too much. Myself, I would have dispatched him by now.'

When de Beaujeu spoke these words, a rumbling noise

escaped from the grotesque figure on the floor, and a grin
broke through the thick and bushy beard. Falconer was regaled
with a row of broken and blackened teeth. The thought of
being sent to meet his maker clearly pleased de Reppes.
Falconer was inclined to assist him all he could. But first he
needed to ask some questions of this wreck of a man. And
hope he could get some sense out of him. Perhaps his mind
was as broken as his body.

'Can I speak to him alone?'

Guillaume waved a hand at the prisoner.

'Of course. He is chained by the arms and legs to the floor,
so he cannot be a danger to you. Even if he had the strength
to be so. I will wait outside.'

After de Beaujeu had exited the stinking room, Falconer
pulled the door closed behind him. The smell from de Reppes'
body and the dirty hole in the floor that must serve as his
toilet became more palpable. But Falconer swallowed hard
and steeled himself. Some of the things he had to say were
not for the Grand Master's ears. He squatted down beside the
skeleton that was hunkered down on the floor and looked into
the man's eyes.

'Odo de Reppes, do you remember me? My name is William
Falconer, and I am from Oxford. It was but a year ago that
our paths crossed. I need to ask you about that time, and the
earlier events leading up to the murder in Viterbo. I need to
know the truth, not for myself, but for others.'

The prisoner's eyes closed, and for a moment Falconer
thought he had died or at least fallen asleep. But then they
opened again. This time they had no spark in them, though.
Falconer feared he had lost his chance, but he urged the
man on.

'There is an old man in Oxford whose wife died, and he
thinks you were somehow involved. I need to convince him
otherwise.' He waved a hand to encompass de Reppes' plight.
'Surely the truth can do you no harm now.'

The skeleton before him stirred, and the chains clanked,
scraped on the floor and resettled. De Reppes attempted to
clear his throat. It was a painful rasping sound, and it took
Falconer a few moments to make out what he was saying.

'Water.'

Falconer cast a glance around the room, but there was

obviously no barrel or jug in the cell. He rose, his knees aching, and went to the door. Pulling it slightly open, he peered out at de Beaujeu.

'Can he have water?'

Guillaume looked exasperated at being taxed with such a menial chore and sighed.

'Very well, I will go back down and send someone up to you with a jug.'

Falconer watched until his back had disappeared around the curve of the stairs, then he returned to the filthy cell.

'Has he gone?'

Falconer was surprised by the firm tones of the man on the floor. Perhaps Odo was not as far gone as he seemed. He had asked for water merely to get rid of the spy at the door.

'Yes, he has gone. You can speak freely.'

'Where do you want to start?'

'That day in Viterbo, when the brothers murdered Henry of Almain in church, were you there too?'

Falconer recalled Humphrey Segrim's insistence that he had seen de Reppes with bloodied hands in the church. The Templar nodded, his eyes fiercely shining once again.

'Yes. I helped them kill him. We had all drunk much wine together, and we were excited and driven by passion. Strangely so, in a way I had never been in battle before.'

De Reppes hawked and spat on the floor.

'I curse the day I fell in with the de Montfort brothers. They were an intemperate bunch after their father's death with nothing to lose. And wild-eyed too, as if they were possessed by demons.'

Falconer wondered if de Reppes also had been possessed by the same demons. He was reminded of the demons that had controlled John Fusoris. Not Devils but drugs. He shrugged off the distraction and pressed on with de Reppes' witnessing of events. It would not be long before Guillaume or one of his minions came back, and the man might then clam up.

'Why did you get involved with them?'

'My family. King Hugh of Cyprus was of the line of the Counts of Poitiers, and my family has always served his family.'

He groaned and shifted his long legs, causing the chains to clank again. His story came in short bursts as his voice faded with the effort of speaking. He had probably not had the chance to talk to anyone for months on end.

'The order has turned against Hugh, and is for Charles of Anjou as King of Jerusalem. The de Montforts played on my divided loyalties over this. They convinced me that King Henry of England also lined up with the Templar hierarchy. That I should ally myself with them. Of course, they really planned to kill him and his family in revenge for what had happened to theirs. The Barons' War in England was a bad time, and many enmities were made between families that last still.'

His voice tailed off as he spouted a litany of Norman-French family names who had become the disinherited – a legion of families who lost everything because they had sided with Simon de Montfort in his abortive battle against Henry of Winchester for the soul of England. Some of the names surprised Falconer, but he needed to keep Odo on track.

'And Segrim, did you pursue him back to England in order to dispatch him?'

De Reppes opened his mouth, and an awful sound emanated from between the rotten teeth. Falconer realized he was laughing.

'That old duffer who pretended to be on Crusade? Why should I be scared of him? He never even got to the Holy Lands, staying on instead in Cyprus. Did he return to England so soon?'

'Yes, he did. Did you never see him there?'

Falconer recalled Segrim's story of being dogged by the Templar and being seen by him in Berkhamsted the day Richard of Cornwall died. He was not surprised that it was all a fantasy in Segrim's fearful mind.

'No. I went to England for another reason, concerning my sister. And no, I did not see the old man there.'

Falconer decided to give Segrim's story one last trial.

'And the death of Richard of Cornwall at Berkhamsted? Was that down to you too?'

De Reppes glanced slyly at Falconer.

'I did go there to kill him at the behest of the de Montforts. He was King Henry's brother, after all, and part of the same nest of vipers. But when I got there, I found I had no need to do anything. No, God will not punish me for that death.'

Both men heard the sound of someone ascending the stone

staircase up to the cell. De Reppes grabbed Falconer's arm with a bony hand and pulled him closer. Falconer could see a tear in the corner of his sunken eye. The Templar whispered in his ear with a breath that stank of death.

'The de Montfort brothers are Devils incarnate – beware of them.'

Falconer shook his head.

'I have no need to fear them. Simon is already dead, and Guy is long missing, so I am safe.'

De Reppes shook his head, and Falconer could see the lice crawling through his hair.

'No. They are not the ones to fear. The runt of the litter is the worst – the pious one. You would think that butter wouldn't melt in his mouth, but he is the very Devil.' He hissed out his final warning. 'Look out for Amaury.'

TWENTY-ONE

The shadows were lengthening in the upper room of the medical school, driving the sunlight into the furthest corners. The precious books still lay untouched where they had been yesterday, when Thomas Symon had sneaked into Adam Morrish's solar for a search. This evening, he was accompanied by Roger Bacon, who observed, as he had done, that the master of the school had scant regard for the value of his texts. He bent down to pick up the book on the floor.

'This is ibn Ridwan's commentary on Galen, and he treats it like rubbish.'

Thomas was nervous.

'Should we not leave it where it is so that he does not learn that we have been here?'

Bacon snorted.

'From the look of the room, he doesn't know where anything is to be found. And I must save Galen from neglect.' He wiped the book over with his palm and laid it gently down on the edge of the table. 'What we can see here does not surprise me. His lecture was so poor that I feel his mind is as untidy as this room.'

It was true, thought Thomas. They had arrived at Morrish's school that morning to begin their agreed plan. Thomas would stay in the background, and Roger Bacon would get to know the students and see if he could discover anything about misuse of drugs. Both he and the friar had sat at the back of the schoolroom as the fresh-faced Morrish had taken the students through one of the standard medical works. Galen's commentaries on three Hippocratic treatises should have been meat and drink to him. But he had seemed nervous at the presence of Roger Bacon, eventually stopping his own lecture and inviting the friar to lecture to the clerks instead.

It had been just in time, for those assembled in the room, which had included Hellequin, de la Casteigne and Malpoivre, had become restless. Fidgeting in their seats, they had looked as though they could not wait for the end of the lecture. Bacon walked to the front and changed all that. He was not a tall man, and looked quite unassuming in his Franciscan robes, but the moment he stood up before the unruly students he had their attention.

'Medicine, astrology and alchemy are special sciences. But the greatest of these is *scientia experimentalis*. Experiment and personal experience of knowledge.'

He winked, and the students leaned forward eagerly, ready for what he had to tell them. Thomas saw Adam Morrish slink out of the room and wondered where he might be going. He followed and watched him leave by the front door. Thomas heard laughter from the schoolroom and knew that the friar had his audience in the palm of his hand. He slipped out of the front door himself and began to follow Morrish.

Unfortunately, his efforts proved useless. He managed to hide in the throngs of people in Paris's bustling lanes as Morrish made his way towards the Ile de la Cité. Thomas wondered if he was making for the Royal Palace, or perhaps the cathedral. But first his quarry had to cross the Petit Pont. The bridge was quite narrow, and there were few people crossing just at that moment. Thomas knew he would be exposed if Morrish happened to look behind him as he crossed. So he decided to wait, and watched as Morrish wended his way over the bridge. Once the man was on the far bank, Thomas chanced his arm and started to cross too. But his way was barred by a sudden flurry of people coming in the opposite direction, and by the time Thomas had stood to one side and allowed them to pass, Morrish was nowhere to be seen. He had disappeared into the maze of streets on the island. He wandered around for a while but could not see the man anywhere. He must have gone into one of the houses, or carried on over the plank bridge that Falconer had almost been tossed off and across to the Right Bank. He wandered back to the medical school, deep in thought, and climbed up to the top room to hunt some more.

His search had centred on the chest, but look as he might he had not been able to find a key to fit the lock. Its contents remained firmly hidden from him. In fact, he had been so absorbed in his task of discovery that he had lost track of time. Fortunately, Morrish had not returned to catch him trying to open the chest. In the end he had given up and waited for

Bacon to finish his lecture. It had taken all morning and part-
way into the afternoon. But eventually the students had
dispersed, and Bacon had joined him in the upper room, there
rescuing Ridwan from its ignominious position on the floor.

Now the friar was continuing to deprecate Morrish's skill
as a teacher.

'His students are sorely ignorant, and know little beyond
the Trivium and Quadrivium. And those subjects they would
have graduated in under someone else at the university in
order to progress to medicine. I don't know what he has been
teaching them this last year.'

Thomas was more anxious to know if the second part of
their plan had borne fruit. Whether Bacon had learned anything
from the students about Hebborn's and Fusoris' behaviour that
suggested the misuse of potions and preparations.

'Did you speak to any of them after you had finished your
lecture?'

Bacon patted Thomas's arm and smiled.

'I did indeed. I avoided the ones you mentioned to me –
Jack Hellequin and the hangers-on around young Malpoivre.
You were right about him, by the way. Geoffrey Malpoivre is
no more than a lazy scion of a noble family, idling his life
away and buying friends with his largesse. He is the very sort
that corrupts Paris and Oxford, making them stink.'

Thomas had rarely seen the friar so angry. But Bacon soon
regained his calm and carried on with his tale.

'Forgive me. His type annoys me. But I am digressing. I
avoided that dissolute bunch on the principle that the two dead
boys were part of it. Even though Hebborn had been bullied
by most of them. I didn't think I was likely to get the truth
from their own mouths. But I did ask a couple of the more
studious pupils to stay and talk to me. Eventually, they told
me some very interesting things about Malpoivre and his
coterie.'

Thomas listened hard as Bacon related the story he had
been told. It seems that Malpoivre had become the source of
preparations from the school's pharmacy. His close group of
friends had begun to enjoy the sensations provided by misusing
these purloined drugs. Particularly popular were khat leaves
and small stones of opium.

'The Assassins' drug!' blurted Thomas.

'If the stories are to be believed.'

The friar was more dubious than Thomas about the rumours circulating concerning the clique that had formed around Hassan, the Old Man of the Mountain. Especially as their fortress at Alamut had fallen to the Tartars many years previously.

'I am not convinced that they needed drugs to carry out their tasks. Though it is true that the sect still survives and will work as mercenaries for outsiders as well as Muslims. In fact, some say that Richard Lionheart himself commissioned them to kill Conrad de Montferrat. But we are not talking about Assassins in Outremer now, but young students in Paris. And of them we have only tales, and no proof.'

'But we do have proof.' Thomas eagerly broke in on Bacon's lament, before recalling what Falconer had made him do with the hashish stone. 'That is, we did have. Only the proof now lies at the bottom of the Seine.'

He explained to Bacon what he meant. How a lump of hashish had been found by Falconer in Paul Hebborn's scrip, and how it had been placed beyond use in the river. He looked glum, but the friar was more optimistic.

'It matters not that you no longer have the evidence, only that both you and William saw it. And that you know John Fusoris chewed on khat leaves.' He paused, thinking through what that all implied. 'Of course, if we have evidence that both the dead boys were eating drugs that would affect their judgement, it draws into question the very premise that they were murdered. Hebborn may have been in much the same state as a drunk and simply fallen off the tower. And Fusoris could have fallen in the river and drowned while still befuddled by khat.'

Thomas shook his head.

'No. I cannot be certain about Hebborn, for I never saw his body. But if he was fuddled by drugs, why was he high up on Notre-Dame's tower? However, I can be certain of Fusoris. After I left William at the Petit Pont the other morning, I went back to where his body lay at the convent, and I examined it again. Before, I had seen only his face cleansed of the river mud. But once his whole body had been washed, it was obvious how he died. There were bruises all around his neck. If I had been able to anatomize him, I would no doubt have found that the little bone in his throat, which is shaped like a Greek upsilon, was broken. He had been strangled for sure.'

Bacon nodded, convinced by this serious and studious young master that they were indeed embroiled in a double murder and not simply wilful wrongdoing. He pointed at the chest now lying at Thomas's feet.

'Is this where Master Morrish keeps his potions?'

'I would guess it is. I have searched this room and have found nothing else. But it is locked, and even though the lock is scratched as if someone has tried to open it and failed, I cannot see how Malpoivre, or anyone else, might have gained access to its contents.'

Bacon knelt on the floor and examined the lock closely, seeing the scratch marks that Thomas referred to. They radiated from the keyhole, suggesting someone had indeed tried with the end of a knife to prise the lock open. He rubbed them with the end of his index finger.

'These are old marks. They feel smooth to the touch. If they had been made recently, their edges would be rough. And their very presence would have alerted the owner of the chest that a thief had been at work.'

Thomas blushed at having missed the obvious, and knelt beside Bacon. He was embarrassed that the clue had been picked up by someone like the friar who was a novice at deduction of a crime instead of himself. Bacon, though, seemed unconcerned by the young man's error. He rubbed a hand over his tonsured pate.

'It does, however, tell us one thing. That whoever took the potions from inside – if potions there be – had the key. And that means that someone knew where the key was hidden. Or that Master Morrish was complicit in the deed.'

This revelation from Roger Bacon had two immediate results. The first was predictable – Thomas rose to his feet and nodded with excitement. Bacon was right about his suppositions. The second result was unexpected. Just as Thomas was about to speak, both men heard a crash from outside the door. Thomas ran across the room and opened it, peering down into the darkness. The front door stood wide open, and whoever had been there had gone. Bacon appeared at his side.

'Too late for us to know who it was who was spying on us now. However, I think we need to speak to our disappearing master, Thomas. But first let us open the box of delights for ourselves.'

Bacon was hugely pleased by the look of puzzlement on Thomas's face that was caused by his suggestion. He took Thomas by his arm and led the young man back into the upper room. The chest still stood in the centre of the floor, locked and untouchable. Or so Thomas assumed.

'What do you mean? How can you open it without the key?'

Bacon grinned mischievously.

'Did you not know that I was an alchemist and in league with the Devil? Or so my detractors would have it. Well, then, let me perform a little magic.'

He dug into his purse and produced a long, thin bar of metal bent at right angles at the end. Its dull yellow colour suggested to Thomas it was made of brass. Bacon waved it in the air, and Thomas truly began to think the eccentric friar was indeed an alchemist and magician. But then Bacon knelt down before the box and poked the rod into the keyhole. He jiggled one way and then the other, his ear cocked as if he was listening for a particular noise. Eventually, it came. With a heavy clunk, the lock was opened. Thomas was astonished.

'How did you do that?'

Bacon tapped the side of his nose.

'That is a secret between me and the thief who taught me. But I have for too long been subjected to incarceration not to want to find a means of escape now and again. It is also why I had no objections to my great works being locked away. I learned how to pick locks a long time ago. It is a useful skill.'

He bent down and eased the chest's lid open. Inside was a cornucopia of pots, glass vials, little wooden boxes and folded leaves. The leaves themselves were simply protective layers wrapped around various dried plants. Bacon unfolded a few and was quick to identify each, pointing to them one by one.

'He has adderwort, beewort, lions' foot, great wort, woodruff, horehound, yarrow, elder, and this—' he picked up a dried root '—is mandrake.'

Thomas looked at the dried and blackened object.

'Yes, I have seen that, though I have not learned its uses.'

'Hmm. I am not surprised. Its usefulness owed more to magic and superstition than practicality. It is supposed to ensure conception, but take too much of it and you will be poisoned.'

'Then what is it doing in the chest of a university-trained

physician? It sounds more like it should belong to a folk-healer. What else is there in the chest?'

Bacon rummaged around, peering closely at the glass vials, some of which had faded labels attached to them with cord.

'Cateputria, bryony, laurel berries. This is more interesting, as they are all poisons.'

Thomas was disappointed. Many physicians had poisons to hand, for they could be used in small quantities for quite inno-cent purposes such as to kill flies. Pliny himself recommended the careful use of belladonna as a specific against earache.

'Is there nothing else?'

Bacon ignored Thomas's impatient question and continued to calmly delve through the pots in the chest. He opened one after the other, examining the contents.

'Ah, what do we have here?'

He held up a small circular clay pot, from which he had removed the wooden lid for Thomas to see. Inside were what looked like several small whitish stones. They were a perfect match for the one Falconer had found in Paul Hebborn's scrip. Thomas was curiously relieved by the discovery.

'Hashish. Then Morrish is the source of the opium the students are using.'

'If no one else has a key, I suppose he is.'

Bacon closed the lid of the chest and jiggled the lock so that it snapped shut again. Thomas pushed it back under the table. But the efforts at concealment seemed pointless.

'Who do you think that was outside the door? Morrish, or one of the students?'

The friar smiled gently.

'We shall know soon enough. In fact, it may have helped precipitate matters nicely. Though I would advise you to watch your back over the next few days, Thomas Symon. If it was the killer of the two boys, he will not hesitate to kill again to keep his secret.'

Thomas felt a shiver run up his spine.

'But what about you, Master Bacon? Your safety is at risk too.'

'Oh, I shall be safe enough in the friary. It is a virtual prison – as I know only too well. What successfully keeps people in will also be well able to keep others out.' He grasped Thomas's arm to emphasize what he was saying. 'But you must be altogether more careful. Keep to the abbey tonight, and tell William what has happened. It is as well you sleep in the same room at St Victor's.'

Thomas refrained from saying that he wasn't sure if Falconer would even be in the abbey tonight. That Saphira's charms might keep him elsewhere. But he nodded his head.

'I will do so, sir.'

'And another thing, Thomas. I think we behave as normal tomorrow. If we meet here and I lecture, and then we carry on with the preparation of the compendium, we will be in the best position to see who is absent or troubled in any way.'

'Agreed.'

They trooped downstairs, and Thomas locked up. Then, with a fearful look over his shoulder, the younger man hurried down the street towards the St Victor Gate. Bacon, though just as concerned about every shadow and sound, took a deep breath and made himself calmly walk back to the sanctuary of his friary.

TWENTY-TWO

Thomas Symon, hastening back to the abbey before it got too dark, was surprised to see Falconer standing in the Place Maubert. And with him was the comely person of Saphira Le Veske, locks of her lively red hair escaping from her snood as they always did. Falconer touched her arm and spoke as Thomas approached them.

'There, I told you that, if we waited long enough, Thomas would pass by.' He winked at her. 'I think he can't resist the charms of the tavern of the Withered Vine.'

Thomas fell into the trap before realizing he was being teased.

'I most certainly can do without the filthy vinegar such a place sells in pretence it is wine. I . . .' He took a deep breath, and began again, bowing his head to Saphira. 'I am most pleased to see you again, Mistress Le Veske.'

'Oh, please, Thomas, we don't need to be so formal, do we? William was only just saying how much more relaxed you had become since discovering the joys of unwatered red wine.'

Thomas began to blush, and would have protested had he not seen the broad smile on Saphira's face. He was not going to be caught out again.

'Indeed, Saphira. Though I cannot compare in consumption of such a treat as my good drinking companion, Master Falconer. Do you know the gentleman?'

Saphira gave a little curtsey.

'I believe I have heard of the fellow. A ruffian, by all accounts.'

Falconer held up his hands in defeat.

'Very well, I am rebuffed. But there is a purpose in our waiting to intercept you, Thomas. We need to talk, but I think here is too public to discuss what I have in mind.' He cast a glance at Saphira. 'Perhaps you can accommodate us in Pletzel?'

Saphira nodded her agreement.

'That would be acceptable, good sir. Though I have not got enough wine on tap to satisfy two such great topers as I see before me.'

Falconer waved his finger at her.

'Take care or what you jest about may come to pass. This errand of the king is becoming more and more exasperating. It is enough to drive a pious cardinal to drink.'

They all three walked back the way Thomas had come towards the bridges across the Seine. The young man was curious.

'Pletzel? Where's that?'

Falconer smiled at him.

'You will see.' Noticing they were passing Adam Morrish's school, he asked Thomas about his progress. 'Have you determined if the clerks have been dabbling with substances they shouldn't?'

'Yes, we have. Friar Bacon helped me find hashish stored in Master Adam's chest.' He gazed at Falconer as they crossed the Petit Pont. The sun was dipping below the buildings either side of the bridge, and it felt suddenly cold. 'He's an extraordinary fellow is Friar Bacon. For a pious man, he has much devilment in him.'

Falconer burst out laughing at Thomas's bewilderment.

'Roger is an enigma and a genius rolled into one. Never underestimate him.'

Having crossed to the Right Bank, they walked through the hiring square, which was now almost empty of people. Falconer and Thomas then followed Saphira through a maze of lanes until they stood in a neat courtyard hard under the walls of Paris. Saphira held her hands up.

'Pletzel.'

'The Jewish quarter,' explained Falconer, indicating that Thomas should follow Saphira into the house outside which they stood. The kitchen fire was already lit, and it banished the chill of the encroaching evening. Saphira broke some bread and poured three goblets of red wine.

'It is watered a little, Thomas. Though, as it is Le Veske wine, it is far superior to the vinegar purveyed at the Withered Vine.'

Thomas took the proffered goblet and sipped cautiously. It was a delicious wine. Falconer settled down in a chair by the kitchen fire and drank deeply of Saphira's wine. The others sat too, and a companionable silence ensued while they drank. Finally, Falconer spoke.

'I would like to hear about your findings, Thomas. And any conclusions you may have come to. I have ignored Hebborn's and Fusoris' deaths too long. And Saphira may have some insights to offer too.'

Thomas might have been offended at William's suggestion that he couldn't solve the case on his own. But truth to tell, he was floundering and was glad to have someone else examining the evidence. It may help to unravel the knots. He repeated all he knew about the deaths, concluding with his suspicions about the students with whom Hebborn and Fusoris had consorted.

'There is a group of them who definitely ate potions that affected their minds, and perhaps their actions. The same type of opium was in Master Adam's chest as that which we found, William, in Hebborn's scrip. But whether the master allowed the hashish to be used, or it had been stolen from him by Malpoivre, I don't yet know.'

It was Saphira who leaned forward first to throw a question into the ring.

'Hashish, you say? The Assassins' drug?'

Thomas nodded. After all, that was the very response he had made to Bacon a little earlier. Saphira turned to Falconer, a quizzical look on her handsome face.

'And you still say these cases are unrelated?'

Falconer frowned and stared hard at Saphira.

'I still cannot see it.' But yet there was something that troubled him, and he decided to tell the others what he had learned from Odo de Reppes. 'It is true that Edward was attacked in Outremer by an Assassin behaving wildly. However – and this is almost certainly a false direction to go in concerning the students – let me tell you what I know, and what the Templar said to me today.'

He told them all he had learned before speaking to Odo de Reppes about Edward's close encounter with death at the hands of Anzazim. He then summarized all that de Reppes had said about the de Montfort brothers.

'He said that he and the brothers had drunk too much wine before the murder of Henry of Almain. That afterwards it all seemed to happen in a dream.'

'Could they too have been drugged?'

It was Saphira's question, and it demanded an answer. But Falconer was not certain enough what the answer should be.

'I once ate khat leaves by accident. I don't think I could have killed a fly in the state I was in afterwards. Besides, why would the brothers need to eat hashish in order to carry out the murder, if as is said they were angry enough anyway?'

Thomas threw his question in then.

'Would they have been so incensed as to do something so openly outrageous and stupid? Why kill Henry so publicly? Would they not have needed someone or something to egg them on?'

Falconer remembered Odo de Reppes' final words before Guillaume had returned with his water. The warning about the other brother – Amaury de Montfort.

'I keep coming back to the thought that someone has been manipulating things without revealing himself.' He looked at Thomas. 'What do you know of Amaury de Montfort?'

'The youngest brother?' Thomas racked his brains – he had been a youth during the Barons' War ten years earlier. 'He must be thirty years of age by now. He was a clerk, not a warrior, certainly, and his father made him treasurer of York. But it was an empty appointment, for soon after the Battle of Evesham King Henry denounced it and replaced him. When he fled to the Pope to plead his case, I believe he continued his studies, but I don't know where.'

Falconer filled in the gaps.

'I do. It was at Padua, and he went in for medicine. The rumour in Oxford was that he was so lazy it took him two years to get round to returning three medical treatises he had borrowed from the abbot of Monte Cassino. But the name of de Montfort was not a popular one in university circles by then.'

This piece of information gave Thomas an uneasy feeling in his gut, but before he could speak out Falconer carried on.

'Talking of names, Odo de Reppes told me something else that would have meant nothing to him, but struck a chord with me. He was telling me of the disinherited – those families in England that lost everything due to siding with Earl Simon – and one of them was Hebborn.'

Thomas was startled by the revelation.

'Paul Hebborn's family lost everything during the Barons' War? No wonder he was struggling to finance himself at the university here.'

Saphira chipped in too.

'And from what you tell me, it is no surprise, then, that he allied himself with the young moneybags, Malpoivre, despite being bullied unmercifully by him. He did it just to survive.'

Both she and Thomas looked expectantly at Falconer now, imagining he had some revelation to offer concerning the coincidence. Falconer, however, simply shrugged his shoulders.

'Don't look at me like that. I cannot make any more of the information than you can. I merely mentioned it in case it has some significance to Thomas's investigations. It surely has no bearing on mine.'

'What conclusions have you come to concerning your travels down those cold trails?'

Thomas was reminding Falconer what he had said when first he had been asked to look into the assaults on Edward's family, scattered as they were throughout the world and time, the oldest being already some years in the past. Falconer smiled ruefully.

'That it is far more difficult to determine the cause of death of an old rotting corpse than one that is still warm. The Assassin Anzazim may have been in de Montfort's employ, but I have no way of proving that as I have only hearsay to go on. And the words of a soldier to boot who owes his allegiance to Edward and may therefore have fed me lies.'

Saphira poured them all another goblet of wine and asked the obvious question.

'Why should he lie to you, when it was his master who set you on your course in the first place?'

Falconer drank deep of the good wine and wiped a dribble of it off his chin.

'That is a good question, Saphira. But let me go on a little further first. My next nuggets of information came from Odo de Reppes and concerned his part in the murder of Henry of Almain. He too implicated the de Montforts, and more specifically Amaury, hinting he egged his brothers on in some way. But I saw the Templar only by courtesy of his Grand Master, who himself once fought with Edward in the Holy Lands.'

'But you say that Guillaume de Beaujeu is your friend.'

'Yes, Saphira. But he is no longer just my friend. He is Grand Master, and obliged to consider the good of his order over all other things. And he was more uneasy with me yesterday than I have ever seen him.'

Saphira sat back down and stared pensively into her goblet of wine. Falconer continued his story.

'Odo also told me of the death of King Henry's brother, Richard, in Berkhamsted.'

'Which Sir Humphrey Segrim said de Reppes was the cause of.'

'Yes, Thomas. Segrim says he saw Odo at Berkhamsted Castle, and that he was pursued by the Templar all the way to Oxford. De Reppes, on the other hand, has another story. He claims barely to remember Segrim and that he didn't even know he lived at Botley. He also reminded me that Richard was half dead anyway, being paralysed down one side.'

Thomas was indignant.

'That does not excuse him from guilt. He killed the old man, even if he was near death already.'

'And it seems Amaury was implicated in it as the prime mover. Whoever I speak to tells me to seek out Amaury de Montfort.'

'Then your case is proven, and you can go to the king and tell him so.'

Thomas was emphatic, but Saphira still had a question for Falconer.

'And what of the king's son, John? Have you learned anything of his death? After all, it was that death that seemed to have affected Edward most strongly from what you have told me. That is what started off this enquiry of yours.'

Falconer pointed a finger at Saphira in triumph.

'Exactly. Everyone I have spoken to has given me just what I wanted in the case of the other three murders – or attempted murder, in Edward's case – but no one has yet spoken a word about Prince John. I should like to learn more about his death, and whether Amaury was involved in that too, before I go to Edward. And where is Amaury now? I have never before been unable to speak to the chief suspect in a murder. If I could trace him, I might learn the truth finally.'

Thomas was hesitant about speaking up now. He had a dread that the seed that had been growing in his mind was nothing more than a fantasy. But then he could not ignore it, could he? What if he didn't say what he thought and it turned out to be true? He had been leaning back in his chair, almost in shadow, while Falconer and Saphira eagerly debated points about the other killings. He was deeply involved with Paul Hebborn's death, and more recently John Fusoris'. Did he now see a link between them and the heady matter of the death of kings that obsessed Falconer so much? William had begun by asking him about his enquiries, but he had soon enough got sidetracked back on to his own investigation. As if the deaths of a few noble-born men were more important than those of a couple of simple students. A few years ago, William would not have thought so, but it seemed to Thomas as though his mentor's head had been turned by his association with kings. He resolved to determine the truth of his growing fears before he risked Falconer's derision if he were wrong. So he just smiled when Falconer spoke to him.

'Thomas, you are very quiet. Thinking about what you will do next about your own case, I would guess. Listen to Roger; he will come up with something, I am sure. And when I have unburdened myself of Edward's case, I will help you too. Saphira has persuaded me to tell the king what I have learned so far, so that I can find out more about his son from him. So we are going to the Royal Palace tomorrow.'

Saphira sat up with a start.

'We? I didn't say I would come with you. Don't you recall what happened last time I met the King of England? I almost got accused of murder myself.'

Falconer waved his hand dismissively.

'That was Henry. His son is younger and more open-minded. Besides, I need you to talk to Eleanor, if it can be arranged.'

Saphira laughed out loud at Falconer's nerve.

'So we are to walk into the palace of the French king and ask to have a word with their royal guest from England. And while you chat with Edward, I am to get up and say, "Just going to have a gossip with your wife"?'

Falconer looked at her with wide, innocent eyes.

'What a good idea. I wish I had thought of that.'

TWENTY-THREE

T he next day the sun was shining brightly, and the streets of Paris were teeming with people. Last night Thomas had returned to the abbey to sleep, leaving Falconer and Saphira in Pletzel. Now he wished he had remained in the city, for it was well-nigh impossible to negotiate the crowded and narrow lanes. At least the flow of people was in the direction he was going. If he had had to force his way against the crowd, he reckoned he would have failed to make headway. Everyone was funnelling on to the Petit Pont, and he was glad to turn down the quieter tributary of Rue de la Bûcherie. But when he got there, he found Friar Bacon and a small huddle of students standing uncertainly outside the medical school. Bacon strode up to him.

'I am glad to see you, Thomas Symon. It seems that Master Morrish has abandoned us for the market.'

Thomas's puzzled look drew a response from Peter de la Casteigne, who had followed the friar.

'It is market day in Les Halles today. That is why everyone is anxious to cross the bridge and get to the Right Bank, where the markets are to be found. It is one of the days when the Flanders weavers come to sell their wares.' He grinned sneeringly. 'Perhaps the master has gone to buy some scarlet.'

Thomas glanced down at his own drab robe, knowing that Morrish too invariably wore black. In contrast to de la Casteigne and some of his noble compatriots, who favoured particoloured surcoats and bright stockings. He had no reply to the youth's jibe, but walked over to the group of students, noticing that Hellequin was not among them. He suggested they take the day off from their studies.

'It seems that Master Adam is indisposed. But I suggest you pay close attention to the next section of Johannitius, so that you are ready to . . .'

He was unable to finish his discourse before Malpoivre and his hangers-on took him at his word and began to walk away. Thomas heard a few disparaging comments about the unlikelihood of Johannitius being opened and sighed at his apparent lack of authority. Bacon patted him on the shoulder.

'Never mind, Thomas, they are a lost cause. Besides, we have much to do today. I reckon our best defence is attack.'

Thomas watched as the last of the students filtered into the crowds of people passing the end of the lane, obviously intent on enjoying their unexpected free day. He turned to the friar.

'Yes. I had the idea that we could confront Adam today, but it seems he has anticipated me. If he is hiding from us, then we shall have to go and seek him out.'

'Do you know where he lives?'

Thomas shook his head.

'No. I followed him as far as the Ile de la Cité, but then lost him. However, I am sure the rector of the university knows. Or Master Gérard de Osterwiic, dean of the medical schools. We will start with him, as he knows me already.'

It turned out that locating Adam Morrish was not going to be as simple as Thomas thought. In fact, having met de Osterwiic, the mystery of his whereabouts began to get stranger. The dean explained that a master who had the right to teach could open a school wherever he pleased, and there were several schools on the Ile and the Left Bank.

'But how does a master get the right to teach?'

De Osterwiic answered Thomas's question in the vaguest of terms.

'There are age limits and courses of study to be undertaken to teach arts or theology, and the courses must be under the tuition of an existing master. Of course, purity of morals is just as important in issuing a licence.'

'But what about medicine?'

Thomas was becoming more and more exasperated as de Osterwiic prevaricated.

'A licence is granted gratuitously without oath or condition. Masters' rights are defended strongly in Paris.'

Thomas wondered about students' rights to be taught well. He was about to press Gérard to be more specific about Morrish, but Bacon touched his arm. He fell silent, and the friar bowed courteously, thanking the dean for his clarity of explanation. Once they had left the room, Thomas could contain his anger no longer.

'Clarity? He told us nothing.'

Bacon nodded.

'Exactly, and there must have been a reason for that, don't you think? There is something he wanted to keep secret concerning Adam Morrish.'

Thomas's doubts and concerns from yesterday began to rise to the surface again.

'I was thinking that Adam Morrish is not who he claims to be.'

'Then hold on to that thought, for we may be able to discover more about him from a friend of mine. If he had not been a proponent of Aristotle like Falconer, he would have prevailed in his battle to be rector of the university here. But he was defeated in the elections by Alberic de Rheims, who was a much more convenient nonentity of a scholar. And therefore more suited to the way of thinking of the Church, which is in control here.'

Siger of Brabant was a tall, stooping individual in his middle years. When they entered his solar, he was bent over a parchment carefully colouring a manuscript. Physically, he gave Thomas the impression of being weak and doddering. But mentally he proved to be sharp and sure of himself. After a little badinage with Bacon over the interfering Bishop Tempier, he came straight to the point.

'You want to know about Adam Morrish, then. I am certain that Gérard de Osterwiic has given you the runaround, or you would not have come to me.'

Both Thomas and Bacon nodded their agreement.

'What is the mystery surrounding him?'

Siger chortled.

'The mystery is who he claimed to be in order to get his licence to teach.'

Bacon held up his hand to stop his friend revealing the truth immediately.

'Is it safe for us to know?'

He was looking at Thomas at this point, and the object of his attention knew the friar was trying to protect him. But he could not bear to be excluded from the divulging of the secret. He blurted out what was on his mind. What had in fact been boiling in his brain for some time.

'It is a person whose family name carries opprobrium with it, isn't it? Someone who has studied and earned the right to teach medicine, but who needs to keep his identity secret. Especially from King Edward.'

Siger of Brabant, while giving nothing away, indicated with a turn of his wrist that Thomas should continue.

'It is Amaury de Montfort, isn't it?'

Again Siger said nothing but simply looked at Thomas in a way that told the young man that his guess was correct. Thomas pressed on with his next question.

'And do you know where Amaury lives?'

Siger pulled a face.

'That I cannot say.' Then his face lit up. 'But I can tell you that Adam Morrish lives on the Ile de la Cité. His house sits between two churches and faces directly on to the towers of Notre-Dame Cathedral.'

'From where Paul Hebborn fell to his death recently.'

Thomas's comment was made under his breath, but its import caused the old man's face to cloud over.

'I can tell you no more. In fact, I have told you too much already. You must go – both of you. And Brother Bacon, I would appeal to you as an older man to hold your young friend's zeal in check. The de Montforts are not a family to meddle with lightly.'

Bacon gave Siger a sideways look that revealed his own stubbornness.

'But we are not seeking out a de Montfort, Siger. We merely wish to ask Adam Morrish – a simple scholar – a few questions.'

Siger shook his head sadly and, picking up his brush, began to fill an ornate letter 'O' with red ink. The friar and Oxford master retired from his solar and returned to the thronging streets of Paris. Many people had already been to the market and were now returning with their purchases. Thomas was almost knocked over as a merchant bustled past, followed by his servant carrying a large bolt of scarlet cloth under his arm. His angry cry brought no apology but just the sight of the rich man's opulently clad, fur-trimmed back disappearing down the narrow lane. Thomas was tiring of the rudeness of the denizens of this city, where business took precedence over courtesy.

'I shall be glad to return to Oxford.'

'But I have barely begun my compendium, Thomas Symon. We have much to set down yet. So let's get on and see what

Adam or Amaury has to say for himself. Then I can turn my attention to the study of optics.'

Thomas groaned but followed Bacon towards the Petit Pont and the island that stood at the heart of the city.

Falconer and Saphira Le Veske had already crossed to the Ile and were on their way to the Royal Palace. He had sent word ahead that he wished to speak to the king on urgent business. So when they arrived at the gates, Sir John Appleby already awaited them. He scowled at the sight of the woman accompanying Falconer, however.

'You did not say you had a . . . companion. She cannot come into the presence of the king, you know.'

Saphira took Appleby's meaning as it was intended, and scowled. She was getting tired of being taken for a whore when on William's arm. She was about to storm off, but Falconer held her firmly by the elbow and reprimanded the garishly dressed courtier.

'Mistress Le Veske is an important woman of business in both France and England. Many nobles are indebted to her, and if she cannot be introduced to the king then I have no time today to speak to him. Good day.'

Appleby gasped at Falconer's audacity, but as the master turned to go he stayed him with an outstretched hand. He could not afford to anger his lord and master. Let Falconer himself earn the king's wrath by bringing a strange woman before him – he would not be held responsible.

'Not so hasty, Master Falconer. I am sure the king will be glad to make the acquaintance of one of his loyal subjects. And one so pretty too.'

Saphira smiled sweetly, while still feeling sick to her stomach at being brought before the English king. This popinjay of a courtier nauseated her too, but in another way. She could not stand the obsequiousness of such individuals. Oblivious to her reaction, Sir John made a vague, loose-wristed sign in the air with his hand.

'Follow me, please.'

Falconer and Saphira were led to the same tapestried room where he had met the king before. The room was empty this time, and they were asked to wait by Appleby, who hurried away to warn the king of Saphira's presence. They waited patiently, and Saphira examined one of the tapestries closely. She was just about to touch the intricately stitched image of a unicorn when a man entered. She was immediately struck by the aura that surrounded him. He was a tall, broad-shouldered and good-looking man with a droopy eyelid that somehow attracted her to him. She gasped, suddenly realizing who he was. Swiftly curtseying to the king, she felt a hot blush creep over her face. He was quite unconcerned, probably used to the effect he had on women. He took her hand.

'Mistress Le Veske. I am told you are a woman who runs her own business, and that it is a success. My wife would like to meet you.'

Saphira looked at Falconer and would have burst out laughing but for the situation. What had they been talking about before? Her meeting with the king and asking to go and chat with the queen. Edward, unaware of the sideways look, went on.

'She is jealous of independent women who manage their own affairs. She complains to me that all she does is produce children. I have told her it is a queen's fate, but still she rails against it.'

Saphira swallowed and spoke out.

'It is the fate of most women in this world, sire.'

Edward nodded his head, his hair flopping across his eyes.

'Yes, and I love my wife for her sacrifice. She is heavy with child right now. I have forbidden her to travel to Castile to see her family, but she is determined. Eleanor is a very determined woman. Would you talk to her, mistress, and try to dissuade her? Appleby will show you the way.'

Saphira knew she was being dismissed, but with such gentleness she could not resist. Besides, she was intrigued that what Falconer had mockingly suggested had come about. She was being given a chance to 'gossip' with the queen, and would tease him with it later.

'Sire, I will try, but if she is as determined as you say, I may have to agree with her.'

She bowed gracefully and left the room with a sour-faced Sir John in attendance. Edward turned to Falconer.

'An intelligent and beautiful woman, Master Falconer. You are a lucky man for a celibate scholar, if I guess rightly. A pity she is a Jew, though.'

Falconer didn't like the implication of Edward's tone of voice. But before he could say anything, the king taxed him about his investigations.

'Now you have found who was responsible for the attacks on my family?'

Falconer patiently explained the evidence he had gathered around the deaths he had investigated. How the attack on Edward himself could have been commissioned by a Latin, which may have been a de Montfort, though he had no direct evidence. And what he had learned from the Templar, Odo de Reppes, concerning the scandalous murder in the church in Viterbo. And then he described Odo's subsequent visit to Berkhamsted, where he probably killed Edward's uncle. He had one caveat, however.

'I have not been able to look into the circumstances of your son's death yet, sire. I would have to go back to England to puzzle the evidence out about that one.'

Edward waved his hand dismissively.

'There is clearly no need to take this further, Master Falconer. I think you have come to a conclusion about who is responsible, have you not? He will no doubt also be guilty of causing the death of poor little John. A boy who would have been king after me, if he had not died so young. You have a name?'

Falconer nodded, a little surprised that Edward had dismissed the investigation of his son's death so abruptly. But then, he was probably keen to know what Falconer had concluded and needed no further evidence of treason.

'Everything points to Amaury de Montfort being the prime mover behind all the deaths, and the attack on yourself.'

Edward's eyes opened wide in surprise.

'Amaury? Surely it was the older brothers who were responsible? I know Simon is dead now of a tertian fever, but Guy still lives. He has protected himself by marrying the Tuscan Red Count's daughter, but I can ask the Pope to intervene. He cannot hide behind the skirts of Margherita Aldobrandesca forever. Surely he is more likely to have perpetrated the murders than little Amaury? The boy is barely old enough to be such a villain. And he is a more a scholar like yourself, is he not, than a warrior?'

'Sire, he is already thirty, though I am told his face barely shows his years. It is perhaps because he looks so young that you cannot believe he is so evil. But everything I have learned points at him. He has no need to be a fighter – he uses others to carry out his wishes.'

Edward looked pensive, stroking his beard and pacing up and down by the window.

'Amaury, eh? And have you located where he might be? Does anyone know?' Edward struck his right fist into his palm decisively. 'If not, please keep searching, Master Falconer. I would not be surprised if he were in Paris right now, plotting against me once again. You have been so persistent so far, I am certain you will find him, if you carry on.'

Falconer shook his head.

'I am afraid I cannot say where he is at this time. No one seems to know. And I may only drive him back into hiding if I carry on.'

'No.' Edward was insistent. He strode over to Falconer and grasped his arm. 'I will speak to Philip and turn Paris into a trap for him. No one will sneak out.'

Falconer wondered for a moment who this Philip was, until he realized Edward was talking of the French king. Such was the familiarity of great men. Edward, meanwhile, had more to say to him.

'In the meantime, you will dig deeper, and you will find him.'

With that command, he exited the room, leaving Falconer to wonder what he might do next. He did not yet know that Thomas Symon had the very information he was charged with uncovering.

TWENTY-FOUR

The great sturdy blocks of the two towers on the western façade of Notre-Dame cast a shadow over Thomas Symon and Friar Bacon. Thomas could not tear his eyes off the tops way above, as he pictured the unfortunate Paul Hebborn plunging to his death from one of them. For a moment his head spun, and he closed his eyes tight. Bacon touched his arm gently.

'I prefer the towers of Oseney Abbey for their grace and charm.'

He was referring to the abbey just outside the walls of Oxford town. It also had two towers, the western one housing a ring of bells. Thomas could hear them now in his head – the peals of Hauteclere, Douce, Clement, Austyn, Marie, Gabriel and John. It brought back a flood of homesickness. He clenched his teeth and turned his back on the dark towers. Opposite stood the home of Adam Morrish, squeezed in between two churches. It seemed an inappropriate place for a Devil-like Amaury de Montfort – if that's who Adam really was. The house's windows were shuttered and all appeared silent. Determined to find out the truth, Thomas strode over to the front door and banged on it with his clenched fist. The sound of it echoed inside the house. Bacon's mild, calm voice spoke from behind his shoulder.

'It would seem the bird has flown. It was probably Morrish who spied on us at the school when we were tinkering with the medicine chest. He has been forewarned.'

Thomas's shoulders slumped, but just as he was about to turn away the door sprung open. But the person revealed was not Adam Morrish, though he was very familiar to Thomas.

'Jack Hellequin! What are you doing here?'

Jack grinned in that laconic way of his, his young face creasing in wrinkles.

'I may ask the same of you, Master Symon. And I would guess we were seeking the same fellow. I came here to see if my education – and that of my fellow students – was to progress any further. Most of them have paid what few shillings they could afford to be taught for the year by Adam. Now it appears he has skipped with their money.'

Thomas turned to the friar in disappointment.

'I think we are too late. He has gone. And we now have nothing to tell Falconer.'

Hellequin pricked up his ears at the mention of the name.

'How is the master? Recovered from his close call on the bridge, I hope?'

Thomas nodded his head.

'Oh, yes. It would take much more than almost falling to his death to shake William off his pursuit of justice.'

'And I thought he was a simple scholar. Who has he been pursuing, then?'

Thomas winked conspiratorially.

'The same person we have been seeking, as it turns out. His enquiries have taken him to the Royal Palace and the prison inside the Paris Temple. But he doesn't yet know about Adam Morrish, or to be more precise . . .'

Thomas was about to reveal what they had learned about Morrish's true identity but felt Bacon tap him on the sleeve of his robe. He looked quizzically at the friar, who intervened smoothly.

'Thomas has a theory that Adam was responsible somehow for Paul Hebborn's death. But it is too fanciful for my liking. But tell me, young man, do you know if some of your friends were stealing from your tutor? I am thinking of pleasant substances that it may on the surface appear harmless to dabble in.'

Hellequin looked down at his well-worn shoes. They were scuffed, but of the finest leather. He appeared to be examining them minutely before he found a response.

'I am embarrassed to tell you. But you are correct in part of what you say. Yes, they have been . . . dabbling, as you suggest. I too have . . . dabbled. But the opium was not stolen. Master Adam gave it to Geoffrey Malpoivre to distribute only to his favourite pupils and in secret. He actually encouraged them to try it. He said it was a necessary part of learning about poisons and drugs. It got a little out of hand, that's all. I think Paul fell . . .' He looked up at the towers looming over them. 'He must have fallen when too drugged to know where he was.'

Thomas winced at the thought of stepping off a tower into space, imagining the ground was still under your feet. It was a gruesome end to contemplate.

Saphira had been fearful of meeting Eleanor when she had been led into the woman's private chamber. But once they had begun speaking, she had lost all her inhibitions. The dark-haired queen, very big with child, had motioned for Saphira to come closer to her chair. She had been hovering uncertainly in the doorway. But when she saw Eleanor's swollen ankles, lifted up on a footstool in front of her, she behaved like any woman would.

'My dear, what we women must go through for our men.'

She knelt at the queen's feet and slowly massaged her legs. At first, Eleanor had protested, but, as she felt the relief, she relented.

'That is so good. Are you trained in medicines?'

Saphira dipped her head.

'I am following the ways of a wise man called Samson, who is teaching me all he knows.'

Eleanor accepted the obvious conclusion to be drawn from the man's name, but did not bridle at Saphira being a Jew. She knew her own husband's prejudices but did not share them. Instead, she spoke gently of the perils of childbirth, patting her stomach.

'This will be my ninth.'

Saphira feigned astonishment.

'Really? And you barely out of your teens.'

Eleanor giggled, aware of her own beauty but knowing too that she was beginning to show her thirty years. It was true she had been a child bride at ten years, when Edward was fifteen. But they had waited until she was eighteen before conceiving. And had supplied almost a child a year since. Saphira smiled too, and carried on rubbing the queen's ankles.

'Alas, I have only one son. Menahem looks after the family business and is a good boy. I did have a daughter, but she was stillborn.'

As she spoke, she could not believe she had said that. Not even William knew about that little sadness in Saphira's life. Eleanor patted her arm.

'My first three were either stillborn or died before they

reached their first birthday. And another one the same when we were in Acre. I was beginning to feel we were cursed, until John came along.' She sighed. 'And then he died aged only five.'

It seemed natural for Saphira to ask her about the death of John, though she felt a little pang at doing so. She was motivated mainly by wanting to help William's investigations. But she didn't want to cause Eleanor to fall into a melancholy. She bit her lip, not daring to look at the queen, as she asked her about her dead son.

'What happened? Do you know?'

'We were told it was a fall from a horse. John was in the care of his uncle Richard at the time. He had probably badgered the old man to let him ride a horse too big for him. Richard gave in and was leading the horse by the rein with John up on its back. Apparently, the horse shied at some noise or other, and John fell. Even then he might have survived, but he was hit by one of the hooves.' She shuddered. 'Richard never forgave himself. His guilt must have contributed to his own illness, for it was not long after that he got the half-dead disease. He was paralysed down one side of his body, and he died four months later.'

'Your husband must have been devastated.'

Eleanor winced and shifted uncomfortably in her chair.

'The strange thing was he didn't show any emotion. Not like when his father died. When Charles of Anjou asked him about that, Edward shrugged it off, suggesting that a father was irreplaceable, but a son was not. And talking of sons . . .'

Eleanor gave a moan and clutched at Saphira's hand.

'You must help me, Mistress Le Veske, and employ some of that medical skill you claim. I think my baby is coming.'

Saphira rose and made to go to the door, saying that she would call a midwife. But Eleanor grasped her arm in a grip of steel such as only a warrior and gravid mother might possess.

'Too late. The midwife and nurse have been sent on to Castile. I was to follow them but got delayed.'

Saphira knew what had caused the delay – the matter of Falconer's investigation. Now it seemed that she was to reap the consequences. She took Eleanor's arm and led her over to her bed. The queen slumped back on the beautifully embroidered coverlet. Saphira prayed such a marvel would not be ruined by the blood and waters of childbirth. She must have looked anxious, because Eleanor raised her head and smiled.

'Don't worry, mistress. You may not have attended the birth of a child before, but I have done it eight times before. I think I can remember what to do. Now, if you look in that chest by the fire, you will find a vial with a preparation of birthwort in it. That will ease the child out.'

Saphira knew of birthwort as both an aid to birth and a means of getting rid of an unwanted child. She rummaged in the chest until she found what she was looking for. It was a green glass vial with a fluid in it. She pulled out the stopper and held the vial to Eleanor's lips, praying she did not exceed the safe measure. Next, carefully but with determination, she slid the embroidered cover from under Eleanor and eased her back on clean white linen. Then, with a moan from the queen, the birthing began in earnest.

Thomas decided he had to inform Falconer of his uncovering of Adam Morrish's identity as soon as he could. Knowing Falconer was probably seeking a de Montfort in connection with his own mission, he saw they were on converging pathways. His first instinct was to make for the abbey and hope William was not with Saphira in the Jewish quarter. But when he reached the St Victor Gate, Thomas was confronted with a peculiar sight. Instead of there being a steady flow of people in and out of the gate, there was total confusion. Crowds of angry citizens milled around the archway, pushing and shoving each other in their desire to pass through. It was apparent, however, that no one was being allowed out of the gate. Thomas could not see what the obstruction was until he too had elbowed his way closer.

Four soldiers stood impassively under the arch, blocking it completely, while a sergeant-at-arms argued with those pressing to leave the city. One by one, people were being permitted to pass, but only after close scrutiny by the sergeant. And only if they were elderly men, or women of any age. Men of Thomas's age were being turned back, and most of them were becoming increasingly angry at the situation. One young man, his age evidenced by the wispy hair that grew on his upper lip and chin, forced his way red-faced through the throng. Thomas ventured a question.

'What is going on?'

The youth spat on the ground.

'You tell me. They will not let us out of the gate. And I have tried the Ste-Geneviève Gate too. It's the same thing.'

Someone piped up from just behind Thomas.

'And at St-Germain, and St-Michel also. We are locked in the city.'

The two speakers seemed ready for a fight, and Thomas discreetly slipped away from the growing angry mob. He decided to head for Saphira's house, hoping that the bridges over the Seine were not similarly blocked and that he might find Falconer there. He had no need. Suddenly, a strong hand grabbed him and pulled him free of the milling crowd and up a side alley that was quieter than the main thoroughfare. It was Falconer, who had been waiting for him for some time.

'Thomas. Where have you been? I have been hanging around here for ages in order to waylay you. Come with me to Saphira's, and we can talk in safety. Paris will be like a tinderbox tonight.'

As they hurried through the streets and across the Ile de la Cité, Falconer explained the reason for the closing of the city's gates. Edward had persuaded King Philip to undertake it in order to trap Amaury de Montfort. He thought Edward's efforts would prove to be in vain.

'He will never find Amaury in this way. In fact, he has probably warned him off, and the man will lie low for a while in a safe place. Heaven knows where that will be.'

Thomas grinned in delight at knowing something William didn't.

'I think I can help you with that conundrum, William.'

He began to explain his suspicions about Adam Morrish's identity. How his history matched up with that of the youngest de Montfort brother through his education at Padua medical schools, and his disdain of the value of books.

'It was your remark about his not caring about returning those medical texts that put me in mind of the discarded books in Adam's solar. And Friar Bacon and I were able to confirm my suspicion with a man called Siger of Brabant. He had been rector of the university when Adam proposed opening up his school. It seems it was known to only a few that using the name Adam Morrish was a way of Amaury concealing himself.'

As the two of them entered Pletzel, Falconer became quite excited by the revelations.

'Perhaps he was not just hiding away from Edward but lying in wait for him. It was inevitable that the king would come to Paris on his way back from Outremer. It would offer Amaury another chance to attempt to kill him.' He stopped abruptly in the little alley that led to Saphira's house. 'You said you might know where he could be hiding. Where would that be?'

'I know where Adam . . . Amaury . . . is living.' His face fell. 'But he was not there when Bacon and I went round.'

'We have to assume that Edward's closing of the gates has kept him in the city, though. He doesn't know yet that we have discovered who he is pretending to be. He is most likely to have gone back to the house to wait for the hue and cry to die down.' He grasped Thomas's shoulder in a firm grip. 'We have to try it. Show me where this house is.'

'It is close by Notre-Dame. But shouldn't we speak to Mistress Le Veske first?'

Thomas pointed at the house before he realized it was in darkness.

'Or at least leave a message.'

Falconer waved his hand dismissively.

'I am afraid Saphira has other more important matters to attend to. It appears she is assisting in the birthing of a child for Edward. If it is a boy, he is to be called Alfonso.'

Thomas stood stock-still, dumbfounded at this unusual turn of events. But Falconer was already walking back down the winding lane. He beckoned impatiently at Thomas.

'Come, Thomas, show me where this house is. We will loiter in the precincts of the cathedral and see if our quarry turns up.'

TWENTY-FIVE

As it turned out, Falconer and Thomas Symon had no need to hide away when they reached Notre-Dame. The great arched entrance to the cathedral, topped with the new rose window, was thronging with people. Thomas wondered if it was because of the trouble at the gates to the city. Would the angry crowd turn into an uncontrollable mob? But the mood of those passing in and out of the cathedral was of joy and calm, not anger. Falconer stopped a cheerful-looking matron, who was bustling towards Notre-Dame, and asked her in French what the occasion of all the activity was. She grinned broadly and replied in an English that placed her as coming from the Essex marshes, east of the English capital.

'Bless you, sir. Haven't you heard? Our king, Edward, has another child. I am going like all these others to pray for his soul. Poor Eleanor has lost children before. We must ensure this little boy survives.'

As she scurried away to light a candle for Alfonso, Falconer turned to Thomas.

'Then Saphira truly has had her hands full today. The boy is born, and Edward will be mightily pleased.'

A voice called out from behind them.

'Another English prince, then, Master Falconer. Your king is hedging his bets over breeding an heir.'

Falconer and Thomas looked around and saw a figure outlined against the yellow glow of the candles inside the cathedral. As he stepped towards them, his features resolved themselves. It was the youthful face of Jack Hellequin, and his eyes seemed quite on fire.

'This is his second male child.'

Falconer nodded in agreement.

'A king cannot be too careful when it comes to ensuring his line. One day, we may have a King Alfonso.'

Hellequin cocked his head to one side.

'He is to be called Alfonso? After Eleanor's half-brother, I suppose. Let us hope he will be as wise.'

Alfonso of Castile was known as 'the Wise' and had indeed wisely ceded Gascony to the feisty Edward, along with his half-sister, Eleanor, in an arranged marriage. Which unusually had become a love match. Hellequin spoke to Thomas.

'Are you here to seek out Master Adam?'

'We are.'

'Do you really think he will return? Is he not far away by now?'

Falconer smiled.

'Not if King Philip's soldiers have had their way. All the gates to the city are barred to all but the elderly and women.'

Hellequin looked as though the information was news to him.

'Really? Then would you mind if I waited with you? We students are keen to recover our money from our former master.'

Falconer held out a hand in welcome, which Hellequin grasped.

'You are welcome to share our vigil. Though it may not be a long one after all. Look.'

Falconer pointed to a shadowy figure skulking in the darkness cast by one of the churches opposite. His eyesight was not of the best, but even he could see whoever it was did not want to be spotted. If they had not been on the lookout, the man may have been able to gain access to the narrow-fronted house that was Adam Morrish's without being seen. The three observers moved gently back into the crowd milling around the entrance to the cathedral and watched as the figure slid across the front of the church and into the house next to it by the front door. Falconer whispered in Hellequin's ear.

'There is no other way out?'

The young man shook his head.

'Then I want you to go to the Royal Palace and alert King Edward to this man's presence.'

Hellequin's eyes widened in shock and surprise.

'I am to go to King Philip's palace and speak to your English king? How am I to do that? And why should he want to know about Master Adam anyway?'

Falconer calmed him down immediately.

'They will listen to you. You have only to say that you have been sent by me, William Falconer, and that I know where the man we seek is to be found.'

'Can't Thomas Symon go in my stead?'

'No. I need Thomas here to bear witness to what we may

find in the house. We will not let the man go until you have returned.'

Hellequin had a worried look on his face but did not see how he could refuse Falconer. Reluctantly, he left the precincts of the cathedral and made for the river bank and the palace at the other end of the island. Thomas looked puzzled as they watched Hellequin leave.

'Are we going to go into the house and confront Amaury? What if he resists us, as he surely will if he knows he is cornered?'

Falconer patted Thomas's shoulder.

'Don't worry. We are not going to go in until Edward or his men arrive. I just did not want Jack Hellequin to become directly embroiled in a confrontation. That is all. Now let us settle down and wait.'

Falconer tucked himself into the corner of one of the grand doorway arches, leaning unceremoniously on the feet of one of the apostles. Thomas began to pace anxiously backwards and forwards, until Falconer grasped his sleeve and pulled him into the shadow of the arch alongside him.

'You will give the game away, Thomas. Now relax and wait for the endgame to start.'

The time slipped by, and Falconer was beginning to wonder whether Hellequin had carried out his task or not. A beam of candlelight had flared briefly behind one of the window shutters of the house opposite. But that had been the only sign of anyone being inside. Falconer was getting anxious. If Amaury escaped by another route, he would look a fool. Worse than that, he would appear incompetent in the eyes of the king, who might not tolerate such a failure. But just as he was about to suggest to Thomas that they enter the house after all, a familiar figure appeared on the pathway beside the river. Despite the black cloak Sir John Appleby was wearing, his gaudy clothes stood out in the gathering gloom. And his jaunty stride made him look like a cockerel in a pen of dowdy scratching hens. Behind him loomed four heavily armed English soldiers.

Falconer groaned and told Thomas to wait where he was. He hurried across the open square that was now emptying of people. In the developing circumstances, he did not want the occupant of the house alerted by such obvious and unusual activity. He managed to stop the small invasion before it could come into view from one of the loopholes in the shuttered windows. He hissed at the courtier.

'Sir John, I see you have come prepared. But we must not alert our quarry, in case he flees.' He cast a glance around. 'Is the king not with you?'

One of the men-at-arms tilted his helm back off his face, and Falconer recognized the droopy-eyed visage of Edward. The king put his finger to his lip to silence Falconer.

'I could not resist being present at such an event as the capture of Amaury de Montfort. But it is safer for me to be unrecognized, don't you think?'

Falconer nodded and beckoned for the group to follow him. Across the square he could see Thomas nervously hovering by the cathedral doors. He held his hand up to indicate that the young man should stay where he was. And out of any danger. Unfortunately, Thomas must have misunderstood his signal, for he ran over towards Falconer and the little knot of soldiers. A few people in the square glanced with curiosity at the group. But as soon as they saw the weaponry being wielded by the men-at-arms, they soon scuttled away. Falconer realized that if Amaury-Adam was looking out through the shuttered windows, he would now be aware that something was wrong. There was no more time left.

He led the soldiers up to the door of the house, leaving Appleby and Thomas Symon in his wake. He pushed at the door, but it resisted his effort. It must have been barred since the occupant had gone inside. One of the soldiers – Falconer thought it might have been Edward himself, but he could not be sure – eased him aside. He charged the door with his shoulder, and the wooden bolt gave, splintering the door in the process. The soldier winked at Falconer and forced the door open on its broken hinges. All four large men squeezed through the gap created and pushed into the house. Falconer clambered over the shattered door after them.

Inside, the dark hall was eerily silent except for the sound of heavy breathing coming from the soldier who had forced the door. He turned back to Falconer and lifted his helmet. It was Edward, and his face was contorted in a grimace.

'I swear my shoulder must be broken, it aches so much. I should leave this sort of work to those who are better built for it. However, now we are in . . .'

He drew his sword and swung it experimentally. Satisfied that his sword arm was not as hurt as he first thought, he motioned for his three companions to search the house. With a swish of steel three more swords were drawn, and the men crossed the darkened hall, poking under tables and toppling chairs with the tips of their weapons. Edward laughed quietly, then called out.

'Amaury? Come out now. We will find you.'

The men moved into the back of the house, where the kitchen was located. Soon, the sound of breaking pottery suggested that their search out there was unsuccessful too. The three men returned, shaking their heads. Edward sighed and slashed at a water jug standing on the table in the centre of the room. It shattered, and water splashed over the tabletop. Falconer felt a hand clutch at his arm, and he spun around only to be confronted by a wide-eyed Thomas. He had slipped in through the door just in time to see Edward's petulant swordplay. Though he was used to the sight of dead bodies, and had cut several open to examine them, he wasn't so used to the violence that usually caused them. Falconer gave a whispered reassurance.

'Just stay back and let them get on with it.'

Edward was pointing grimly at the staircase that led up to the upper part of the house. The steps creaked as the chain mail-clad men crept up them. Falconer stood in the hall for a moment, then he could not resist it. He crept up the stairs too, followed closely by a frightened Thomas. They got to the top of the stairs just in time to hear a wail and scuffle from the solar at the top of the house. The triumphant Edward came out on to the landing, followed by a soldier dragging a body across the floor by one leg. If the prostrate figure had not been wriggling, Falconer might have thought that Edward had had Amaury dispatched there and then. But he was very much alive, though he was face down, and his cries of fear were muffled. Edward smiled at Falconer.

'We have him. The coward was hiding under the bed. Now let us see him face to face.'

One of the other soldiers emerged from the room with a lighted candlestick in his fist. Edward kicked out with his leather boot, rolling the captive over, as his fellow soldier thrust the candle in the man's face. Edward groaned.

'Damn it all. This is not Amaury de Montfort.'

TWENTY-SIX

Adam Morrish lay pinned down on the table in the ground-floor hall of the house in Paris. His tearful face was bloated with fear, and Edward was pacing up and down beside his prostrate figure. Falconer leaned over him and asked him to tell the truth about himself.

'The rector of the university, and the Church authorities who pay you, think you are secretly Amaury de Montfort. Why do they think that, Adam?'

Morrish sucked in a deep breath, but, before he could reply, Edward grabbed his right arm and extended it over the side of the table. He forced it down, making tears start in Morrish's eyes. Edward pushed his face into Morrish's.

'I swear I will break your arm, and then I will have one of these men with me chop it off, if you do not speak.'

Morrish looked wide-eyed at the soldier who stood at Edward's shoulder. He was grinning and lifting his double-edged sword into the air. The captive wailed.

'I meant no harm. I was a student of medicine at Padua when de Montfort became a master. I was envious of him despite his family history. I did not have the money to continue, you see.'

Edward snorted in derision.

'You did not have the brains, you mean. So you stole his credentials and purported to be him here in Paris. The Pope and the Church, which pays your wages, were taken in. You knew they favoured his family over mine, so were inclined to keep the secret, weren't they?'

Morrish nodded, his features contorted with fear and pain. Edward did not release the pressure on his arm, however.

'But the Church didn't know what secret they were keeping, eh? They thought they were hiding Amaury from me, when in reality they were colluding with a charlatan. A faker who passed himself off as a master for his own vanity.'

Edward bore down on Morrish's arm, and the man shrieked in agony.

'Yes, yes. It's true.'

Falconer stepped in and lifted Edward's hand from the defeated Morrish.

'This is pointless, Majesty. If you should punish anyone, it should be me. I said I had found Amaury right under your nose, and I was wrong. All we had was Adam Morrish after all.'

Edward kicked the table in his frustration, and Morrish flinched, nursing his aching right arm. Thomas drew Falconer to one side and whispered in his ear.

'William, do you think we could ask Master . . . er, well . . . Morrish whether he was responsible for giving his students potions, or if they stole them?'

Falconer frowned and glanced at the angry figure of the king, who was now conferring with Appleby. The courtier had stood in the background while Morrish had been savagely interrogated, and even now had a greenish cast to his face.

'I am not sure this is the right time, Thomas.'

'But look at him. He still has something to hide. He looks so shifty.'

At Thomas's insistence, Falconer took another look at Morrish. The man's agonized face did indeed look strained, and he could not bear to look his captors in the eyes. Was it because he was merely in fear for his life, though? He shrugged.

'Go ahead. There can be no harm in it. And he may be afraid enough to confess.'

Thomas walked over to the table and stared hard at the cowering figure of the spurious master.

'I want to ask you a question on a different matter.'

Morrish looked up, his eyes dulled with pain.

'What could matter now?'

'I just want to know the truth about Paul Hebborn.'

Suddenly, Morrish's eyes were not as dulled as before. Thomas could see a glint in them, and a shiftiness that suggested there was more to find out about Adam Morrish. Thomas pressed him on the matter.

'How did the students get their hands on the opium? And why was Hebborn at Notre-Dame in such a state?'

A groan was wrenched out of Morrish's throat.

'It was not my idea.'

Falconer stepped up behind Thomas's shoulder.

'No one said it was. You were being asked if you gave your

students opium, or if they took it for themselves. And what that had to do with Hebborn's death.'

By now, all the eyes in the room were on Morrish, and he looked fearfully around. But there was no escape for him. He put his head in his hands and rocked backwards and forwards on the tabletop.

'You know, don't you? I overheard you and Friar Bacon talking, and I knew the game was up.' He paused and drew a deep breath. 'He made me do it. I could not stop him. He knew, you see.'

Thomas was puzzled, not understanding anything that Morrish was saying.

'Hebborn was responsible for the theft of the opium?'

'Noooo. He took it reluctantly in order to be one of the group. That night at Notre-Dame, he didn't know where he was. He should have fallen, but he didn't. So I had to give him a little push.'

A hush fell over the room at Morrish's confession. But he had more to say, pouring out his wretched soul.

'John Fusoris was harder work. I had to hold him under the water until he stopped moving.'

He looked up at Falconer, pleading with him but knowing his fate was sealed.

'He made me. He knew who I really was.'

Falconer finally made the connection.

'It was one of the other students, wasn't it?' He stared coldly at Morrish. 'Someone who knew you weren't who you said you were, and played on it.'

Thomas broke in on Falconer's questioning.

'It was Malpoivre who passed out the opium. I found that out myself. He is the guilty one.'

Falconer frowned.

'No. It could not have been Malpoivre; he hasn't got the brains or the nous to plan such an evil act. Nor could it be de la Casteigne and the rest of the hangers-on. They are followers, not instigators. Nor can I see any of them actually causing Hebborn's death, or that of Fusoris. Baiting him and being cruel maybe, but not murdering him. There is only one man who could take pleasure in leading others astray and stand by to watch the consequences. His name has made fools of us all along.'

Thomas gasped, recalling the meaning of the name of the person Falconer was talking about.

'The demon who pursues the damned to hell.'

'Yes. Jack Hellequin.'

The man of whom Falconer was speaking was at that moment strolling along one of the passages in the French king's Royal Palace. On his way to the palace on the errand for Falconer, he had stopped off at the medical school by the Petit Pont. Inside the upper room, he had retrieved the key to the potions chest from the ledge up the chimney where Morrish habitually hid it. He had picked out some harmless pots of unguents and pills, and added arsenic and a paste made from laurel berries. These he put in a large pouch, which he hid under his cloak. Once at the palace, he put on the appearance of a distraught young man with an urgent task to perform. He begged the guard at the gate to convey a message to the English king from Master William Falconer. He even slipped a coin into the guard's hand to ensure the message was passed on.

When the overdressed courtier came to the gate, he reiterated his story, emphasizing how urgent and important it was. It did not take much to convince the old man, who clearly was expecting such a tale. He ushered Hellequin inside the palace, asking him to wait in a side room. In the hubbub that ensued, it was not difficult for him to slip away and hide. He'd seen the courtier looking briefly for him, but then he had rushed away, obviously with more important tasks to attend to. Hellequin had been forgotten.

Now he had produced the pouch from under his cloak and tied it prominently around his waist. From within the pouch, he pulled out a pair of eye-lenses and perched them on his nose. The glasses were plain, but they gave him a look older than his years. With the dark cloak disguising his youthful and colourful surcoat, he was now every inch the physician he wanted to appear. No one gave him a second look as he walked freely around the palace. He had once in a former life been in the palace, but now he could not recall precisely where the guest quarters were located. He finally had to admit to himself that he was lost, and he stood at a crossing of two passages wondering what to do next. Hearing someone approaching, he put on his most severe mien and waited. When a maidservant came around the corner, he stopped her.

'Child, tell me where Queen Eleanor is to be found. I am a physician called urgently to her bedside. The child will be in danger if I do not reach her in time.'

The girl looked a little puzzled. She had been outside the queen's room when the boy had been born. The red-haired woman had been present and had said everything had gone well. She herself had been sent for clean sheets. She shrugged her shoulders. Perhaps something had gone wrong in the meantime. The doctor seemed most anxious by the look on his face. She pointed back the way she had come.

'The room is just at the end of this passage, master. You cannot miss it. I am to fetch clean linen for the queen's bed.'

'Then go about your business, child.' He waved her away and called after her as she fled. 'There is no rush for linen, though. Take your time, for I will need to examine the queen first.'

The girl slowed her pace, glad not to have to rush after all, and disappeared around the corner. Hellequin grinned and walked off the way she had first come, sure the servant would not hurry back now. It would give him some extra time for what he had in mind. He paused momentarily outside the chamber door, adjusted his glasses and walked abruptly in. Before him in the bed Eleanor, Edward's queen, sat propped up by cushions. She looked tired but well, and the new child lay snuggled against her bosom. Eleanor looked up at him, a smile of satisfaction on her face.

'Ah, doctor. You are too late, I fear. The baby is delivered, and I am quite well. Saphira has gone to . . .'

Hellequin was not interested in the maidservant's whereabouts. He knew she had gone on her errand for linen and would take longer than the queen imagined. He quickly interrupted.

'Majesty, let me be the judge of your well-being. It is what I have trained all these years for.'

Eleanor was amused by the physician's severity. He looked so young, but she assumed, if Philip or Edward had sent him, he must be competent. There would be no harm in him making sure she was well.

'Please. Carry on, master.'

The doctor fussed around, peering close into her eyes through his eye-lenses and enquiring after her bodily functions. He then lifted the child up, noting it was a small but healthy boy. For a moment, while he had the boy in his hands, he wondered about dispatching it there and then. He could just dash its brains out on the floor. But he knew he would then be unlikely to escape from the palace without being caught. Self-preservation demanded a subtler approach. He gave the child back to Eleanor, who settled him down on her stomach again. Laying his glasses on the bed, he rubbed the bridge of his nose where they had pinched.

'I would like to examine a sample of your urine as soon as possible, Majesty. In the meantime, I want you to take these pills regularly, as they will give you strength.' He lay the pot with the arsenic pills on the bed at Eleanor's elbow. 'And this paste you can put on the end of your finger and let the baby suck. He is a little thin, and this will help his growth.'

The pot of laurel berry paste was placed beside the arsenic. Hellequin rose from where he had perched on the edge of the bed and stared solicitously at the baby.

'In fact, you could try him with a little now. I can see he is desirous of suckling.'

Eleanor dipped her finger in the paste and held it up before her face. She thought the concoction looked most unpleasant. But the doctor smiled encouragingly. Saphira, who had been discreetly clearing the mess caused by the birth, came back just as Eleanor was easing the baby into a position where it could suck her finger. She paused and looked up at her new friend.

'Saphira. This is the doctor sent by Philip to see if I was well. Have you located Edward yet?'

Saphira nodded an acknowledgement to the young physician and stepped towards the bed.

'Not yet, Eleanor. It would seem he has been called away on an urgent matter.' She went to sit on the bed and moved the eye-lenses that lay there. Then she spotted the two pots. 'What are these?'

The physician smiled indulgently.

'Mistress, it is nothing to bother your head about. I have suggested some potions for the mother and child.'

Saphira, who had learned much about herbs and medicinal

preparations from a fellow Jew, was not to be put off by the man's supercilious nature. Besides, she was suspicious of him for another reason. The eye-lenses were fakes. William Falconer had need of lenses for his poor eyesight, and the curved glass distorted things when she looked through them. These lenses were clear glass. She picked up the pot of paste and held it to her nose.

'This is laurel berry.' She looked at Eleanor. 'You have not taken this, have you? It's poisonous.'

Eleanor paled and drew her finger sharply from the child's lips. Fortunately, little Alfonso had not sucked it yet, and she wiped her finger clean on the edge of the bedlinen. Hellequin snarled and took a step towards the bed, but Saphira stood in his way, preventing him from reaching Eleanor and her newborn. She slid the little knife that she kept hidden up her sleeve from its sheath and brandished it in the doctor's face. When Hellequin saw it, he backed off towards the door. Opening it, he spun around and fled the room, leaving Eleanor trembling and clutching Alfonso so tightly to her that he began to bawl.

TWENTY-SEVEN

The sight of heavily armed men lumbering through the narrow streets of Paris caused the few who were out and about to scatter. It had been a strange day, with gates closed to all but women and the old, and now soldiers were barging their way towards the Ile de la Cité. Some wondered if an English invasion was in the offing, but consoled themselves with the thought that the English king was safely tucked up in King Philip's palace. Those who saw the soldiers would have been shocked to know that one of their number was that very king. Edward was deathly afraid for the safety of his wife and newborn, whom he had not yet even seen. Having left Morrish in the custody of one of his men-at-arms, he and the two other soldiers ran as fast as their chain mail allowed them to. Edward's battle-hardened legs almost kept pace with the unencumbered Falconer and his assistant Symon. In the end, though, he had to give best to the Oxford masters, who, accompanied by Sir John Appleby, ran on ahead.

Falconer reached the Royal Palace first and had to wait while Appleby caught up with him. The guards on the gate would only allow them access once the well-known face of the courtier had arrived. Appleby was exhausted and waved Falconer and Thomas on once they were through the gate.

'The guest quarters are on your right.'

'Yes, I remember where they are.'

Falconer and Thomas rushed onwards, driven on by the fear that Saphira might also be in danger from whatever Hellequin intended for Edward's family. They need not have been afraid. The passageways of the guest quarters were now teeming with servants and soldiers, all in the garb of King Edward. In fact, they found themselves barred from penetrating very far into the warren of rooms, and coming under suspicion themselves of being would-be killers. It was only when one of the guards recognized Falconer as someone who had been in the presence of the king earlier that they were allowed under escort to proceed. The bedlam of noise and feverish activity spoke more of servants being seen to be doing something than actually being effective. But they finally passed through the chaos into a quieter enclave at its centre. It was like being in the eye of the hurricane. The door they knocked on was opened cautiously, and Saphira stood before them. Falconer was relieved.

'Thank goodness you are safe.'

As he and Thomas were allowed in to the room, he noticed the flash of a blade disappearing up Saphira's sleeve. He said nothing, happy in the knowledge that she was well able to take care of herself. He grinned at her and squeezed her arm, feeling the blade in its secret sheath. She smiled back, understanding his acknowledgement of her self-assurance.

'He was here – whoever he was – but I persuaded him to leave. The king should know that Eleanor and his child are safe.'

Falconer realized for the first time that there were others in the room. On a large and comfortable bed, propped up on cushions, reposed the Queen of England. And close to her bosom, in a bundle of fresh linen, lay the new prince, Alfonso. Falconer bowed.

'Majesty, the king is on his way. It is only his armour that has made him a little slower than me or Thomas Symon.'

Thomas blushed at being introduced to the queen and bowed low, unsure of how to behave. Eleanor smiled sweetly.

'I thank you for your attentions. And I am relieved to know that Edward is coming soon. Do you know who this madman was? And what his intentions were?'

Saphira broke in, holding the two pots left by the intruder in order to show Falconer.

'He purported to be a physician sent by the French king. He tried to persuade Eleanor to take these pills.' She held out the first pot. 'They are a preparation of arsenic, and very poisonous. They would have killed Eleanor slowly but surely, and before she died she would have transmitted the arsenic in her milk to the child. That was evil enough, but to be sure of his purpose he gave Eleanor this pot for the boy to suck off her finger.' She produced the second pot. 'It is a paste of laurel berries. Equally poisonous. William, who would do such an awful thing to a child?'

'He calls himself Jacques or Jack Hellequin.'

Saphira, French by birth and aware of the legend, frowned. 'Hellequin? Jack the Demon?'

'Yes. I took it as a coincidence at first. An unwelcome family name that he made a joke of. But now I am convinced it was a joke on us.'

Outside the room there was a clatter, then Edward burst into his wife's chamber, tossing his helm away as he crossed the room. He discarded his chain mail gloves and tenderly stroked his wife's head, gazing fondly for the first time on his newborn son.

'Thank God you are both safe. So this is little Alfonso, eh?'

Saphira touched Falconer's sleeve, and all three of them slipped out of the queen's chamber together, leaving the regal family to console each other. Outside in the passageway, they spoke in hushed tones, Saphira asking the first question.

'What did you mean in there about the man's name being a joke on us?'

Despite their lowered tones, Falconer drew his two companions further away from the door. He didn't want Edward to overhear what he was about to say.

'I have been thinking about Jack Hellequin, and how he is always around when things go wrong. He seems to chase death around just like his name suggests.'

He was about to tell Saphira of his mishap on the bridge, and how he now thought Hellequin was the perpetrator before becoming his saviour. But he didn't want her to hear how close he had come to death. He was now convinced that the fleeting glimpse he had got of a youthful face inside the hood of the man who barged into him was that of Hellequin. No one had seen his attacker leaving the bridge for one very good reason. Hellequin had turned back to check that his actions had resulted in Falconer falling into the river. Confronted with his victim hanging on for dear life, and surrounded by witnesses, he had had no alternative but to save the man he had wanted to kill. And as the attack had been close on Falconer's visit to the Paris Temple and his request to speak to Odo de Reppes about the Templar's foul deeds in Viterbo, there had been good reason to try to kill him. Falconer also wondered if his uncanny feeling of having been watched while leaving the donjon tower was to do with Hellequin lurking in the vicinity. It occurred to him that even Odo de Reppes himself may be at risk from such a demon. Saphira interrupted his reverie.

'William, explain yourself.'

'Hellequin was hiding himself in Paris. Such a youthful-looking person would find it easy to secrete himself in the student community. It is a chaotic assemblage, with young men coming and going without too much scrutiny. He probably attached himself to Adam Morrish's medical school because he knew much about medicines already. I think he wanted access to the drugs Adam stored in his medical chest. And he found he had a hold over Adam, thereby gaining access to the chest. With it, he amused himself by dispensing some of the more interesting drugs to the other students. It was something he had done before.'

'What do you mean?'

Falconer shrugged in response to Thomas's question.

'I am only surmising. Perhaps he took the drugs only in order to confuse the mind of Paul Hebborn, so that he could arrange for Morrish to kill him more easily.'

Thomas gave a yelp that Falconer quietened with an admonitory finger to his lips.

'Quiet. Edward must not hear us.'

'But why do you think Jack Hellequin arranged the death of Paul Hebborn? Why would he want him killed? And what about John Fusoris?'

'Oh, yes, he certainly had Fusoris killed too. And for a similar reason.'

Saphira's face broke into a soft smile of realization. She could see where Falconer was going with all this, but she let him continue. She did not want to steal his thunder.

'He had a hold over Morrish and got him to kill Hebborn because of a curious coincidence.' He grimaced. 'You know how I hate coincidences. But in this case they form the cause and origin of all this mess. Paul Hebborn was just unlucky to have been caught up in it.'

'It has to do with Hebborn's family being one of the disinherited ones after the Barons' War in England, doesn't it?'

Falconer nodded eagerly at Saphira's supposition.

'Exactly. Not only did Hebborn know who Hellequin really was, but Hellequin also knew who Adam Morrish wasn't.'

Thomas could contain himself no longer.

'This sounds more complicated than the Gordian knot. Do I have to cut through it myself, like the great Alexander? Tell me what you mean by it.'

Falconer patted Thomas on the arm.

'Hellequin knew Adam wasn't Amaury de Montfort, despite the rumours, for a very simple reason. Hellequin himself is Amaury.'

Thomas took a deep breath and continued Falconer's line of thinking.

'And poor Paul Hebborn knew Hellequin was Amaury because he had seen him, albeit at a distance, in the medical school in Padua.'

'Yes. Maybe he wasn't sure at first. It may have taken him a while to figure out why he recognized Hellequin. But when he realized, he must have inadvertently let Hellequin know the truth. If the game of taking opium had already begun, it would have been easy for Hellequin . . .'

'Amaury.'

' . . . For Hellequin-Amaury to feed Hebborn opium and lure him to the tower of Notre-Dame for a secret meeting. He was hoping Hebborn would merely step off into space while his mind was befuddled.'

'But he made sure Morrish was there, just in case he didn't fall. And when he didn't, the faker pushed him.'

'Either way, Hellequin . . . Amaury . . . damn it, I have known him as Hellequin too long to change now . . . *he* was responsible for Hebborn's death. And he was equally responsible for Morrish killing Fusoris. He no doubt feared that Hebborn had spoken to him and told him his secret. If Hebborn had a friend among the students, it was Fusoris. And sadly that was his death warrant.'

Thomas's face looked as though it had been carved in stone. He remembered that Hellequin had known of Thomas's interest in Fusoris, because he had asked Jack how to find him. A sense of guilt hung over him like a dark cloak. He had been duped by Jack Hellequin, whom he had liked. Amaury de Montfort's youthful looks had stood him in good stead in his guise as a student of medicine, who would have already spent several years studying the arts. As Thomas had done so recently himself. It turns out he was thirty years of age and adept at dissimulation and deceit. From what William was suggesting,

his distribution of opium had not begun with the students of
Adam Morrish.

'When you said Amaury had done this before in relation
to using opium, what did you mean?'

'I was recalling what Sir Humphrey Segrim had said to me
before we left England. He had sworn that Odo de Reppes
had been wild-eyed when he saw him in the church in Viterbo.'

'At the murder of Henry of Almain.'

'Exactly. Odo said the same thing when I questioned him.
He said he had felt euphoric both before and during the foul
deed. And the two other de Montfort brothers had apparently
behaved wildly too. It is not beyond the bounds of possibility
that Hellequin made them feel quite reckless with opium then
incited them to do what they did. It was a bloody and a crazy
act. He then made sure he was well out of the way when it
all came to a head, and therefore innocent of complicity. It
was the same with Adam Morrish. He kept his own hands
clean and had someone else perpetrate the deeds we have been
investigating.'

Saphira touched William's arm.

'But if Hellequin is indeed Amaury de Montfort, do you
not want to tell the king and let him deal with it?'

Falconer shook his head.

'Edward is too engrossed in his feud with the de Montforts
to use a clear head. He will blunder around, throwing men-
at-arms at the problem. Meanwhile, Amaury will slip away.
No, we must try to find him ourselves, quietly and discreetly.'

'Where do we start?'

It was Thomas's question, and Saphira answered it.

'If the gates of the city are still closed, and there are guards
on the bridges, then the only way out of the city is by the
river itself.'

'Exactly.' Falconer shepherded them further down the
passageway. 'And we should get to the river bank as soon as
possible. Hellequin has had a head start on us already.'

They hurried along the labyrinth of corridors in the Royal
Palace and out into the street. There they stopped, realizing the
enormity of their search. Boats lined both sides of the Seine,
though it was from the Right Bank that most of the craft plied
their trade. The area around La Grève was where many
seagoing vessels loaded and unloaded. Falconer suggested

that would be where Hellequin would make for. But Thomas disagreed.

'True, it is busy, and he may be able to hide in the crowd. But the Left Bank is more familiar to him, and fewer boats mean fewer people are likely to see him. He also knows some of the sailors who drink in the Withered Vine, which is close by where they moor up.'

Saphira agreed.

'Thomas is right. A hunted animal will always run to ground in familiar territory.'

Falconer flung up his hands in defeat.

'We have no more time to debate this. You are probably right. Let's try the Left Bank.'

They crossed the Petit Pont, pushing past the two men-at-arms on the southern side. The soldiers, taxed with looking for Amaury, gazed suspiciously at Thomas. But they let him pass when Saphira smiled and professed that the boy was her son, and not who they were looking for. Thomas blushed in embarrassment, mumbling to Saphira that she needn't have said that. She pinched his cheek.

'Are you ashamed to be taken for my son, Thomas?'

'If that makes me in some way William's stepson too, yes I am.'

Falconer aimed a swipe at Thomas, who quickly led them along the narrow lane running parallel to the river and past Morrish's one-time medical school. They first tried the tavern where the ships' captains often passed their time waiting for the right time to sail down to Rouen and catch the tidal flow. The Withered Vine was unusually quiet, so Falconer asked the landlord if he had seen Jack Hellequin recently. The landlord was a cheery, red-faced man, who obviously imbibed too much of his own stock. It also made him incautious with his knowledge.

'Why, yes, as a matter of fact. But you have missed him. He went with Georges Fouarre on *La Sylvie* some time ago. That is why there's hardly anyone in here. He and his crew have set sail for the coast and Antwerp.'

All three companions rushed down to the sandy river bank, close to where the body of John Fusoris had been found. But when they got there the strand was bare, and the river empty of craft. Amaury de Montfort had flown the city.

TWENTY-EIGHT

Falconer sat on the quayside at Honfleur staring across the water that separated France from England. The compensation of his short-sightedness was that his long vision was good. But still he could not see the cliffs of his native land. His shoulders slumped, and he peered at the rough cobbles at his feet. He felt that his time in France had been wasted. Not only had he signally failed to understand the attack on Aristotle initiated by Bishop Tempier, which had been supported by the lily-livered tutors at the University of Paris, but he felt he had failed in bringing the true killer of the king's family members to justice. He had caused the apprehension of the perpetrator of the Paris murders – Adam Morrish – and the unfortunate man had been hanged for his crimes. But Amaury de Montfort had escaped, and it was now rumoured that he was under the protection of the Pope. So he was also beyond the grasp of King Edward. Falconer's only consolation was that he had found Saphira again.

Arriving like a mummer picking up a cue in a miracle play, Saphira came up behind him. He knew it was she because he could smell her scent. She placed her warm, soft hands on his dejected shoulders and squeezed.

'You have done all you could, William. One killer is hanged and another is only safe courtesy of your Christian Pope. He is as good as in prison, and should he dare to venture beyond the papal reach he will suffer the consequences.'

Falconer was not consoled. Amaury had been made a papal chaplain, and he had even persuaded the Pope to withdraw the sentence of excommunication that had been passed on his father, Simon, Earl of Leicester, for his rebellion against King Henry. It would take a bold monarch to stand up against the Church. Saphira tried to rouse William from his torpor. She pointed along the quay at a sturdy, round-bellied cog that bobbed eagerly on the lines that held it to the quayside. The boat looked anxious to be on its way.

'Look, the ship is ready and waiting. It is loaded with good red wine from Bordeaux. And it will soon carry us both across the Channel and back home.'

Falconer smiled, liking the sound of that. It would be good to get back to Oxford, especially as Saphira was accompanying him thence. He was missing Thomas, though.

'Do you think Thomas will be safe in Paris?'

Saphira laughed heartily with that strong, bubbling laugh that had first attracted Falconer to her. That and her shapely figure that he had first been able to admire coming down a drainpipe. The girlish act had been carried out to escape from a locked room in Bermondsey Abbey, and the wind had caused her dress to cling close to her curves. Her pretty calves had been on view too. The breeze off the sea caught her dress now and flattened it against her belly and hips. She stared at William, knowing what was going on in his mind.

'Thomas is a grown man now and is quite capable of finding his own way in the world without your help. In fact, you have not been much of an example to him, breaking your vows of celibacy as you frequently do.'

Falconer grinned.

'Yes, but I blame this temptress with red hair for my frequent falls from grace.'

As if summoned by his comment, the wind caught Saphira's hair and tugged it loose.

'Thomas Symon will learn much from Friar Bacon and will probably make a finer scholar than you ever could be, William Falconer. You chase your dreams too much to be a serious scholar.'

'You are right. Thomas will do very well. And he has promised to return to Oxford, should Roger ever be allowed to come back to the university.'

He saw the black-bearded captain of the ship waving at them.

'Look, it is time to go.'

Eleanor was finally able to leave Paris for Castile and her family. Edward still did not like the idea, however. His fussing was beginning to annoy her.

'First, you do not want me to travel because I am about to give birth. Now you do not want me to travel because I have given birth. Edward, dear, I have been giving you children year after year since we married, and in that time we have travelled to the Holy Lands and back.'

Edward stroked his wife's face with the back of his hand.

'I don't want to be apart from you.'

'Don't become all silken-tongued now, my dear. You go away when it suits your warrior instincts. Tell me exactly where you will be going soon whether I stay or not.'

Edward grinned sheepishly.

'I must go and put down this revolt by Gaston de Béarn in Gascony. If I do not show my face, we stand to lose the territory. And I can tie it closer to us by making treaties for the future marriages of our children.' He chucked the baby on his wife's lap under the chin. 'Even for little Alfonso here.'

Eleanor was not to be diverted from her argument.

'And may I remind you that, if I had travelled to Castile before your new son's birth, I would not have been here and at the mercy of Amaury de Montfort. So I am going before anything else goes wrong.'

Edward paced anxiously back and forth across the chamber. The shaft of morning sunlight coming through the window sparkled on the chain mail shirt that he still wore. He was in warlike mood and found it difficult to be countermanded by his own wife. But in the end he sighed and gave in.

'Very well. But you must take care. Amaury may have scuttled off to hide under the Pope's skirts, but he is quite capable of having others carry out his tasks. As we have seen so clearly.'

Having triumphed, Eleanor now looked a little wistfully at her husband.

'I will take care, my darling. I just wish Saphira was still here. I felt so safe in her company.'

She was thinking of the dagger hidden up the woman's sleeve that had sent Amaury scurrying off. But Edward was of a different opinion about Mistress Le Veske.

'She is a Jew, and Falconer's bed companion. Such a woman at your court would be unseemly. When we reach England, we shall both be under scrutiny.'

Eleanor squirmed at her darling's dislike of the Jews. It was one of his faults that set her teeth on edge. But she knew he was right about one thing. They would have to fit into other people's ideas of what made a king and queen when they landed on England's shores.

'When shall we be there, Edward?'

'Oh . . .' Edward was already thinking about his forthcoming campaign in Gascony and how long that might take. 'Next year some time. A king no longer has a need to fight for his birthright, and the Archbishop of York and Robert Burnell are both coping well in my absence. The coronation can wait a while.'

The Feast of St Henry the Pious, the Thirteenth Day of July 1273

The journey towards Oxford had taken a lot of time. It was a wet summer, and the roads were muddy and difficult to negotiate, even on horseback. Having landed at Dover, Falconer and Saphira Le Veske had broken their journey for a while in Canterbury. Saphira, who had friends in the large Jewish community in the town, had once thought of settling there. Then she had met Falconer, and her plans had changed.

Having spent a few days in Canterbury, refreshed they had struggled along the road towards London. Crossing the Thames by London Bridge was a struggle. The bridge had buildings and shops cluttering both sides, and this narrowed each of the two lanes to no more than six feet. Crowds of people on foot were pushing to get from one side to the other, while others were lingering in front of the shops examining the wares on offer. The shop signs in the form of the articles sold within were hung just high enough for Falconer and Saphira on horseback to clear them. They followed the north shore of the river west and out beyond the city walls. They rode down the Strand to pick up the old Roman road called Akeman Street, and the route took them close by the Royal Palace on the river bank.

Around the Palace of Westminster there was already building work going on. Masons and carpenters were busy constructing temporary halls around the sides of the palace. When Falconer asked them what they were doing, one of the masons briefly stopped his chiselling of a piece of stone.

'This is for the coronation of the new king. Extra rooms for the princes and nobles to banquet in.'

Falconer and Saphira thanked him and rode off on their hired rounceys, not wanting to tell the mason that he could take his time about the building. When they had left France, Edward had been on his way to Gascony, not England.

They stayed only one night just outside London, preferring to reach Oxford and home as soon as possible. But further along Akeman Street, approaching a hamlet unknown to Saphira, Falconer pulled up his horse and stared across the river valley and marshes to their right. Looming over the little town they were approaching was an old Norman motte-and-bailey castle. It gave the impression that little had changed in this neck of the woods since the arrival of William two hundred years ago. Saphira didn't know why William had suddenly become so pensive. She wheeled her horse around and trotted back to where he sat on his horse.

'Where is this, William? And what on earth is going through that cluttered mind of yours?'

Falconer pointed at the old castle.

'Thomas Becket once held this castle. It is said to have bankrupted him.'

'Very interesting. Shall we get going?'

Falconer remained stock-still.

'Eventually, Richard of Cornwall took it over.'

'The king's uncle?'

'Yes, and he died here.' He paused. 'And so did young Prince John.'

'Ah.'

Saphira now knew what was on William's mind. She knew how he hated loose ends and unresolved puzzles. It was not enough that he had pulled together all the facts about the other deaths connected with Amaury de Montfort. He would have to resolve the mystery around Edward's son John or it would be like a worm nibbling at his brain forever.

Falconer kicked his rouncey's flanks and trotted into the hamlet of Berkhamsted looking for an inn. He wanted to stay in the same place Sir Humphrey had told him about. He only knew that it overlooked the River Bulbourne and had a view of the castle, and that the innkeeper's name was Roger Brewer. Saphira followed him, knowing better than to ask William any questions at this stage. He would only become taciturn and clam up. She knew that, if she let him brood, he would explain everything to her eventually. But she did wonder why he rode past three perfectly good and clean-looking inns, only to settle on a drab and ramshackle place hard by the river. It promised to be a damp, uncomfortable night.

Falconer knew it was the inn because of its location, with the keep of the castle looming over it just as Segrim had said. For propriety's sake, they took two rooms high in the eaves of the inn. But Saphira soon bustled into the dark, damp cupboard that was William's quarters. She sat expectantly on the low pallet covered with a straw mattress, watching Falconer look out of the unglazed window at the castle opposite. Eventually, he turned back into the tiny room.

'This is where Segrim saw Odo de Reppes pass by on the night that Richard of Cornwall died. The interesting thing is that the Templar didn't use the main highway . . .' He pointed to Akeman Street that ran beyond the wall on the opposite side of the room. 'Instead, he sneaked down there . . . the back lane between the inn and the river.'

'But as he had killed Richard, would that not be the normal way of a murderer?'

Falconer frowned, something niggling at his memory.

'Perhaps. Though I don't see de Reppes as one who skulks. And there is another problem.'

'What is that?'

'I am not sure he did kill Richard.'

'But did he not admit himself, when you questioned him, that Amaury had commanded him to murder Richard?'

Falconer fidgeted from one foot to the other. The room was too small to accommodate both him and Saphira, and he loved to pace when thinking. He moved to the door.

'Let us go outside and walk along the lane. There is a thought in my head, and it won't come out when I am so confined.'

The grass along the back lane, which was no more than a rough path along the river bank, was wet, and the hem of Saphira's dress was soon soaked. But she bore it in order to hear what William had to say. He pursed his lips, as if trying to force out the hidden fact that worried at his brain.

'Odo told me that when he got to Berkhamsted, Richard was as good as dead. He said he had no need to do anything himself.'

'Surely he said that Richard was as good as dead because he had suffered a stroke?'

Falconer shook his head.

'That is what I took him to mean at first. But then I got to thinking. Richard was stricken by the half-dead disease around the Feast of St Mawes of Falmouth in December. He didn't die until April, so Odo could not have imagined his victim was near death. He had already survived four months. I now think that Odo meant that when he entered the castle to kill Richard, he found him already dead. By another's hand.'

TWENTY-NINE

After an uneasy night, Falconer and Saphira Le Veske met the next morning in the gloomy parlour of Brewer's Inn to break their fast. They had slept in separate rooms as neither of their pallets was wide enough to accommodate more than one body. In fact, in Falconer's case it did not even achieve that, and he spent the night with his feet sticking out over the end of the bed. Saphira sipped on the weak ale in the battered goblet set before her, thinking longingly of sweet red wine. A wooden bowl of dry bread was placed in front of them by a surly young lass with crossed eyes and boils. Falconer eagerly dipped the bread in his ale to soften it and began to eat. With a sigh, Saphira proposed that William explain himself further.

'What evidence do you have for supposing someone else killed Richard? And who do you think it would be?'

Falconer put a finger to his lips and hissed.

'We should keep our voices down. Richard was the lord of the manor here, and some may not take kindly to suggestions that he was murdered.'

Saphira looked pointedly around the parlour. It was empty of people other than themselves and an old man snoring loudly beside the ashes of the previous night's fire. It was just as well that the fire had died, because his feet, wrapped in rags, were stretched out perilously close to the heap of ashes that had once been a cheerful blaze.

'We should have to shout very loud to be heard in this place. Though I dare say, if you asked for the bill in a whisper, the landlord would be here soon enough.' She smiled sweetly. 'Shall we try?'

Falconer knew better than to cross Saphira when she was sounding so reasonable. It had been almost disastrous once. He did not want to annoy her again.

'It may be a good idea to call for Roger Brewer. He might be able to tell us about the night Richard died, and something of what the people thought of him when he was alive.'

Saphira was correct in her assumption. As soon as Falconer called for the bill, Roger was bustling around collecting the leavings of their sparse breakfast. Whisking the coins Falconer offered into his purse, he seemed at first amenable to Falconer's questions.

'Poor Lord Richard. Yes, I remember the day he died. We were all in this very parlour when Paul Crouch came in and broke the news.' He hooked a thumb in the direction of the castle across the little river. 'That place was a curse to him and his family. It's a good job his son, Edmund, stays away.'

'A curse? In what way?'

Roger pulled up a three-legged stool and sat leaning close to Saphira and William, his beery breath wafting over them.

'He had three wives, and two of them were soon dead. First there was Isabel Marshal, who died giving birth right there in the castle. That must be thirty years ago now. Then there was Cynthia of Provence, who died about twelve years ago. Also in the castle. Then not so long ago he married that Beatrice, who was barely sixteen to his sixty.'

'You forget his mistress, Roger Brewer.'

The hoarse, throaty voice was that of the old man seated by the embers. Falconer looked across the room at him. He had barely stirred, his eyes still gazing absently into the fireplace, as if recalling the warmth of the fire that was no longer there.

'You can hold your tongue, Guy Fordbridge.'

Brewer was clearly incensed that the old yeoman should speak so harshly of the old lord of the manor. But the old man merely hawked and spat into the embers.

'Joan de Valletort gave him three kids and lasted longer than all his prissy noble wives. Earl Edmund takes after his mother – all foreign and full of airs and graces. He wouldn't live in that shitheap of a castle if you paid him.'

Brewer was about to apologize for the old man's crude tongue, but Falconer cut off his protests.

'Fetch the old man some ale, and the best red wine you have for Mistress Le Veske.'

Falconer had noticed that Saphira had hardly touched her ale and prayed the wine would be better. He produced another coin from his dwindling supply, and the landlord sloped off, mumbling curses under his breath. Falconer beckoned to Guy Fordbridge.

'Come and join us. The fire is cold, so you will not be missing much.'

The old man heaved himself up and tottered over to the table where Falconer and Saphira sat. He slumped down on the stool Brewer had vacated, wheezing after his exertions. He took the pot of ale that Roger banged down at his elbow and stared at him until the landlord took the hint and left. He took a swig and wiped his mouth with a tattered sleeve.

'Roger's all right, as landlords go. He feels he needs to be polite about the lord's family to strangers, that's all.'

Saphira posed a question for the old man.

'What do you think killed Richard?'

Fordbridge took a deep draught of ale before he replied.

'Some say it was the half-dead disease as got him at last. Others that it doesn't matter what he died of – he was better off dead. He couldn't speak, you know, after he was struck down. And he had been such a vigorous man.' He chuckled. 'He would have had to have been with three wives, the last one only sixteen, and a mistress or two tucked away. One of his sons by Joan is a priest hereabouts – Philip Cornwall he's called.'

Falconer was anxious to keep Fordbridge on track and to learn more about Richard alive than dead.

'A vigorous man. And was he liked?'

'Liked? How does that signify? He was the lord; he didn't have to be liked. And he knew it, as he was fearsome harsh sometimes. He had a temper on him, you know. He would lash out at anyone near him, if they angered him in any way. There was a story . . .'

The landlord, who must have been eavesdropping, came in with a goblet of wine for Saphira.

'That's enough, Guy. You've abused my hospitality too much already. Besides, your son will want to know where you are. There's work to do in the fields.'

Grumbling, Fordbridge prised himself off the low stool and shambled out of the room. Saphira took a sniff of the wine that Brewer had brought and studiously pushed it to one side. The landlord apologized for the old man's behaviour.

'He likes to run down the earl's family. They take a high rent off him for his farm. Don't pay any attention to him. Now, if you are ready, sir and mistress, I have your horses in the yard for you.'

There seemed to be nothing more they could learn in the inn, so Falconer and Saphira gathered up their simple belongings and went out to the horses. Once on horseback, they turned them through the arch and on to Akeman Street once again. Falconer had one final question for Brewer.

'Is there anyone living in the castle now?'

Brewer shook his head.

'No, sir. Only some caretaker sort sent by the old king to look after the property for Earl Edmund while he is in France.' He laughed. 'He must have done something awful bad at court to be exiled over there. He's a young chap too, by the name of John Zellot.'

Falconer thanked him and urged his horse on with a jab of his heels. Once on Akeman Street, he turned back south. Saphira called after him.

'That's the wrong way, William.'

'No, it's not. This is the way to the castle.'

Saphira gave a deep sigh and followed him down the lane towards the river. A low wooden bridge took them over the river and led them towards the castle. Both the outer and inner drawbridges over the two moats were lowered, and they rode straight into the heart of the castle unchallenged. In the bailey, which was split in two sections, there were apartments, chapels, workshops and stables. But the big, open space was devoid of servants, save for two men digging down the side of a flint-stone wall. They seemed to care nothing for the two intruders, studiously continuing their labours. Falconer descended from his rouncey and called over to them.

'Where is John Zellot? I wish to speak to him.'

One of the men looked up from his trench and gave Falconer an odd sideways glance.

'He's in the hall over there.'

He pointed briefly to the large building on the western side of the bailey then returned to his work. He said something, and they both laughed. As he turned, Falconer saw that his left eye was clouded completely over and as white as a boiled egg. Saphira had dismounted and was at his side as Falconer walked across the muddy courtyard.

'I knew as soon as you heard the name Zellot that you would not be able to let matters lie.'

John Zellot was a young courtier, who had been eagerly

making his way in King Henry's court a few years ago. He had been sent to bring Falconer to the king with a rare stone that the king coveted. Falconer had taken Saphira with him, and Zellot had earned due reward for services rendered. But now it looked as though he had fallen out of favour with the old king and his son, Edward. Banished to this backwater, he had lost some of his shine. When they entered the dark, dusty hall in search of Zellot, they heard the clatter of metal on metal and an accompanying curse. Beyond the fireplace, they found a rather drunken figure swinging his sword at an array of battered goblets standing on a long oak table. Some lay on the floor and had obviously been hit by the swinging sword. The rather bloated-looking man's next effort, however, missed and took a gouge out of the already savaged table. Another curse rent the air.

Falconer called out to him.

'John Zellot, you are ruining the edge on an otherwise perfectly serviceable sword.'

The figure turned and almost fell over. He clutched at a chair, then slumped into its embrace. Zellot peered drunkenly at the two intruders.

'Why, it's the Oxford sage and his paramour.'

Falconer took a step towards the young man.

'Have a care how you speak of Mistress Le Veske, Zellot. I am not too old to tip you up and spank you, especially when you are in this state.'

Zellot waved a tipsy arm at Saphira, who was finding the male posturing quite amusing.

'My apologies, sweet mistress. You are evidently not who I thought you were. I did not see you clearly.'

John Zellot had not fared well in his new role. Boredom had turned him into a drunkard, who was beginning to neglect himself. When he and Falconer had first met, he had been elegantly dressed and trim around the waist. His clothes were now grubby and torn in places. And his waist had expanded, stretching his shirt and surcoat to their limits. His once-trimmed beard was long and straggly. Nervously, he began to pull at it, twisting strands of it around his fingers.

'I must apologize for my appearance. I rarely see anyone these days. You see me reduced to the role of a caretaker who has nothing to take care of.'

'Hence your game with the goblets.'

'Yes, Master Falconer. But now you are here, I shall tidy myself up and provide you with the hospitality you deserve. And you too, Mistress Le Veske. See, I do remember your name. How could I forget one so beautiful, after all?'

Saphira laughed gently at Zellot's tipsy attempt at chivalry and at righting the wrong of his earlier comment.

'Unless you can supply me with some decent red wine, I think I must say no to your invitation, John Zellot.'

Zellot leaped to his feet and begged his visitors to stay a while, a pleading look in his red-rimmed eyes.

'Good wine is the one comfort I can supply. Don't go away.'

Falconer and Saphira stood for a while, and then a while longer. Zellot was taking a long time, and they were uncertain what to do next.

'William, what are we doing here? Zellot will know nothing about Richard's death, or John's. He could not have been here then.'

Falconer grimaced.

'I had hoped that we could speak to some of the servants who might have been around at the time. But there does not appear to be any.'

There was no sound from outside the hall, no noise of the normal bustle you would expect at a lord's castle. No sound of horses being cared for and saddled, or the smells of food being prepared. The only sound was the dull and monotonous thud as the two men outside dug their hole. It was a dead, brutish noise that made them both imagine that the castle was indeed cursed. They were about to give up their quest and leave, when Zellot came hurrying back into the hall followed by two old women, one bearing a flagon of wine and the other some cuts of cold meat on a large trencher.

'Forgive me, but I had to tidy up, and it took longer than I expected. Meg, Annie, serve our guests.'

The two women, happy to have something to do for once, cleared the battered goblets from the table and laid out the food and drink. Saphira could see that Zellot had indeed taken care with his appearance, even to the extent of wetting down his formerly tangled hair and beard. He waved them to the table, and they sat down together. To Saphira's surprise, the wine was sweet and full of flavour. The women fussed around like mother hens, sharing the cold meat out on pieces of the bread trencher. Zellot would have sent them away, but Falconer stayed his hand.

'With your permission, John Zellot, I would like to ask a question or two of Meg and Annie.' The two women blushed and giggled, exposing their toothless mouths. Zellot looked puzzled, but he acquiesced.

'By all means, Master Deductive.'

Falconer recalled the name he had been saddled with at Henry's court, and he nodded his head in wry acknowledgement. He was indeed going to play the part of deductive, seeking facts and comparing them in order to come to the greater truth. The two old servants gaped open-mouthed at him, not at all sure what the title he was given meant, but certain it was very significant.

'Meg, Annie, I want to talk to you about Lord Richard.'

Their looks suddenly became very solemn, and their eyes flickered between the two men and the red-haired woman. Falconer thought they looked scared.

THIRTY

John Zellot ran his fingers through his thick, unruly hair, teasing away nervously at the tangles. He stared at Falconer and drew his tongue slowly across his lips.

'What are you going to do with this information?'

Falconer laughed softly and exchanged a look with Saphira.

'Why, nothing, of course. It is meaningless without corroboration. And I strongly suggest you do nothing with it either.'

He could imagine Zellot making use of what they had learned from the two old women in order to further his career at court. But it was a very dangerous piece of information that might explode in his own face like one of Roger Bacon's gunpowder firecrackers. Falconer had once nearly lost his fingers with one of the real items, mixed from a recipe provided by Bacon. Zellot could lose his life, if he misused the story the women had told. Somehow, though, Falconer knew he would have to delve further. And if he ascertained the truth, he would be obliged to tell Edward. Saphira looked at him, knowing what was going on in his head, and gave her tacit approval for what he was bound to do.

'What else can we do, William?'

It was Zellot who cut in with a warning.

'You must leave well alone, Falconer. God knows what you will learn if you delve any further.'

Falconer ignored the advice, speaking instead only to Saphira.

'The king must know the truth. He charged me with investigating the instigator of several murders and attempted murders. But the start of all this was the death of his son, John. That is what began the cycle of events I was supposed to look into. And my conclusions led to the accusation of Amaury de Montfort as being the guiding hand. Now it looks as though he had nothing to do with the act we supposed was the first in the sequence.'

A gloomy silence descended over the room as all three people reconsidered the testimony of the two old serving women.

It had begun quite innocently with Meg being bold enough

to suggest that their former lord had been a hard taskmaster. Annie had screwed up her wrinkled face and snorted in disgust.

'Hard? He was unfair, and that's the truth.'

'You shouldn't speak ill of the dead, Annie.'

'The truth is the truth.'

Annie saw that neither Zellot nor the two visitors were about to reprimand her, and she was emboldened enough to go on.

'Lord Richard had a temper on him. If he didn't get his own way, he would lash out. And not at just the servants neither. Family members got it in the neck too. Many's the time I've seen bruises on poor young Beatrice's face. And her barely sixteen. It seemed the younger they were the less well they fared, as if he couldn't stand the children's playfulness. Look at poor John . . .'

There was an awful silence at this point, and Annie's red face suddenly went very pale. Falconer urged her to continue.

'What about John?'

Annie backed away a little and looked pleadingly at Meg, wanting her to come to her aid. Meg, the shorter and fatter of the two women, pulled at Annie's arm.

'Now look what you've gone and said.'

Zellot broke in, speaking sternly to the servants.

'Whatever it is you meant to say, Annie, it is too late now to stop. Nothing will come back on you concerning what you say. I promise you.'

But Annie was too fearful to continue, hiding her face in her hands. It was Meg who broke their silence, staring defiantly at Falconer and ignoring Zellot. He was no more than an upstart caretaker, and she didn't respect him. But the grey-haired man in black looked like someone with authority. Someone she could trust.

'It is only a story, mind, spoken of between the servants. We didn't see it happen.'

Falconer nodded.

'I understand. Tell me what you have heard.'

There followed a tale involving enmity and unjust punishment meted out by Richard to his nephew, John. Despite his great wealth – he was said to be the wealthiest man in Europe – and his title of King of the Germans, Richard was jealous of the little five-year-old. The boy's grandfather, Richard's

brother, was King of England. His father Edward would be
the next king, and then John would be king in his turn. None
of Richard's offspring could aspire to be King of England,
and it rankled. The boy was chastised for the merest slight,
and given a cuff with the back of Richard's hand. A hard and
calloused hand that was used to fighting in battle. And more
than that – the child was pushed into training as a knight,
performing exercises that were far beyond the capabilities of
a small child. Richard justified his acts by maintaining that
the child needed to be hardened up for the tasks that lay ahead
of him. And when he inevitably failed – in lifting the smallest
of swords and completing a set of thrusts and parries most
adults would tire doing – Richard would beat him.

'And then he took it too far.' Meg now had a determined
look on her face. Nothing would stop her now. 'The Lord
Richard was set on putting poor John on horseback.'

But it had not been a quiet rouncey he had selected, but
Richard's own skittish and enormously powerful destrier. The
massive horse he himself rode into battle. All the servants
present could see the fear in the little boy's eyes, but there
was nothing they could do. The destrier had been brought
from the stables by one of the stable-hands, and it stood in
the centre of the courtyard. As it danced nervously on the end
of its rein, its iron hoofs struck sparks off the hard stone slabs
under it. Richard himself lifted the boy on to the horse's back,
where for a while he perched like a wart on an old man's
face. Then it happened. The horse reared and threw John to
the ground. Everyone could see he was dead, for his neck was
horribly twisted, broken by the fall. Richard just walked away
in silence.

Annie was weeping, and Meg's voice had broken in the
telling. Falconer was a little disappointed. Saphira had already
told him the story Eleanor had told her about John's death.
This just seemed to confirm a sad accident, caused by Richard's
foolishness. But then Meg had a final thing to say.

'It was put down as a terrible accident. But Tom the stable-
hand swears that he saw Lord Richard rake the pommel of
his sword across the horse's flank just after he put John in
the saddle. It was deliberate, he says.'

A deathly silence had followed this revelation, and the
women were swiftly dismissed. As Zellot and his guests

considered their next actions, the sky darkened and large drops
of rain began to fall. The castle felt cold, damp and gloomy,
as if it had been in mourning for the dead for years. Falconer
knew he had to check the women's story in case it was just
rumour.

'Is Tom still a servant here?'

Zellot looked up at Falconer, his eyes reddened from the
wine he had consumed since hearing the terrible tale. He
nodded his head.

'He is the only one left in the stables. There are not many
horses to look after now. And yes, before you ask, you can
speak to him. Offer him some reward, if you have to. God
knows he needs some help in the stables. But don't tell me
the result of your interrogation. I don't want to know. Then
I can pretend what I heard was all servants' gossip.'

'We will leave immediately after we have spoken to Tom.'
Falconer patted Zellot's arm. 'You are a good man, John Zellot.
Stick to your task, and you will be rewarded.'

Zellot was not so sure, but he stood and shook Falconer's
hand and kissed Saphira's. She had one bit of advice for him
as they departed.

'Don't drink too much, Master Zellot. And practise your
swordplay at the lists, not on defenceless goblets.'

As she and Falconer walked across the courtyard, heads
bent against the relentless rain, she asked him a question.

'Do you really think Zellot will be rewarded for baby-
sitting this old castle?'

'I'm afraid not. Poor man, he was so ambitious when we
last saw him at Westminster. I fear he will now be forgotten
in this arsehole of a place.'

Entering the run-down stable that stank of horse piss and
rotting straw, Falconer spotted a bent-backed old man lovingly
rubbing down their two rounceys. He called out.

'Tom?'

The old man straightened his back with a wince of pain
and peered at the two people who had entered his domain.
He was ashamed of its state, but he was too old to look after
it properly by himself. In its heyday, the castle had a dozen
stable-lads running around.

'I am Tom, sir. What is it you might want? I have looked
after your mounts as well as I could, sir.'

'You have done a good job, Tom. As I am told you have for many years for Master Zellot, Lord Edmund and his father Richard before him.'

Tom squinted suspiciously at the black-clad man. He was not used to flattery, and when it came he was sure something awkward was to follow. He shuffled his feet waiting for it. He did not have to wait long. The red-haired woman hung back in the shadows, and the man asked the question Tom had been fearing for the last two years.

'Meg and Annie have been telling us about the death of poor Prince John. They said you told them something about it. Something you saw.'

Tom poked at the dirty straw with his sandal.

'Those two blabbermouths should keep their traps shut. I saw nothing.'

Saphira stepped forward, touching Tom's arm gently.

'There is nothing to fear. No one will know it was you who told us. And John Zellot will reward your honesty. He might even be persuaded to find a stable-lad to make your work here a little lighter.'

She could sense that the old man was weakening. He wanted to tell his tale to someone. She held her breath, and finally it tumbled out.

'I did see something. It was unmistakeable, especially when I tell you that the boy used to argue with the master all the time. And Richard hated being crossed by anyone. But even more so by young John, who never stopped reminding the master that he would be king one day. Even so, the master shouldn't have put the little lad on such a wild and large animal. He had no hope of controlling it. Then I saw Lord Richard hold the scabbard of his sword at the top and poke the pommel in the horse's flank and rake it down. He must have intended the boy some harm, but God alone knows if he meant to kill him. But kill him he did.'

Saphira thanked the old stable-hand and took the reins of her rouncey from his hand. She and Falconer led their horses out into the rain and mounted, gathering their cloaks around them. It would be a miserable journey onwards to Oxford. As they plodded towards the castle's inner drawbridge, Tom called out after them.

'I think he was remorseful afterwards – Lord Richard. I

reckon that is what brought on the attack that led to him suffering from the half-dead disease. And his eventual death.'

Falconer checked the progress of his horse, thinking of how to ask his question.

'Did you expect Richard's death, when it came? Was he too ill to survive?'

'No, that's the funny thing. Master hated the state he was in, but that had made him even more cantankerous. He wasn't frail, or near death. So it came as a surprise when he died in his sleep like that.'

The rain beat down, and Falconer and Saphira bowed their heads and rode off westwards.

THIRTY-ONE

The Feast of St Edward the Confessor, the Fifth Day of January 1274

Falconer had been waiting months for some news from Paris. It was a reply to an enquiry he had sent for the attention of Grand Master Guillaume de Beaujeu. He had expected and hoped that it would come soon, for it would have concluded his long-drawn-out enquiry into the lethal activities of Amaury de Montfort. Once known to him as Jack Hellequin. Falconer wanted Guillaume to question Odo de Reppes once again about the night Richard of Cornwall died. He was still convinced that Odo had meant him to understand he was not responsible for Richard's death. That Amaury had desired it, but that the Templar had been too late to carry out his task. Someone had beaten him to it. Falconer needed Odo to tell him all he knew about that night. But in lieu of travelling once again to the Paris Temple at the Marais, where Odo was incarcerated, he had to rely on Guillaume being his agent. Now months had passed without a reply to his letter, and he felt very frustrated. His only consolation was that King Edward was still tied up in Gascony and had not returned to England to be crowned.

Wandering the water meadows to the west of Oxford, he rehearsed in his head the events surrounding Prince John's and Richard's two deaths. There was no doubt that Uncle Richard had caused the death of the child, leaving the sickly young Henry as Edward's only male heir. And the gossip was that he might not last out the year either. And the next male child – Alfonso – whom Saphira had helped bring into the world was barely a year old yet. Babies' lives were so perilous. Edward could only hope that, with Amaury still at liberty, one of his boys would survive him. But the question for Falconer still remained. If Amaury, through the agency of Odo de Reppes, did not kill Richard, who did? And for what reason?

His wanderings around the water meadows, with the spiralling towers of Oseney Abbey rising out of the mist, gave him no answers. But when he returned to Aristotle's Hall, one of his students was waiting for him with news. Peter Mithian had been glad to see Master Falconer's return. Brother Pecham, who had been left in charge of maintaining Aristotle's Hall and of teaching Falconer's students in his absence, had been dull and of a strict nature. Falconer was an uncompromising taskmaster, but he was always entertaining and never predictable. Everyone was glad he was back.

'Master, there are two visitors waiting for you in your solar.'

'You allowed them up into my private quarters, Peter Mithian? How many times have I told you not to let strangers in there.'

Mithian feigned repentance, hiding a smirk behind a raised palm.

'I am sorry, master, but they insisted.'

Grumbling under his breath, Falconer hurried up the rickety stairs to his solar set high in the eaves of the narrow tenement. He was sure some meddling envoy of the king had barged his way in and would be disturbing the perfect disorder of his room. He swung the door open and called out as he entered.

'I hope you have not touched anything, or I shall be searching forever.'

The familiar voice he heard shocked him to his core.

'You do not surprise me, William. This table looks as disordered as your mind.'

Squinting into the sunlight that hung low outside the narrow window arch, Falconer strove to make sense of what he saw. Before him stood the slight figure of a tonsured Franciscan monk who had not been allowed in Oxford for years.

'Roger? Is that you?'

'Put your eye-lenses on, William, and you will see that it is I. And I have brought you back your able scribe and assistant.'

Falconer looked to his right for the first time, recalling that Mithian had said he had two visitors. Standing to one side, in the shadows, his hands modestly folded in front of him, was Thomas Symon. He strode over to him and took one of his hands, shaking it vigorously.

'Thomas. It is so good to see you again.'

Symon could not repress a huge grin, and he extricated his hand from Falconer's only to rub the top of his head with it in embarrassment. Falconer then clutched Roger Bacon to him and gave him a hug, whispering in his ear.

'They have set you free at last, then?'

Bacon freed himself from his friend's clutches and smiled.

'My order has seen fit to permit me to return to Oxford, where I may teach and write. So long as I show my completed writings to my Father Superior. My three volumes are still under lock and key in Paris, however.'

Falconer glanced at Thomas, who was still grinning from ear to ear.

'And the task Thomas and yourself undertook in Paris?'

Thomas opened the flap on the satchel slung over his shoulder. Delving inside, he pulled out the corner of a substantial bundle of parchments. Bacon waved a hand.

'Our little conspiracy continues, and Thomas works on recording my . . . lectures. How industrious of him. But we have something else for you. I nearly forgot in all the welcoming hugs. Thomas.'

Thomas nodded and slipped a single letter out of his tightly packed satchel, handing it over to Falconer. He took it, examining the hand that had scribed his name on the outside of the folded document. He didn't recognize that, but then a clerk will have written it, because the wax seal on the edges of the parchment was clearly that of the Grand Master of the Order of the Poor Knights of the Temple. Guillaume de Beaujeu could write, but his hand was slow and awkward. He had dictated a letter to one of his clerks and sealed it not with his personal ring but with that of his office. Falconer had a sense of impending doom about this communication from his old friend. He broke the seal and moved to the window to read the letter.

William

I have to give you bad news. You have asked me to inter-rogate the prisoner Odo de Reppes concerning his complicity in the death of Richard Cornwall, King of the Germans. I am sorry to inform you that de Reppes is dead. Quite soon after you left Paris, one of the guards appointed to keep an eye on him entered the chamber where he was confined alone. The guard found de Reppes hanging from the wall loop that held his chains. Somehow, Odo had managed to wind a short length of the chains attached to his wrists around his own neck. He had then used the weight of his own body to choke himself to death. It was a sore

*ending to an unhappy life, but I cannot help but feel he is
free from the oppression forced on him by my predecessor
and his own iniquity. I have prayed for his soul.*

> *I also pray for the success of Edward's future reign
> as King of England.*
>> *Guillaume de Beaujeu*

The signature was Guillaume's own hand, but the sentiment
rang untrue to Falconer's ears. It was the letter of a Grand
Master, and in the reading of it Falconer sadly realized he had
lost a friend. He also had the uneasy feeling that Odo de
Reppes had been dispatched by someone seeking to hide the
truth. And not by his own hands.

'Is it bad news, William?'

Roger's solicitous enquiry brought Falconer back to the
present.

'In a way. It marks the end of the enquiry I was following.
My report to Edward – when he deigns to return to these
shores – will have to be incomplete. Still, let us not dwell on
that. You are returned to Oxford. Will you reopen your tower
at Grand Pont?'

Falconer was referring to the tall building resembling a
watermill that stood beside the river and the main bridge
over it to the south of Oxford. The Franciscan friar had built
quite a reputation for black magic when he had last occupied it due to late-night experiments within its upper room.
Bacon shook his head.

'I fear it is too damp and crumbling to be inhabitable.
Besides, I have to exist under the watchful eye of Father
Superior in the friary itself until I have proven myself to be
totally innocuous.'

'Quite some time, then.'

The three men laughed, but there was a hollow ring to the
jollity expressed by two of them. Bacon would be under surveil-
lance because of his beliefs, and Falconer had been deliberately
thwarted in his investigations into the death of Richard of
Cornwall. Only Thomas Symon was unencumbered by the pressure from those around him. Falconer hoped that his natural
optimism would not also be crushed as that of his companions
had been. They each took leave of the other, with Bacon returning
to the Franciscan friary just outside the southern walls of the

town, and Thomas to Colcill Hall, next to Aristotle's, where he would temporarily reside before finding his own teaching post.

Falconer sat alone in his solar, staring at the message from Paris. He felt there was something hidden in the words of Guillaume's missive. But rack his brains as he might, he could not see it. He lay back on his bed until he heard his charges down below in the hall leaving Aristotle's for a night of roistering in the low taverns of the town. Some of his students were too poor to buy anything but the cheapest watery ale. But Oxford offered them nothing other than inns and the bawdy houses of Grope Lane to pass the hours of a long summer's evening, and beer was cheaper than a whore. They would come back even poorer and have sore heads in the morning, and they would not have learned a lesson, doing it all over again the next night. Falconer remembered his own student days in Oxford and then Bologna. He must have been a disappointment to his friends, for he would prefer to study a text by Aristotle than drink with them. But he had no more money then than he had now. Yet what he did have was a fierce determination to transcend his background as an orphaned farm boy funded at the university by a local priest. He knew nothing of his father other than the name he inherited, and little about his mother other than as a pale, drawn face that had disappeared from his knowledge when he was a small boy. The priest had been a severe presence in his young life, giving him no love, and Falconer learned his distrust of the Church from that time. He had been very surprised that the priest had eventually paid for his studies. But all that had been going on forty years ago. Now he had other charges in his care, and he would make sure they were brought up right. Including letting them get drunk now and again.

As silence descended downstairs, Falconer became aware of the creaking of the old timbers of the house. And of his own solitude. He thought of Saphira only a few minutes' walk away in Jewry. Convincing himself that he should consult her about Guillaume's letter – that she would see through the text to the core of it – he scooped it up and went out into St John Street. Avoiding the already noisy taverns lining Shidyerd Street and Grope Lane, he crossed Vine Hall Lane and hurried down the dark narrow alley of Jewry Lane. Saphira's house was just across Fish Street, and he let himself in. As he quietly closed the door, she called out from the back of the house.

'William. I thought you might come. I have just taught Rebekkah how to make charoset. We are in the kitchen.'

Used to Saphira's acute hearing and uncanny way of knowing his every move, Falconer made his way to the rear of the house. In the kitchen, sectioned off in the proper Jewish way, stood Saphira and her servant girl. Both had their sleeves rolled up, and Rebekkah had something stuck to the tip of her nose where she had rubbed it as she worked. Saphira spotted it and wiped it off, causing the girl to descend into a fit of the giggles. Sternly, Saphira told her she could go home now, as she would no longer be needed. Rebekkah looked at Falconer and started giggling again, before running off. The slam of the front door announced her departure. Saphira sighed.

'One day I will teach her to be quiet in all things. Now sit down, William, and eat while you tell me what you have come here concerning.'

Falconer grinned and took a wooden spoon and dipped into the bowl of the delicious-looking dark concoction. He swallowed the sweetness and enquired what it was made of.

'Nuts and apples chopped up, cinnamon, sweet wine and honey. The honey is for you, as the great Maimonides says honey is good for old people.'

Falconer took a swipe at her with the sticky spoon. But she was too quick for him, and he contented himself with taking another big helping from the bowl. Relieved to be back in favour with Saphira, and with their former relationship restored, he produced the letter and passed it over to her.

'What do you make of this?'

Sitting across the table from him, she read it by the light of the candle that stood between them. She sighed.

'Odo was your main hope for enlightenment about Richard's death, wasn't he?'

Falconer nodded.

'Yes. And I have once again spoken to Sir Humphrey Segrim since returning home. He tells me the same story. Of seeing the Templar sneak out of Berkhamsted under cover of darkness on the very night Richard died. Why would he have done that other than because he had killed him?'

'Did you reassure Segrim that Odo hadn't been aware of his presence in Berkhamsted also on that night? That that could not then have been the reason Segrim's wife Ann was killed – as some form of warning?'

'Yes, he now accepts that he was not unwittingly the cause of her death.'

'Good. Now tell me again what Odo told you when you spoke to him in the Templar prison.'

Falconer closed his eyes in concentration, picturing that horrible cell and the ragged skeleton that was all that was left of the once-strong and powerful Templar. He could see again how the man had been chained down to the floor apparently without the strength to lift up his burden. He strived to recall the words Odo had spoken.

'He said he did go there to kill Richard at the behest of the de Montforts. He explained that he was King Henry's brother after all, and what he called that same nest of vipers. Then he said . . . that when he had got there, he found he had no need to do anything. That God would not punish him for that death.'

Falconer opened his eyes and looked at Saphira.

'I took him to mean that Richard's stroke had already done that for him. But now I think he intended me to know that he had been beaten to it. That someone else had killed Richard, who up to then had apparently survived the stroke quite well.'

Now something else was trying to wriggle to the surface of Falconer's mind, a piece of information Saphira had almost caused to surface. She looked at the letter again.

'I wonder why he added the line at the end about praying for Edward's success?'

'I suppose because it is a formal letter, not a personal one. That is what I found odd in the first place. It is so unlike Guillaume.'

'But now he is Grand Master of his order, he has so great a responsibility that personal friendships may not survive it. It is also odd that he says he prayed for Odo's soul, and that he thought he was now free. Is it not a sin in Christian eyes to commit self-murder?'

Falconer suddenly saw again the picture in his mind of Odo on the floor of his cell, and he knew what Guillaume had been trying to tell him. What a fool he was – it had been in front of his eyes all the time. He leaned across the table and gave Saphira a honey-laden kiss.

'Thank you, Mistress Le Veske. You have solved the case.'

THIRTY-TWO

*The Feast of St Magnus Martyr, the Nineteenth Day of August
1274*

The Palace of Westminster was abuzz with activity. Every
kitchen available had been commandeered to prepare
a feast of swans, peacocks, cranes, oxen, swine, sheep,
goats, chickens and rabbits. A silken canopy hung with silver
bells had been set up above carpeted paths running from the
palace to the Abbey Church. It was the day of Edward's coronation, and yet among all this bustle he had found a moment
for himself. Away even from Eleanor, his queen. Only a short
while ago, a harassed Sir John Appleby had come to him with
a message. The courtier was gaudier than ever on this auspi-
cious day, but his face was ashen.

'Majesty, I am truly sorry to disturb you at such a time.
But Master Falconer says he must see you as a matter of
urgency. I tried to put him off, insisting that you could not be
interrupted in your preparations for the coronation. But he
said to tell you it was about . . . Prince John.'

Edward's face had fallen, and he had told Appleby to bring
Falconer to him in his private chamber. Now he awaited the
meeting wondering what information the Oxford master had
concerning the death of his child. He did not have long to
wait, as almost immediately footsteps could be heard outside
his chamber. They stopped outside the door, and there was a
brief silence, presumably while Appleby plucked up the
courage to knock. Edward spared him the anguish and called
out his command.

'Send Master Falconer in, Sir John. We will get this over
with, and then we can concentrate on the coronation ceremony.'

The door opened, and Falconer stepped in the room, his
normal shabby black robe in marked contrast to the king.
Edward wore a deep-blue, voluminous cloak clipped with a
golden brooch on one shoulder so it hung on him like an
ecclesiastical cope. Under it was a white linen shirt, which

was edged with motifs embroidered in gold thread. He was newly clean-shaven, and his hair was carefully arranged. He beckoned for Falconer to enter and called out to the hovering Appleby.

'Sir John, go and see if the queen is ready. You may close the door.'

With a palpable sense of humiliation in the air, the door was closed behind Falconer. Smiling, the king waited until he heard Appleby's footsteps retreating down the passage. Only then did he turn back to Falconer and ask him to begin.

'We will keep what is said between ourselves I think, Master Falconer. What have you to tell me that could not wait until after my coronation?'

'Sire, I wished to complete the task you set me in Paris last year.'

'But you did all I could ask of you. You identified Amaury's involvement in the attempt on my life, in the conspiracy that killed my cousin Henry, and in the murder of my uncle. It was no reflection on your skills that Amaury slipped through the net. And you did help foil his attempt on the life of Eleanor and Alfonso.'

'Well, that was thanks to Saphira more than myself. And I never did connect de Montfort with the death of your son John.'

Edward looked at the floor, sadness in his eyes.

'Ah, well, that is a forgivable omission, when you were in Paris and the events had taken place in England. We shall say no more of that. Sons, after all, can be replaced.'

The king was ready to dismiss him, but Falconer was not going to be diverted from the path he had chosen to tread. A path he had determined on months earlier in Oxford. Pursuit of the truth and its revelation held sway over all other considerations. Even his own personal safety. He took a deep breath and continued relentlessly.

'Yes. That may well be. But as I returned to England soon after failing to locate Amaury, I could not fail in my duty again. I took the opportunity of passing through Berkhamsted to see if I could uncover anything about his death. And that of your uncle, Richard.'

Edward lifted his gaze from the floor and fixed it on Falconer. But he said nothing, and Falconer went on.

'You see, I had doubts anyway about Richard's death. In

fact, on reflection I was uneasy about the whole investigation
I conducted in Paris.'

'In what way?'

'The paths that all led to Amaury de Montfort were all too
easy to follow. I had the feeling I was being led by the nose.'

Edward smiled wistfully.

'You are no fool, are you, Master Falconer? I think I under-
estimated you. It is true I aided your investigations by pointing
you at the right people – my own men-at-arms, and my wife.
But I made a mistake when I led you towards Odo de Reppes.
I did not know then what he knew about my uncle. Still, that
has all been rectified.'

Falconer knew he had just had his suspicion – his greatest
fear – confirmed. His friendship with Guillaume de Beaujeu
was shattered to pieces. The Grand Master must have agreed
with Edward to silence Odo in return for future influence in
worldly affairs. He could imagine what had happened in Odo's
cell.

*Guillaume took the key of the tower from his sergeant and
dismissed him. He climbed alone up the narrow spiral staircase to the top and unlocked the heavy cell door. Taking a
deep breath, he pushed open the door. Odo stirred under his
burden of chains, which pinned him to the floor. He was weak
and parched from lack of food and water, which had been
deliberately withheld for days. Still his eyes sparkled, and
when he saw the Grand Master alone, he knew. He parted
his cracked lips.*

'It is time. Thanks be to God.'

*Guillaume stepped swiftly over to him, turning him so Odo's
back was towards him, and grabbed a loop of the chains on
his wrists. He looped the chain around Odo's windpipe and
pulled it tight. Odo emitted a stifled choking sound, and his
feet drummed on the floor of the cell. Guillaume held on long
after the body had gone limp, then let it fall. Feeling sick
inside, he left the chamber with the door ajar; de Reppes was
not going anywhere but to meet his Maker.*

Falconer knew Odo had not killed himself, because in his
letter to Falconer Guillaume had referred to a loop high on
the wall that the Templar had been chained to. There had been
no such loop, and Falconer knew that only too well once he
had envisioned the scene at Saphira's instigation. And she had

been right about the other matter. Guillaume would not have prayed for the soul of a self-murderer who was condemned to Hell. The missive had been a sort of confession by Guillaume to salve his own conscience.

Falconer stared calmly back at Edward. He was not intimidated and laid out what he knew.

'You got de Beaujeu to dispatch Odo, but it was too late. The Templar had already told me that he was not responsible for the death of Richard. So I had to ask myself who was. Who had the best reason to kill him? Then I saw it. It all came back to the death of your son, didn't it?'

Edward suddenly flew into a rage, stomping around the room and scattering gilded goblets from the table in the corner with a sweep of his arm.

'The bastard killed my son. He was supposed to be caring for him while Eleanor and I were in Outremer. So he stuck him on a horse too powerful for John, and then made the animal shy and throw the boy off. The beast trampled John underfoot, and Richard just walked away. He was always jealous of his brother, my father, knowing he would never be king. Even that petty courtesy title of his didn't help. King of the Germans was not enough for him. He had to have his revenge. Well, I made him pay for what he did.'

Falconer's blue eyes bored into the king's visage.

'You had your uncle killed, didn't you? You couldn't do it with your own hand, but you arranged it to happen. Strangely, it was on the very night that Odo de Reppes turned up in Berkhamsted to kill him on behalf of Amaury de Montfort.'

Edward snarled in frustration.

'Yes, damn him. If I had waited another day or two, I would not have needed to kill him myself. Still, it was sweet to be the cause of his death. That was my revenge. For John.'

The rage that had flooded over Edward was as suddenly gone, and the king was once again calm. He rearranged his cloak and ran his fingers through his thick black hair.

'Now, Master Falconer, I must thank you for your persistence, but I have a coronation to attend.'

Falconer sat brooding over a goblet of sweet red wine that Saphira had put before him. They were lodging in London's Jewry in a house on the corner of Milk Street and Cheapside.

The streets outside were quiet, as almost everyone was thronged around Westminster Hall, where Edward and Eleanor were feasting. The coronation had been a great event, and everyone had welcomed Edward as a great and noble king. Falconer groaned.

'I have failed completely. I unearth one murderer in Jack Hellequin, who turns out to be Amaury de Montfort. And he disappears into the protective folds of the Pope's skirts. And then I unmask another murderer in the shape of the new King of England, who is far out of my reach.'

Saphira put an arm around his shoulders.

'You did catch Adam Morrish, and he has been hanged for the murders of Paul Hebborn and John Fusoris. And you were brave enough to confront the king with the truth. I know of no other man who would dare do that.'

Falconer picked up the goblet and drank deep.

'Tomorrow we escape this mad city and return to the small and safe world of Oxford, where all that matters is the debate over the number of angels on the head of a pin.'

Saphira nibbled Falconer's ear, whispering in it.

'And tonight?'

Falconer turned to look at her beautiful face, framed by her tumbling red hair.

'Tonight I will lecture you on anatomy.'

EPILOGUE

Towards the end of 1275, Amaury and his sister – another Eleanor – set sail for Wales, where she was to marry Llewelyn. They travelled by sea to avoid England and Edward, but passing Bristol the expedition was caught by four ships led by a knight called Thomas the Archdeacon. Amaury and Eleanor were captured and handed over to the king. Edward treated Eleanor kindly, allowing her to marry her Welsh prince once he had settled a peace with England. He bore no such sympathy for Amaury.

The last de Montfort brother was imprisoned in the grim fortress of Corfe Castle until 1282. Banished from England then, he never regained his family lands, though styling himself Earl of Leicester still. He made a sad figure, wandering through France and Italy, laying claim to lost titles and privileges. Sinking into obscurity, by 1300 he was dead.

HISTORICAL FOOTNOTE

The perceptive among my readers will identify the secret diary that Friar Roger Bacon was writing in cipher. It has re-emerged in modern times as the Voynich Manuscript. Rumours abound that in the sixteenth century it was sold to Rudolph II, King of Bohemia, by Dr John Dee, astrologer to Queen Elizabeth I, as a text written by Bacon. But it is said that Dee or his companion, Edward Kelley, concocted it as a way of making money. What is certain is that an obscure alchemist in Prague owned it in the early seventeenth century, and it found its way into the library of the Collegio Romano. Then, around 1912, it was sold with other manuscripts to Wilfrid Voynich. It has not yet been fully deciphered, defying amateur cryptographers and code-breakers from the Second World War.